Paper, Scissors, ROCK

PAPER, SCISSORS, ROCK

NICOLE S. GOODIN

Paper, Scissors, Rock (second edition)
Published by Nicole S. Goodin

ISBN: 978-0-473-58776-5

Copyright 2021 by Nicole S. Goodin
All rights reserved. ©

First published September 2017
Cover design by Nicole Goodin
Images purchased from Shutterstock and Canva
Editing by Spell Bound

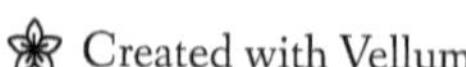 Created with Vellum

This is for everyone; friends, family and people I barely know, who message me or come up to me and say 'oh my god, I read your books...' thank you for your support, your encouragement and for taking a chance on me.

And to my good friends, thank you for not looking at me like I've completely lost the plot when I attempt to explain to you how these characters and their stories appear in my brain – I promise I'm not totally insane just yet.

Nicole xx

FOREWORD

This book has been written using UK English and may contain euphemisms and slang words that form part of the New Zealand spoken word.
Please remember that the words are not misspelled. They are slang terms and form part of everyday, New Zealand vernacular.
I.e: I'm from New Zealand and sometimes we say weird things down here... please try and be cool about it.

CHAPTER 1

Parker

THE ROAR of the crowd nearly caused me to fall backwards as I sauntered out into the centre of the stage, my trademark bad-boy smirk in place.

I chuckled as my heart sped up to a gallop in my chest. Performing live was a thrill that was rivalled by no other.

I live for this shit.

The rest of the fame I could take or leave, but not this. The pure ecstasy of the fans screaming your name, watching the sweat pour off them as they gasp for air, some of them even passing out... I needed it like an alcoholic needs a drink.

I was addicted. One hundred percent hooked on

the euphoria that fifty thousand people screaming your name created.

I bumped fists with Jasper as I approached the mic stand.

This is how it went. He introduced me to the crowd... I introduced the guys... then I did my best to blow their little minds right out of their heads.

"How's everybody doing tonight?" My voice boomed across the huge stadium, causing the level of screams and shrieks to reach an even higher intensity – something I didn't think was possible.

I chuckled deep and low, my skin already prickling with my body's eagerness to begin. Despite the cool air, I was already covered in a fine layer of sweat. By the time this was over, I'd be drenched with it.

"How about we have some fun, huh?" I grinned suggestively.

The high-pitched, female screams ricocheted through my ear drums.

I strummed my guitar and the sound screeched out through the air above the crowd. I strummed a few more chords and turned to face the guys behind me.

I didn't take the band with me everywhere, but when I wanted them, they were there.

"Can you all say hey to my man Ricky on the drums?" I asked the mass of bodies.

The crowd went wild as Ricky pounded out a beat on his drum kit.

"Jimmy on the bass," I yelled into the mic.

His response was just as deafening.

"And Peter 'pumpkin-eater' on the guitar." I chuckled.

The momentum was building – the crowd were hungry for more. They were no longer individuals... they had turned into one screaming unit – a beast in its own right.

I thrust my hips forward and rolled them seductively... it was all part of the show.

I live to feed the beast.

"You ready boys?" I cooed.

I knew they would be. They were always ready – they lived for this shit too. I heard a collective 'whoop'.

"Let's do this."

CHAPTER 2

Charlotte

THE MINUTE I set foot in the club, I noticed him.

He was hard to miss... tattoos, posse... V.I.P. booth, gaggle of underdressed groupies...

Typical rock star.

I rolled my eyes as I typed out a text to Hannah.

"Parker Sloan is here..."

I knew she'd kill me if I didn't keep her informed on the location of her precious rock star.

Her reply was a series of 'OMFG' and 'are you serious?' Followed by an 'I'm on my way'.

Hannah was infatuated with that man – among others. She had been for as long as we'd been friends. I had to admit, he wasn't exactly my type; tall, dark-haired, brooding and covered in tattoos didn't really do it for me, but holy hell he had a way with music.

I couldn't deny the fact that his talent was enough to make him alluring. It wasn't nearly enough to make me want to throw myself at him – but the same could not be said for my best friend.

He was one of the reasons we'd been hanging out in this club for the past year or so; Han was always hoping that he, or one of her other obsessions would be here, so she could get 'her shot' – her words, not mine.

I thought she was crazy. I didn't see what the big deal was – he was just like any other guy in this club. Fame, money and publicity didn't flick my switch the way it obviously did for so many others.

I watched with amusement as woman after woman made their attempt to get up to where he was seated, his arms splayed widely on the booth, bored smirk on his face. Most of them failed, but every now and then, Parker, or one of his boys would nod at their security, and a girl would be given access.

I skirted around the edge of the dance floor, heading for the quiet end of the bar and heard his name mentioned at least ten times on my travels. It appeared my vagina was the only one in here that didn't care to be Parker Sloan's parking space for the night.

I shook my head at their naive stupidity. I never understood the obsession some women, my best friend included, had with the rich and famous. He was known for being untameable – Parker Sloan didn't *do* girlfriends... but these girls obviously thought they could be the one to change all of that.

I don't get it.

I reached the bar and hoisted myself up onto one of the bar stools – no small feat for a girl my height.

I dreaded to think about what Hannah was doing to 'primp' for the evening and I actually shuddered when I thought about what she might deem a good choice of outfit.

I glanced back over to Parker and his friends and found myself watching him, trying to figure out what all the fuss was about.

I honestly didn't see what the big deal was.

He threw his head back and laughed and I begrudgingly admitted to myself that he was easy to watch.

So is a dog doing a trick...

Sure, there was *something* about him...

I guess he is good looking, if that's what you're into...

It wasn't necessarily that either though, he had this magnetism about him... an energy I could feel from even this distance, and for a fraction of a second I could understand why he was such a hot commodity.

Two girls that didn't look more than a day over twenty-one walked past me on their way to the bathroom, and I couldn't help but overhear the topic of their conversation.

"He *only* does blondes," the black-haired one insisted to the blonde one. "You should totally go for it."

The blonde one nodded in agreement. "I read that he's like, a *total* adrenaline junky... if I could get up there we'd *totally* hit it off, right?" she replied with a flip of her hair.

Jesus...

"*Totally*." Her friend nodded enthusiastically.

"Like, totally," I mocked as they strolled past out of ear shot.

Christ, what have I got myself into here...

I shot daggers in Parker's direction.

This is all your fault.

I cursed him and his celebrity status in my mind.

"Damn rock stars," I mumbled under my breath.

I sat back and waited for Hannah to turn up. I cringed just thinking about it. She'd be no better than the two desperate girls I'd just witnessed when she finally did arrive.

I was embarrassed for her already.

CHAPTER 3

Parker

"WHO'S it gonna be tonight, Sloan?" Ricky yelled across the table, gesturing towards the hordes of groupies that had scored themselves entry into our area.

I shrugged – well past bored with the scene in front of me. They were the same type of girls that followed me around everywhere. They might not have been the same women every night – but they were all after the same thing.

Sure, I'd had my fair share of women, but I wasn't interested in these ones anymore... they presented no challenge whatsoever. It wasn't like I wanted or needed to chase women, but these ones came a little too easy for my liking. It didn't stop them from throwing themselves at me whenever the opportunity presented itself though.

These girls, they already knew the answer, but for some reason, they continued to ask the question.

Ricky shook his head at me like I'd lost my mind and went back to the busty brunette that had perched herself on his lap. Guys like him never got tired of banging groupies; 'the more the merrier' was like the motto of his life.

I glanced around again and thought about getting the hell out of here.

Same shit, different day.

"Try not to yawn, you'll damage our rep," Jasper deadpanned as he nudged me in the ribs.

I shot him a look.

Hypocrite.

He looked nearly as mind-numbingly bored as I was.

I frowned and took another shot from the table in front of me.

"Wanna get some air?" He tilted his head towards the main bar and dance floor.

I tossed the amber liquid down my throat and smirked as the burn moved through my body. I lifted my chin in agreement – 'get some air' was code for chase some tail.

———

"We're good," I called to Sammy, my head of security, as we passed him.

I could tell he didn't agree with my assessment in the slightest, but he chose to only nod in response and remain where he was.

I knew as well as he did, that we couldn't stay down here long – the vultures would swoop as soon as they got wind of me mingling without security.

I never needed long anyway.

A tingle of excitement ran down my spine. There was just *something* about pulling some random girl out of the crowd and making her mine for the night. In my experience those girls were always so excited, so willing. I gave them my all too, but only for the night.

They knew the score, I made sure of that. It was just sex – mind-blowing sex most of the time, but that was it. No sleepovers, no feelings, no repeats.

There had only ever been a handful of woman that I'd trusted to have more than one roll in the hay with, but not for years, not since the media circus had stepped up its game.

My life wasn't my own anymore – it was splashed on every tabloid for the world to see. I didn't care what they captured, I had nothing to hide and no one to protect. That thought caused a familiar pang of sadness to shoot through me.

The fact that I had no one to share my life with was something that had been beginning to bug me; it was there, nibbling away at the edge of my subconscious. I'd found myself starting to watch couples... families... and feeling like I was missing out on something. But that was the way it went – nobody could have it all in this world, and the life I lived left no room for that kind of commitment.

"Where to?" Jasper asked, pulling me out of my own head.

I scanned the room, flicking from face to face.

Too much makeup... too fake... too drunk...

Jesus, she may as well be naked...

I paused briefly on a black-haired girl, but moved on just as quickly. She was looking right at me and I had a feeling her and her friend were talking about me like I was some kind of tasty snack.

Hell no...

My eyes landed on a petite, red-haired girl, sitting alone at the bar. Her skin looked like porcelain, and her eyes were wide as she gazed over towards the door.

Her.

"There." I pointed her out to Jasper.

His eyes followed my direction. "The red-head?" he asked, surprise colouring his voice.

I watched her cross one of her sexy, creamy legs over the other as she turned back around to face the bar.

"Yeah." I nodded, my voice inexplicably gruff. "Her."

"Well alright," Jasper replied lazily.

I raised an eyebrow at him in question, but he just smirked and said nothing.

I knew it was popular belief that I was only interested in blondes, I guess the fact that they made up about eighty-five percent of the women I'd ever been photographed with only fuelled that rumour. Truth was, I didn't really have a preference – a beautiful woman was a beautiful woman, regardless of her hair colour.

I glanced at her again and it was as though something was telling me to hurry up and get hold of her. It felt like I was being sucked in.

Like gravity.

There was something special about that girl.

I'm damn well gonna find out what it is.

CHAPTER 4

Charlotte

I LOOKED around behind me again, still searching for Hannah. We hadn't agreed to meet for another hour, but now that she knew her precious Parker Sloan was here, I was expecting her to rock in any minute.

Sell out.

It was when I glanced around that I saw the very man himself, followed closely by Jasper Jones – the guy the media called his 'wing man', and they were heading right for the very bar I was sitting at.

Mingling with the common folk, huh...

Hannah is going to lose her shit.

I rolled my eyes and carried on looking for her, but she wasn't anywhere to be seen.

I gave up and decided to get myself a little less-sober while I waited.

"Vodka tonic please," I asked the bartender, resigning myself to the fact that I'd have to sit here like a loner until my roommate arrived.

He sat the drink down in front of me and I passed him a ten as I took a long sip through the straw.

'The Mack' by Nevada blasted through the speakers and my body swayed involuntarily to the beat.

"Thirsty?" A deep, husky voice to my left took me by surprise. Goosebumps I couldn't explain prickled my skin.

I turned towards the voice, hoping it wasn't some creep I was going to have to fend off.

Ah crap...

The rock star himself...

The minute his eyes met mine, it was like a warning siren went off in my head. 'Dangerous' it screamed, 'evacuate the building while you've still got your panties on'.

He pointed to my drink and I followed the gesture with my eyes to look down at it.

Half empty already.

I laughed lightly as my eyes settled back on him. "Yeah... I guess I was."

He smiled and I found myself unable to think of anything else to say. His ice-blue eyes were looking right into mine.

It was totally unnerving.

Most people averted their gaze every now and then; it was common 'don't make people uncomfortable' practice.

Mr. Sloan apparently hadn't got that memo.

I glanced back to the entrance, looking for Hannah again, suddenly eager to get the hell away from here and the hell away from him – bad-boy rockers were not something I had the patience for right now – that was Hannah's fantasy, not mine.

Dammit... she's still not here...

I sighed as I glanced down at my watch again.

Ten thirty-five.

I saw Parker whisper something to Jasper out of the corner of my eye.

"Are you waiting for someone, sweetheart?" he asked in his gravelly voice, focusing his attention on me again.

I turned my body in his direction, stalling, still trying to figure out why he was wasting his time talking to me. I nodded curtly. "My name is not *sweetheart*, and yeah, I am."

If I didn't know better I would have sworn he frowned slightly.

What's the problem, rock star, not used to a woman who can think for herself?

I took a moment to really look at him – the man from the magazines. He was tall, taller than I'd thought – much taller than me, but that wasn't hard. His dark hair was long on the top and shaved close at the back and sides. The longer strands were flopped forward, half in his eyes. The exposed skin on his arms, shoulders and neck was golden brown and covered in tattoos, and he wore fitted black jeans, a white singlet and beat up old chucks.

I guess rock stars have their own dress code.

He wasn't at all my type, and I shouldn't have been attracted to him, but there was just something there in his blue eyes that made my stomach flip a little.

I hated myself for it.

"I'm meeting my friend Hannah." I told him, the words out of my mouth before I could figure out what had possessed me to specify that little detail.

He visibly relaxed and smirked a cocky grin like he'd had some type of victory. "Is she as pretty as you?"

I resisted the urge to roll my eyes.

Not gonna work on this girl, rock star.

Something inside my brain told me to give him one last chance to have a real conversation.

I reached my right hand out towards him. "I'm Charlotte."

He reached out and took my hand in his, an amused expression on his face as he shook it gently.

His hand felt strange in mine – it was almost familiar.

Jesus... how much vodka was in that drink?

"Are you not going to introduce yourself?" I asked when he didn't speak.

"Oh please," he scoffed, his arrogance coming off

him in waves. "Like you don't already know who I am?"

I raised an eyebrow at him and pulled my hand back.

Cocky bastard.

I would have loved to be able to say no, but I wasn't into lying, and I wasn't going to start purely for his benefit.

"Oh, I know who you are," I confirmed. "Parker Sloan – big-time rock star." I rolled my eyes.

He waved his hand in a gesture that said 'exactly'.

"Knowing your name doesn't mean I *know* you," I stated quickly, narrowing my eyes at him. "I thought that maybe you might have had the manners to introduce yourself properly, but I can see I was wrong."

Jasper punched Parker in the arm as he let out a loud chortle. "I like her," he choked out through his laughter.

I smiled and winked at Jasper.

I held out my hand to him instead, ignoring the perplexed expression of the other man. "I'm Charlotte."

He took my hand and shook it gently. "Jasper." He nodded. His hazel eyes were warm and soft and I decided right there and then that Jasper Jones was okay in my book.

Jasper was nearly the same height as Parker, but with longer blond hair on the top that he had tied up in one of those man buns, and a thick beard growing from his face. His tattoo collection also rivalled Parker's, covering every patch of skin I could see outside of his t-shirt and jeans.

"It's nice to meet you, Jasper." I screwed my nose up at Parker as I took my hand back.

I picked up my drink and swivelled around on my stool to scan the crowd again.

Relief flooded me as I spotted Hannah by the door. My feeling of relief was quickly replaced by shock.

Christ. What the fuck is she wearing?

I downed the rest of my drink as I slid off my stool. I sat the empty glass on the bar and stepped in her direction at the same moment that Parker's hand landed gently on my upper arm.

My skin tingled from the contact, and I hoped to god that he didn't notice.

"That's it?" he asked in disbelief. "You don't want to try for a night with a celebrity? You don't even want me to sign anything?" he asked with a well-practised cocky grin.

I tugged my arm from his grasp. "Seriously?" I asked, in disbelief of my own.

He just stared at me, wide eyed, apparently waiting for an answer.

Oh god... he's delusional.

"No." I shook my head, spelling it out to him. "Parker Sloan – big-time rock star, I *don't* want to sleep with you." I patted down my little black dress dramatically. "And I seem to have forgotten my pen;

so, you'll have to spot me a boob sign next time we meet."

Jasper erupted into laughter again, still watching our little encounter from behind a bewildered-looking Parker.

I laughed and shook my head as I walked away.

Men.

I weaved through the sea of people until I reached Hannah.

Oh my god. It's worse than I thought.

She had the fuck-me heels *and* the fuck-me dress on.

Don't even get me started on that makeup.

"Han, what the fuck are you wearing?" I demanded as I reached her, looking her up and down.

She had on the scantiest dress I'd ever seen. If she were to bend over in that thing the whole club would see what she'd had for breakfast.

Hannah was a beautiful girl; her blonde hair was cut into a long bob and her skin was a pretty, golden tone – not that you could see it from under the foundation she had caked on her face. She had a slim, athletic figure that didn't need to be dressed in skin-tight outfits to look good.

"Lotte, *he's* here. This is it. *My shot...* I had to wear the hooker dress."

"Friggin' hooker dress alright," I mumbled. "And tonight, just might be your lucky night," I added. "He's at the bar, and he's looking to score."

Her eyes darted to the bar like a wild cat laying

eyes on its prey. "How do you know he's on the pull?" she demanded.

"Because..." I groaned. "He just tried it on with me," I replied with an eye roll.

Her mouth fell open and her eyes bulged. "What?"

"Don't even get me started, Han, I'm not equipped to deal with his particular brand of crazy right now," I ground out.

Truth was, Parker had rattled me... he'd gotten under my skin. It was only a little, but that was more than any man had been able to achieve in the past two years.

I sent up a silent plea that the rock star wouldn't give me anymore grief.

CHAPTER 5

Parker

"WHAT THE FUCK JUST HAPPENED?" I asked no one in particular.

Jasper let out a low whistle. "You just got schooled by a mega babe." He took great pleasure in reminding me.

"Fuck," I muttered under my breath.

I couldn't figure out where I'd gone wrong. It *always* worked. I just looked at the girl I wanted and she was putty in my hands – I couldn't remember being turned down once in the past five years.

And I'm not starting now.

Not this girl.

I'd been right on the money when I'd thought there was something special about her.

Charlotte...

She was smart, sassy, beautiful, and possibly the sexiest woman I'd ever laid eyes on.

I wanted her.

I wanted her so badly I could barely think straight.

I gave my so-called best mate the middle finger and began to weave through the crowd, following after her. I ignored the groping hands and screams of my name as people began to recognise me.

I could hear Jasper calling out for me to give it up.

Like hell.

I followed the path I'd watched her take and I didn't stop shoving until I laid eyes on her.

She was standing with her back to me, those sexy damn legs on full display, talking animatedly to some blonde girl who was wearing a barely-there, pink dress, sky-high heels, and about two inches too much makeup on her face.

Cake face's jaw dropped with recognition as she saw me approaching, but I ignored her. She was just like all the other women in here that I could pull without saying a word.

I slid my arm around Charlotte's slender middle and turned her gently around to face me. Her hair brushed past my nose and she smelt so good it almost knocked me over.

She gasped in surprise before her eyes landed on me and frustration set in. She picked up my wrist like it was dirty and dropped it from her waist as she took a step away from me.

She sat her hands on her hips and smirked at me. "Rock star," she acknowledged with attitude thick in her voice. "What can I do for you?" Her full lips were painted the most alluring shade of...

Burgundy?

Fuck if I knew, but it was sexy as hell.

Get on with it, Parker, you're being a pussy.

I stared hard at her, trying to figure her out. She knew who I was; she'd said as much, she just didn't seem to give a shit, and that only made me want her more.

"Riiighht," she drawled when I didn't answer.

She pulled her friend in towards her. "So, since you're so big on introductions, this is Hannah, my friend and roommate. She's a big fan."

I pulled my eyes off her long enough to nod once at the friend and mutter a 'hey'. She looked like she'd all but pissed her pants with excitement.

Why is Charlotte not like that?

"Do you not like my music?" I demanded, all of my attention firmly on the red-haired beauty in front of me.

She shook her head quickly and her eyes softened. "No, I *love* your music."

I got a major thrill from hearing those words from her.

But then what the fuck is the problem?

"I'm confused." I stated.

She reached out and stroked my cheek gently with her small hand, sending tingles down my spine. "Poor rock star, does that happen a lot?" A smart-ass grin spread across her face.

She tugged on her friend's arm and started to walk away from me again, her friend was still staring at me with her mouth open, whilst being dragged away. If I wasn't in such a state of shock, I probably would have laughed.

I was frozen to the spot; her touch had sent shock-waves through my body that I wasn't used to and didn't know how to deal with.

"Come up to my booth?" I called lamely at the back of her head, even though I already knew the answer would be no – it was blaringly obvious that Charlotte wasn't like any of the other women I'd met lately.

Maybe ever...

"Nah... I'm good," she called back over her shoulder, giving me a glimpse of the smirk she had on her pretty face.

She continued to drag her friend over to the dance floor.

Holly? Harper? Or was it Hannah?

I looked over to the bar where Jasper was near doubled over laughing at my expense.

Bastard.

Fuck this. No one says no to Parker Sloan.

It struck me for a moment that perhaps my cocky asshole routine was what was hindering me most right now, but I pushed the thought aside. It was the only routine I had and I was sticking with it.

Some dark-haired bimbo appeared in front of me with a 'fuck me' gleam in her eye. I shifted her sideways with barely a second glance as I strode towards the dance floor – chasing Charlotte again.

There was only one woman I was interested in right now.

I caught sight of her long, dark-red hair and creamy, pale skin swaying to the music.

She had her back to me, so I did the first thing I thought of – I scooped her up into my arms and carried her off the dance floor, newlywed style, and stalked towards where Jasper was still waiting at the bar.

Charlotte kicked and thrashed, yelling a string of curse words the whole way – and I had to give it to her, the girl knew how to make a scene. People were staring, but I wasn't worried. I was a celebrity, no one was gonna kick me out of this shit hole.

"You kiss your momma with that mouth?" I whispered hoarsely into her ear as I slid her body down mine and sat her back on her feet. The feel of her body against mine... her in my arms was just about my undoing.

I need her.

Her face was flushed from all the struggling. "What the hell do you think you're doing?" she cried. "You complete and utter moron." She shoved my shoulder angrily and it was almost comical given her size.

Feisty.

I couldn't help but laugh at how adorable she was when she was pissed off.

Adorable? Jesus...

Since when is adorable in my vocabulary?

"I wanna know why you turned me down," I demanded, getting back to the issue at hand. "You know who I am, you like my music... I don't see what the problem is?" I dipped my head and crouched slightly so we were at level height. Even with her heels on she was tiny next to me.

She turned around and looked at Jasper for help. "Is he on something?" she demanded dramatically.

Jasper just grinned.

She looked back at me. "I'm serious, did someone sell you a bad batch or something?" Her eyes raked over my face like she was looking for clues.

"I don't do drugs," I growled.

She frowned like I was a puzzle she couldn't figure out.

"Okay then, crazy." She reached up and patted the top of my head like a dog. "This is my cue to leave."

Her bewildered friend had followed us over and Charlotte grabbed her hand and pulled her in close.

"Let's just back away slowly." She stage-whispered, her eyes still locked on my face.

She glanced at J. "It was really nice to meet you,

Jasper." She smiled genuinely at him and he smiled back. It took every ounce of self-control I had not to punch my best friend for getting that smile instead of me.

She took a couple of steps back, her friend reluctantly following.

"Rock star..." she acknowledged, her eyes on mine again. "It's been... *interesting.*"

I opened my mouth to reply but they turned and disappeared into the crowd before I got the chance.

What the hell just happened?

I glanced around and noticed that our security had appeared and were keeping the boisterous crowd back away from us, some of them were filming me and I knew without a shadow of a doubt that I looked like a complete idiot in those videos.

How did I not see that before?

"Well that was a blinding success," Jasper drawled from next to me as we turned our back on the cameras and faced the bar.

I smirked at him. "It wasn't a complete failure actually."

"How's that?" he asked, a grin still playing on his lips as he took a drink of his beer.

Smug bastard...

"The part where she walked away from you three times?" he asked with a laugh. "Or the part where she thought you were crazy? Which, might I add, you were doing a mighty fine job of acting." He chuckled.

"Nope." I shook my head. "The part where I got

this." I held up the cell phone I'd pick pocketed out of her bag.

Jasper raised his brows at me. "You know you're meant to get her number right, not her whole phone," he drawled.

Most people would be losing it with me right about now, but not J, he was as cool as they came.

"I had to get creative," I mumbled. "She was making me work for it."

"Ever think that maybe she just wasn't interested, man?" he asked in the most serious voice he could muster.

I shot him a look.

"Then she damn well better get interested." I murmured to myself.

CHAPTER 6

Charlotte

"I DON'T KNOW what's going on," Hannah stated, pure confusion written all over her face. The poor girl had looked completely shell shocked from the moment Parker had grabbed hold of me – and that was saying something, Han was about as un-shockable as they came.

"Me either," I agreed, squeezing her hand. I glanced back over my shoulder as we reached the door of the club, I was half expecting to have been followed again, but I couldn't see *him*, or Jasper either.

Thank god.

We stepped into the cool night air and I took a

deep breath for the first time since I'd been propositioned by a total nutcase of a man.

Crazy bastard.

I looked up at the sky and inhaled another deep breath. There were people milling around and a bunch of photographers that were probably hoping to get a shot of said crazy bastard.

What the hell happened in there?

"Charlotte!" Hannah pulled hard on my hand, shaking me from my thoughts. "What the hell was all that?" she demanded. "Parker Sloan, *the* Parker Sloan was chasing after you like a puppy dog!"

I shushed her and dragged her further down the street, away from nosey media. I rolled my eyes dramatically. "Why do you have to call him *the* Parker Sloan? He's just a man for God's sake."

Her eyes bulged as though I'd just said something totally outrageous.

"You are such a groupie." I laughed.

"I'd be *anything* that man wanted me to be," she said in a dreamy voice.

I made a gagging noise. "That's not only immoral, it's totally degrading."

"Parker Sloan can degrade me anyt—"

I clapped my hand over her mouth and dragged her further down the street. "Hannah! Have an ounce of self-respect for crying out loud."

I felt her laugh against my hand.

"If I let you go, do you think you can keep your sexual innuendos to yourself for five minutes?"

She nodded and I let her go.

"You know I was just playing." She laughed freely. "But my god, girl, how freaking hot is Jasper Jones?"

"Christ woman, keep it in your pants..." I mumbled to myself.

Hannah winked at me.

"I'm calling a cab, my feet hurt," I announced. That, and I wanted to get the hell away from there as fast as I could.

"Good. I can't wait to get all this shit off my face," she whined.

I rummaged around in my purse for my phone.

"Yeah, seriously, I'm not leaving you alone with my makeup *ever* again. I mean this in the nicest way possible, but you look like a cheap hooker."

Hannah erupted into laughter.

My search of my bag was coming up empty.

Where the hell is my phone?

I dumped the contents out on the top of a fence rail.

Mascara, lipstick, credit card...

Where the hell is my phone?

"It's gone," I told her in a panicked voice.

"What is?"

"My phone," I stated, my voice rising another octave.

Shit.

"Here." She pulled her phone from her bra and

offered it to me. "Call it from mine and we can go back to the club and find it."

I was so panicked about having misplaced my cell phone, that I couldn't even find it in me to give her shit about her choice of phone holder.

We headed back towards the front doors as I dialled my number.

I listened as the phone rang in my ear.

"Hello?" a deep male voice answered.

CHAPTER 7

Parker

SAMMY and my other security ushered us out of the low-key back entrance and into my waiting car as quickly and effectively as they could, given the situation I'd created inside. I'd messaged Kelvin to pick us up right after I'd lost sight of Charlotte. I didn't want her coming back, looking for her phone – I needed it as an excuse to see her again.

"Now what?" Jasper inclined his head towards the gold phone I'd sat on the seat next to me.

"Now I wait for it to—"

Ed Sheeran's 'Shape of You' blasted out of the phone, interrupting me. I made a mental note to change her ringtone to one of my songs before I got it back to her.

I smirked at Jasper. "Ring," I finished smugly.

I picked up the phone, 'Hannah Banana' was flashing across the screen. I swiped right to accept the call.

"Hello?"

"Oh, thank god," her soft voice sighed. "You found my phone."

I settled back into my seat. "You could say that," I replied, anticipation already pulsing through me.

"Okay... so I'll just come back inside the club and pick it up?" she asked, her voice a mixture of confusion and hope.

I grinned.

So far, so good.

"Actually... I've just called it a night and headed home."

"And taken my phone with you?" she asked quizzically.

"I can meet up with you tomorrow for a coffee and get it back to you?" I offered.

The line went quiet for a moment.

"Who is this?" she demanded.

I chuckled. "Who do you think this is?"

"Rock star," she ground out, obvious irritation in her voice "Jesus, do you have a problem with speaking your own name out loud?"

I couldn't help but laugh again. My heart was racing and excitement was coursing through my veins, all just from talking to this girl on the phone.

"Why do I have a feeling I didn't *lose* my phone at all?" she snapped.

"What exactly are you accusing me of, sweetheart?" My barely concealed laughter did nothing but anger her further.

"I told you, my name is not *sweetheart*. And you know what? Keep it," she stated angrily.

Shit.

"I'm not keeping your phone, Charlotte," I replied quickly, slight panic seeping into my voice.

"Well, then you'd better turn your off-the-charts crazy ass back around and return it to me," she half yelled down the phone.

Fuck.

I glanced at Jasper for help. He grinned and shrugged, giving me a 'what'd you expect' look.

I was torn. She seemed completely and utterly serious about leaving her phone with me.

"Might be the only shot you get to see her again," Jasper offered quietly.

He was right, she could disappear and I might never find her. The thought of that bugged me more than I knew it should.

"Alright," I agreed. "I'll bring it back."

I held the phone away from my ear. "Kelvin, back to the club," I told my driver.

"Right you are," Kelvin answered quickly, pulling over to turn around.

"I'm not saying thank you," she stated in a pissy voice.

I huffed out a laugh. "I wouldn't have expected you to..." I glanced out the window. "Where are you right now?"

"Out front."

Dammit.

I only had minutes left before we got back there and this game was all over.

"I'll give it back if you let me take you out tomorrow," I bargained, desperately clutching at straws.

She growled. "You're a sociopath, you know that, right?"

It wasn't the answer I was hoping for, but I thought I could hear a hint of humour in her voice... and she hadn't said no, so I clung to it like a lifeline.

When did I get so god damn desperate?

"You do realize you've left me out in the cold, dark night, without a phone to keep myself safe?" she asked dramatically, pulling me back from my thoughts.

"You're with your friend. You have her phone," I stated, not buying into her guilt trip one little bit.

"She went off talking to some guy." She huffed dramatically. "I'm out here all alone."

I knew the club well – there was no way she was alone, there'd be at least twenty people hanging around out front, most of them with cameras, and I was willing to bet that her friend was right there next to her... but still... my skin prickled with unease at the thought of her out in the dark night on her own.

"Stay there," I growled against my better judgment. I couldn't stop my eyes looking out the window again to see how far away we were.

Not long now.

"Ooo look!" she exclaimed. "A dark alleyway."

She wouldn't...

"Charlotte," I warned.

"Oh! There's some men down there, they look friendly... I might go say hi."

I could hear the clicking of her heels on the sidewalk.

She can't be serious...

"Charlotte!" I barked at her as we rounded the corner to the front of the club.

She didn't answer.

I tossed the phone on the seat and swung the door open before the car had even come to a complete stop.

"Parker, what the fuck?" Jasper called after me.

I leapt out of the door and my eyes searched frantically left and right before landing on her, right outside the club door, friend at her side and phone still at her ear.

She winked at me. "Gotcha, rock star," she called as she handed Hannah back her phone.

"Dammit, woman," I cursed under my breath as I prowled towards her.

She sat her hands on her hips dramatically. "Where's my phone?" she asked at the same moment I heard the first call of my name.

"Parker!"

"It's Parker Sloan!"

"Hey Parker, can you sign this?"

Cameras started flashing.

"Shit," I mumbled. "Come on." I reached for her arm, but she shrugged me off.

"Just give it to me already," she demanded.

"It's in the car," I argued.

"Go get it."

"I swear to god, woman, if we don't get out of here, you'll get trampled," I begged.

"They don't want me." She smirked knowingly.

She was right. The only way I was getting her into my car was if they wanted her too.

I grabbed her arm and pulled her flush against my body. "Challenge accepted," I murmured before pressing my lips firmly against hers.

The surprised, breathy gasp she made before I felt her warmth did nothing to ease the hard-on I'd been sporting since she'd come onto my radar. I imagined her making that very noise as I fucked her six ways to Sunday.

My hands gripped her neck and jaw lightly as I kissed her. Her lips were soft and sweet, just the way they looked.

Perfection.

Cameras flashed liked crazy behind me.

Her breath hitched as though she'd only just realised what she was doing and she pulled back abruptly. "What the hell are—"

I cut her off with another kiss, more persistent this time.

I felt the exact moment she gave in to me. Her grip tightened on my arms – before she was pushing me away, now she was pulling me closer. Her lips opened and moved against mine. I slipped my tongue into her mouth, teasing and probing hers. She tasted like lemon and vodka.

All the noise, the grabbing and the cameras fell away. It was just me and her and it wasn't for show anymore. I backed her up against the block wall and pressed the length of my body hard against her.

She moaned in my mouth and I was totally and utterly lost to her.

"Ah, Casanova... might wanna move this party somewhere more private." I heard Jasper's voice, right behind me.

Charlotte sighed into my mouth. I got a thrill knowing she was as disappointed as I was about stopping this.

I begrudgingly looked around – J was right. The crowd was closing in and this mess was about thirty seconds away from getting out of control. There was no way I was having that happen – not with her here.

I'd made a mistake coming back here without Sammy and his team, Kelvin may have been more than just a driver – I wouldn't be stupid enough to go without any form of protection in a situation like this, but still, he was only one man and there was only so much he could do with this swarm of idiots.

"Let's go." I tucked her under my arm and pushed through the crowd towards the car. Surprisingly, she let me lead her without putting up a fight.

"Parker! Who's the girl?"

"Is she your girlfriend?"

Shit.

The questions fired rapidly at us. I felt like a total asshole. I'd just intentionally put her in the middle of my media circus, and all just to get her to take a ride in my car.

Idiot.

"What's your name, honey?" some douche asked Charlotte, shoving his cell phone in her face.

No fucking way.

"Don't even fuckin' think about it. Don't even look at her," I growled. I gave him a murderous glare and he backed up quickly.

Jasper had already got Hannah into the car and he and Kelvin were doing their best to clear a path for me and the tiny woman next to me.

"Get in," I murmured in her ear.

She slid in, with me right behind her.

"And my name is *not* honey!" Charlotte yelled over her shoulder at the dickhead that had gotten in her face.

I slammed the door shut behind us with a chuckle.

CHAPTER 8

Charlotte

THE CAR WAS FILLED with silence for a moment.

Well that was intense.

I didn't know what had rattled me more – the passionate feel of Parker's kiss... or the craziness that followed after.

I took a deep breath and took a few seconds to take in my surroundings. I was sitting next to Parker, Hannah was opposite me, Jasper next to her.

Of course the rock star has a limo.

I glanced around and spotted my phone on the seat between us. I reached for it, but Parker was too quick, he snagged it off the leather and leaned back, holding it in the hand furthest from me.

"Oh c'mon," I whined. "Would you stop being such a pain in the ass?"

Parker grinned and shook his head.

Jasper laughed.

"Is he always this much of a stalker?" I asked Jasper.

He looked at me quizzically for a moment, like he was trying to figure something out.

"Nope," he eventually said with a shake of his head. "Never... I dunno what's got into him."

Honest... I like it.

Parker flipped him the middle finger, but didn't deny it as he continued to tap away on my phone.

I turned my attention back to the man causing me worlds of trouble. "What the hell do you think you're doing on there anyway? And how'd you figure out my pin?" I lunged for my phone but he moved swiftly out of the way.

"Really, Charlotte?" he asked, clearly amused. "One, two, three, four wasn't exactly rocket science. Even for me."

I blushed. "Fine. I'll change it," I mumbled. "Can I have it back now?"

"Just... one... more..." A phone rang from somewhere in the car and he grinned triumphantly. "Done." He handed it back to me.

"Did you just call yourself from my phone?" I asked in outrage as I snatched it from his hand.

He nodded, not an ounce of remorse on his stupid, cocky face.

"Saved my number for you too." He grinned.

"Did you now…" I deadpanned as I clicked on my recent calls.

I couldn't help the small smile that escaped my control. He'd saved his number as 'Sexy Rock Star'.

"You sure think a lot of yourself, huh?" I asked as I tucked it safely back into my bag and away from Parker.

He just laughed.

I glanced up at Hannah and Jasper; they were both regarding us with curious expressions.

"What?" I asked.

Jasper just shook his head in response.

Hannah raised her hand timidly. "Um, I have a question?"

"Hannah, right?" Parker replied as he slung his arm over my shoulders. It was so casual, you'd be forgiven for thinking the two of us were as close as they came, not total strangers. I considered shrugging it off, but decided it was pointless – the man had just had his tongue in my mouth, this was by far the lesser of the two evils.

Hannah nodded in confirmation of her name and blushed.

I rolled my eyes. I'd never seen my best friend blush once.

"Go ahead," he encouraged.

She lowered her raised hand. "Um… well…" She glanced back and forth between us, and then at Jasper.

He winked at her in encouragement which only made her blush more.

Huh... more blushing... interesting...

"Well... what the hell is happening here?" she finally asked.

Parker chuckled. "Here as in..." He gestured between me and him.

She nodded, wide eyed. "You're *Parker Sloan,*" she replied quickly. Her voice caressed his name like he was royalty.

I rolled my eyes again and huffed out a breath.

"And we're in your car," she carried on. "And you're looking at my best friend like she's a tall glass of water and you've been wandering in the desert for days."

Parker and Jasper both laughed and I couldn't help but join them. Han was always cracking me up with the stuff she came out with.

"And you're Jasper Jones." She turned to face him. "You know they say you're the only one who can keep him under control," she stated.

Jasper raised his brows at her. "He just kidnapped you and your friend here, right after he carried her off the dance floor and stole her phone like some kind of caveman..." He pointed out. "Does it look like I have his ass under control?"

Hannah giggled.

"I knew I didn't just lose it." I pointed my finger accusingly at Parker.

I left Jasper to do his best to explain the current

situation to Hannah, even though it seemed like he was nearly as confused about it as she was.

Parker grinned at me, again, totally unremorseful.

Shit...

When he smiled like that it caused a deep dimple in his right cheek that was far sexier than I wanted to admit.

"This isn't normal behaviour, you know that, right?" I choked out.

He laughed loudly and made an attempt to slide me across the leather seat, closer to him.

"Does it look like I do *normal?*" he asked with a hoarse voice, right at my ear.

Nope... nothing normal here...

I twisted my body in his direction and tucked one of my legs up under myself, effectively putting some distance between us.

He frowned at my obvious resistance, but sat back and angled himself towards me.

"You're crazy," I stated.

"You're beautiful," he replied.

Mr. Smooth...

I shook my head at him and tried to hide my smile.

"Do you always stalk women?" I asked.

"Do you always make men work so hard for your attention?" he threw back.

My smile broke free at that question and he grinned back at me.

Damn that dimple.

I studied him hard and finally admitted to myself that I liked what I was looking at.

Dammit...

More than like...

He's not my type... at all.

He was *covered* in ink. Nearly every visible inch of his arms and chest were covered in designs and pictures. An image of a guitar on his deltoid caught my attention.

I couldn't deny it was fascinating to look at, he was like a living breathing piece of art. All that ink made me want to explore and see what else there was to see.

His dark hair was flopped forward onto his face again. His grin was wide and easy, like he didn't have a care in the world, and his eyes were sparkling the same way that they did when he was on stage.

I would know – I'd seen countless pictures and clips of this man singing. Hannah bought every single gossip magazine there was, every damn week, and it'd become habit for me to flick through them. She also wasn't shy about her YouTube habits and was always forcing me to watch one clip or another of her latest crush.

I didn't know why he was doing it, but having him looking at me like that was making me nervous. He was intense. The man was more in tune with his sexuality than anyone I'd ever met. It rolled off him in waves that screamed 'I'll have you, and you won't regret it'.

Maybe I'll let him have me...

"Stop making those eyes at me," I demanded suddenly, shocked at the direction my thoughts were heading.

"What eyes?" He smirked.

"Those rock star eyes." I pointed at him. "Stop it."

"Make me," he replied, still looking at me in the exact same way.

I sighed. "You are bat-shit crazy, boy."

"And you are beautiful, legs." The reply rolled off his tongue, and this time I felt myself blush.

"Legs?" I asked with a frown when I realized what he'd just called me.

He smirked and raked his eyes over the exposed flesh on my legs, nearly making me shudder.

"Those damn sexy legs." He almost groaned.

His reaction did crazy things to my insides. Things I tried to bury deep, deep down.

"Ah... where are we going?" Hannah asked, breaking through the tension building between Parker and I.

I took a deep, steadying breath and tried to get my wits about me as I looked out of the window.

"Home," I replied at the same time as Parker answered, "My place."

"What?" I spun back around. "We are *not* going to your house."

"Ignore her. We're keen," Hannah interrupted quickly.

"Hannah, what the fuck?" I demanded, my new-found anger shifting from Parker to my so-called best friend in a flash.

She just shrugged at me, not in the least bit bothered by my reaction.

I groaned in frustration.

Barking up the wrong tree there...

She's a lost cause.

I looked to Jasper for help, but he was just staring at Parker with curious eyes and a surprised expression.

I turned back to Parker. "Rock star, there is no way I'm going home with you."

He just smiled, but otherwise ignored me.

"Excuse me..." I called to the driver when I realised I was wasting my time back here. "Corner of West and Donohue please."

The man in control of the car glanced in the rearview mirror to meet Parker's eyes.

Parker shook his head at his driver.

God damn rock star.

"I'll go to the press," I threatened him.

"You won't," he replied with a cocky grin.

I suddenly felt incredibly nervous. I knew he was just playing, but I didn't want to go home with him... I didn't want to risk another media frenzy like we'd encountered at the club... I didn't want any drama.

I just wanted to go home and sleep in my own bed. Alone... but he was right – I would never go to the media with anything.

I felt my smile drop.

"Hey," he said softly, noticing the change in me immediately. "I was only joking around."

I peeked up at him.

He reached out and gently stroked the side of my face. "You really want to go home?"

I nodded. "Yes please," I whispered.

He smiled and leaned in, placing a soft kiss on my forehead, completely taking me by surprise. Parker Sloan didn't strike me as the kind of guy that kissed foreheads; he seemed more like the 'screw you hard and fast in a toilet cubicle' kind of guy.

"Kelv," he called out to the driver. "Corner of West and Donohue," he repeated the address I'd given from memory.

I saw the driver tip his head in acknowledgement.

"Say please," I growled quietly and nudged his leg.

I heard Jasper laugh but I didn't look at him.

Parker stared hard at me and I stared right back.

I won.

"*Please*, Kelv," he added.

"Better."

Parker shook his head like he was confused, and ran his hand through his hair.

"What is it about you, woman?" he mumbled to himself.

"Should I be concerned you know where I live now?" I asked, ignoring his comment.

"Probably," Jasper drawled.

Parker shook his head but then shrugged. "I dunno, maybe..." He smirked. "Now I've got your number *and* your address. There's no way you're getting out of our date tomorrow."

My mouth fell open before I quickly regained control and snapped it shut.

"We are *not* going on a date tomorrow," I argued.

"Oh yes we are," he replied, totally unfazed by my resistance to the idea.

The car slowed and pulled over.

I peered out of the tinted glass.

Home.

Thank god.

"Seriously, rock star... do you understand what it means when a woman tells you *no*?"

"I wouldn't know," he replied. "Can't say I've ever heard it."

I laughed, but stopped abruptly when I realized he wasn't joking.

"What?" I choked out. "You've never been turned down?" I asked in disbelief.

"Not in the last five years," he replied in a cocky voice.

Is he serious?

"Got girls lining up to be a part of that show back at the club, do you?" I asked him, suddenly remembering that I hadn't yet made a fuss about the shitty move he'd pulled on me back there.

His smile dropped slightly.

That's right...

"Which, by the way, I never got to thank you for... I'm looking forward to seeing my face in the news tomorrow," I added sarcastically. Truth was, I wasn't looking forward to it at all – I was dreading it.

He shrugged. "It's the price I pay."

The door next to me opened and I turned to climb out. "Well, not me."

"You know I won't just give up, legs," he called after me as I stepped out of the car.

It was both a promise and a warning.

"Thank you." I smiled at the driver, Kelvin, who had opened my door, and he nodded politely in response.

I stuck my head back into the car. "Suit yourself, rock star... but don't expect me to fall at your feet like one of your groupies."

He smirked at me and I heard Jasper laugh.

"Thanks for the ride, Parker," Hannah gushed as she slid out of the car.

Thanks for the kidnapping more like...

I rolled my eyes for what felt like the millionth time this evening and got away from this crazy man while I still could.

"See ya, Jasper," I called over my shoulder as I strolled towards the doors of the building.

"Laters," he called back from inside the dark car.

I rummaged around in my bag for my keys.

Rock star probably stole them and had them copied...

Crazy-ass stalker.

The car's engine started up again and I watched out of the corner of my eye as they drove away.

"Why do I have a feeling that won't be the last I see of that man?" I groaned as I opened the door.

Hannah was virtually bouncing next to me. "Oh my god, Lotte." She swooned. "He's *never* like that with girls... he must really like you... you are totally going out with him... ugh I'm so jealous... oh my god what if you get married..." She rambled, non-stop all the way up to our floor.

"Breathe, Han... remember to breathe," I reminded her.

"Sorry!" she exclaimed. "This is just *so* exciting. You have *the* Parker Sloan's number."

I stopped in my tracks and pointed a finger at her. "I swear to god, you put a 'the' in front of his name one more time and I'm gonna slap you," I threatened.

She ignored me completely and put her hands together like she was praising the lord. "Thank you, god, my girl is finally getting back in the game. And with none other than Parker Sloan, ladies and gentlemen... what a way to come off the bench!"

I rolled my eyes and sent up my own prayer that she'd shut the hell up.

———

I woke to the sound of music blaring.

What the hell, Han?

I groaned as I rolled over onto my side and tried to go back to sleep.

The music stopped abruptly and I sighed in contentment.

It was short-lived.

The music started up again and I recognized the song as one of Parker's.

Make Me Feel Alive.

Jesus, Hannah. Fan girl: level one hundred.

Banging came from the wall to my left. "Shut the hell up, it's early," Hannah's muffled voice yelled from the next room.

Not Hannah then...

My fuzzy brain was slow to catch up.

If it's not Hannah then who...

The music stopped momentarily before starting over again.

I sat bolt upright, only now noticing the light on my cell flashing.

"Rock star," I grumbled, realising exactly what he'd been doing when tinkering around on my phone.

I snatched it up off my nightstand and swiped to accept the call of the self-professed 'Sexy Rock Star'.

"You're persistent, I'll give you that," I stated by way of welcome.

"Charlotte." His caress of my name was smooth and seductive and I'd be lying if I didn't admit it gave me tingles.

I yawned loudly in an attempt to hide my reaction. "I was sleeping ya know?"

"But it's after nine?" He questioned.

"So?" I demanded. "Me and Han have an agreement, no noise before ten on a Sunday. You and your number one hit just cost me the dishes for a week," I complained.

He laughed and the sound made me smile.

"You're a rock star; I thought you only came out at night?"

"I'm a musician, not a vampire." He chuckled.

I scoffed at him.

"So... you know my song's a number one," he stated smugly, entirely ignoring the part that meant I was on cleaning duty because of him.

"Yeah, yeah," I acknowledged. "I wasn't trying to feed your giant ego."

He barked out a laugh. "Do you know you're kind of brutal?"

"I'm aware. Do you know you have psychopathic tendencies?" I fired back.

He chuckled again. "I like you."

"You don't know me."

"Well what I do know, I like," he amended.

I sighed. "Look, rock star, what do you want? I'm not your usual M.O." I flopped back down onto my pillows. "I'm not tall, blonde, sexy and looking for a good time," I explained, just in case he was under any illusions about what I was or wasn't.

There was silence for a moment before he answered me.

"You were the sexiest woman in that club last

night, and you didn't even know it," he growled as though I'd said something to insult him. "You *are* sexy," he added in a gruff voice.

I blushed and was lost for words for once in my life.

"What do you want, Parker?" I whispered.

I heard a sharp intake of breath as I spoke his name to him for the first time.

"I want *you*... I want to take you on a date, I want to see you smile, and I want to look into those pretty blue eyes while I fuck you," he answered. "Then I want to do it all over again."

It was me that inhaled a sharp breath this time.

"And you know what I want more than any of that?" he asked, but he didn't wait for me to answer him. "I want to hear my name in your sexy voice, coming from your soft lips. Again, and again, and again..."

A nervous giggle escaped my mouth.

"So, Charlotte, how about it?" he asked, more light-hearted than before.

I paused for a beat, thinking about the consequences that this could have on my life. Parker Sloan was famous – big-time famous. I knew I'd be in the news already, just from last night alone.

Do I need that drama in my life again?

It was more than that too. He was so intense, and for some reason, that intensity was focused solely in my direction – I didn't know how to handle a man like this.

"Please?" he begged.

I could already feel my resolve slipping.

"You're killing me here," he groaned.

"Alright," I answered quietly, giving in to him. "To the date," I added. "Not the 'looking in my eyes while you fuck me' part."

He laughed loudly.

"Alright," he repeated. "That'll do for now."

———

What am I doing?

I smoothed down my jeans for the fifth time in the last two minutes.

Why am I doing this?

I'd been second guessing my decision from the moment Parker had let me off the phone. I'd accepted that I was already going to be doing the dishes for the week, so I'd gone and woke Hannah up early to tell her the news. She'd been flying around like a tornado ever since.

First thing she'd done was sit bolt upright, grab her laptop, and load up her go-to gossip websites... and there I was, with speculation running rampant.

'Who is Parker Sloan's latest squeeze?'

'Sloan carries mystery redhead across dance floor.'

'Who's got Parker Sloan going all cave-man?'

I cringed as I thought about how many times I'd seen my own face in the last hour.

Hannah was thrilled. She would have loved

nothing more than making the front page of the tabloids. She'd even been able to spot herself in the background of numerous pictures; I'd never seen someone excited about something so stupid.

I wasn't so thrilled. I'd been there, done that, and sworn never again.

Yet here I am.

There were a dozen or so videos of Parker sweeping me up in his arms and carting me off towards an amused-looking Jasper, me cursing and thrashing about. They were all over YouTube; some of them had millions of views already.

Fame is one crazy bitch.

I would know. I'd had an unpleasant brush with it.

Understatement of the century.

I just had to hope that that particular experience would stay firmly in the past.

This thing with Parker was nothing... I had no need to tell him about my past right now. If things went any further, then maybe...

Getting ahead of yourself...

It wouldn't – I was just the latest plaything for a guy like him.

I took a deep breath as I studied my appearance in the mirror.

I'd reminded Parker of the fact that I wasn't his usual type, but the truth was, he wasn't exactly my type either. I had a list – a short list, but a list none-theless, of 'boy next door' type boyfriends – blue eyes, blond hair, tanned skin, muscular and *no* tattoos.

That was my type. Right up until the last one blew up in my face about two years ago.

These days my type was more of the non-existent variety.

Parker Sloan didn't exactly fit my tastes, but the more I thought about him and looked at the photos of us together, the more I felt my preferences shifting – in the bad-boy rocker direction.

The dangerous direction.

Shit.

"It's just lunch. Stop freaking out." Hannah's voice brought me back to the present.

She was standing behind me, pulling my long hair effortlessly back and forth into a stunning, but simple ponytail.

Hannah was a fantastic hairdresser – meeting her at a photo shoot all those years ago had been a blessing. I took care of making faces look perfect, and she took care of the hair – we were a team.

"I wish you'd let me cut this mane," she moaned.

"I like it long," I muttered. "And maybe if you weren't so trigger happy with those scissors, I wouldn't be so strict."

I saw her roll her eyes in the mirror.

"Where is he taking you?" she quizzed me.

"He just said lunch," I answered. "I didn't ask."

"Well you look stunning," Hannah told me as she put one final touch on my hair.

"Thank you," I replied quietly, looking at myself in the mirror.

Since I didn't know where we were going, I'd chosen casual clothes, and I would choose shoes – either Nikes or heels, depending on what Parker showed up wearing.

A knock at the door took me by surprise.

"He's early," I stated dumbly, grabbing for my bag. "Someone must have let him through the front door."

She rolled her eyes. "Of course they did, he's Parker Sloan for Christ's sake... you wait here," Hannah instructed. "I'll text you about the shoes," she added as she flew out my bedroom door.

"Try not to eye fuck the shit outta him," I called after her. "And don't agree to anything stupid, just because he's famous."

Her laugh sounded throughout the living room.

I heard her swing open the door. "Parker!" she cried, sounding genuinely surprised.

She should have gone into acting.

"Hey, come in," she added.

"Hannah?" Parker's voice sounded confused.

I held back a laugh; Hannah looked completely different now than she had last night. She was wearing sweat pants and a tank top and didn't have a stitch of makeup on her face. She looked one thousand times more appealing than she had a mere twelve hours ago.

Silly girl.

Hannah must have nodded in response to his question.

"Oh, I didn't recognise...you look... different," Parker elaborated.

The pang of anxiety I felt, took me by surprise.

What if he made a mistake choosing me?

Hannah was like all the girls he was photographed with; tall, blonde, stunning, slim... everything I wasn't. Well, sure, I was slim, but I was short too, and my pale skin and dark red hair were a far cry from Hannah's beach babe look.

Calm your shit...you're not meant to like him anyway.

My phone chimed next to me and pulled me from my pity party.

"Nikes. Definitely Nikes... god he's HOT"

I smiled. Parker must have been in his usual jeans and chucks get-up.

I grabbed my white Nikes and slipped them on my feet, I rolled up my black jeans a couple of rounds and I was as ready as I'd ever be.

Here goes nothing...

CHAPTER 9

Parker

SHE LOOKED SO beautiful sitting there in my car. Her hair was pulled up in a ponytail, which looked so freaking good on her, but I still preferred her hair loose down her back, like it had been last night.

That wild look is sexy as hell.

I wasn't used to this. I hadn't been on a real date in years. Everything I did these days was all about my career or my reputation. I couldn't remember the last time I did something like this just because I felt like it.

There was this added sense of pressure knowing that I'd had to work hard to convince her to come, she wasn't dying to be here, and if I fucked it up, she'd just walk away and never look back.

I glanced over at her again. I wasn't being sneaky about it. I wanted to look at her – so I did.

She noticed this time and raised her eyebrows at me in question.

"I'm just looking," I explained.

"Well two can play at that game," she replied as her eyes roamed deliberately over my body as I manoeuvred the car around a bend.

I'd chosen to drive her myself, rather than getting Kelvin to do it. I wanted the privacy of being alone with her. I'd also insisted Sammy stay behind – no one was going to bother me out here.

I knew she was trying to make me nervous, but it wouldn't work – her eyes on me was enough to turn me on to no end.

"Well what do you think?" I asked, fishing for compliments.

I still had no clue as to whether or not she was attracted to me. There had been some serious heat in our kiss last night, so I thought the answer was a yes, but I couldn't be sure, and I didn't like the feeling of uncertainty.

"You dressed up," she stated, her tone smug.

I snorted. "Hardly."

I was wearing dark jeans, a black t-shirt and chucks – they were my good chucks, but I wasn't about to tell her that.

"You did." She grinned triumphantly. "Those jeans don't have any holes in them and your shoes have been cleaned."

She clasped her hand over her chest. "Parker Sloan, a man after my own heart..." she squeaked in a put-on girly voice.

If only you knew.

I laughed loudly. This girl was not afraid to take the piss out of me.

It was refreshing.

The only one I could count on for that anymore was Jasper, and he only bothered to give me a good ribbing about once a week these days. Everyone else was more concerned with kissing my ass.

She was playful and carefree. I liked it – a lot.

"So where are we going anyway?" she asked as she glanced out the window.

We had headed out of town. I didn't get to come out here nearly as often as I would have liked, but that was the nature of the beast.

"Somewhere quiet," I answered vaguely.

She nodded her head in response.

"It's pretty out here." She said after a moment of looking out at the passing countryside.

I took a moment to appreciate the trust she was putting in me. Sure, I was well known, and her friend knew she was with me, but still, she was taking a chance on a virtual stranger and letting me take her wherever I wanted – she was trusting me to keep her safe, and that was a damn good feeling.

I reached out for her hand and squeezed it gently. "Thank you for coming with me."

She looked surprised by my gesture, and a sweet smile graced her lips.

"We're going to visit someone special to me. She owns a little diner down by the water," I told her, feeling like I owed her some more information.

"Really?" She crinkled up her nose. "That is not what I was expecting you to say. *At all.*"

I felt my body tense slightly. "What were you expecting?"

I was used to women only wanting to spend time with me to gain themselves a certain status. They wanted to go to the hottest clubs, the most exclusive restaurants... they were out for all they could get. They only wanted to be with me if the whole world saw it. Charlotte didn't strike me as that kind of girl, but I didn't seem to be the best judge of character these days.

She grinned. "A posh restaurant somewhere lame, with over-priced steak and a bunch of idiots with cameras at the front door?" she offered with a grin. "This sounds much better,"

I barked out a laugh and relaxed.

She's not that kind of girl.

"You're not a fan of the limelight then?" I asked curiously.

She shook her head quickly, a flash of emotion crossing her face that I couldn't even attempt to figure out before I had to pull my eyes back to the road.

"Nope," she replied simply.

There seemed to be more to it, but I didn't ask.

"I seem like a strange choice of date considering," I said instead.

She laughed. "Oh yeah, because you gave me a choice?"

"You could have said no," I told her with my best poker face.

She gaped at me. "You're joking, right? You said, and I quote, 'you know I won't just give up, legs.' remember?"

She relayed the words back to me in a piss poor impression of my voice.

"That was terrible, legs." I chuckled, picking the nickname back up in a flash.

She laughed lightly. "Yeah, well we can't all have voices that define our generation now, can we?"

My publicist had shown me the very article that stated that very quote about a month back – Charlotte had done her homework.

I pulled into the small parking lot outside the diner, killed the engine, and twisted in my seat so I could look at her properly.

"What do you do when you're not busting balls?" I asked her curiously. Truth was, I had no idea. I didn't know anything about her. Sammy had been all set to run a background check, like he'd done with any of the women I'd been involved with, but I'd told him not to. Call me old-fashioned, but I wanted to find out about Charlotte, from Charlotte.

There was something about that fact that Jasper had found fuckin' hilarious. He'd tried to spin me some bullshit about meeting 'the one', and I'd wrestled him into a headlock until he'd stopped laughing.

Charlotte wasn't 'the one'. That shit wasn't real. Not in my world anyway. Ninety-nine percent of women – they wanted something from me, and it wasn't my heart.

Money, fame, a good fuck…

There was always something.

"I'm a makeup artist," she answered brightly. "That's how I met Han – on a photo shoot; she's a hairdresser. Now we run our own business."

No wonder she looks so good.

"That's cool," I replied with a nod. "That's awesome actually."

"Yeah, we do okay," she added with a smile.

Now that I thought about it, they lived in a nice place, a *really* nice place. They were obviously doing well for themselves.

"How old are you?"

"You never ask a woman her age," she replied in mock outrage.

I chuckled. "No, you never ask a woman her weight," I assured her.

"Meh, maybe you're right." She shrugged with a laugh. "I'm twenty-five."

She brought her hands together and twisted a large, blue stone ring around her dainty finger.

"How old are you?" She undid her seatbelt and turned to face me, the same way I was.

"Did your Google search not get my age?" I asked with a cocky smirk.

She swatted my leg. "I didn't Google you!" she cried.

I shot her a look of disbelief.

"I swear," she insisted. "Hannah buys all of those stupid magazines and leaves them all over the coffee table. Sometimes I look, and sometimes you're in them."

I raised my brows at her.

"Okay, okay. I *always* look… and you're *always* in them," she admitted.

I chuckled.

"I get bored!" she whined.

"Nothing wrong with reading a gossip mag, legs," I reassured her.

She rolled her eyes. "Just tell me how damn old you are, rock star."

There she was again, calling me rock star. I wanted to hear her saying my name, not this nickname she'd labelled me with.

"Twenty-eight," I stated. "And call me Parker."

"Ahh… he is capable of speaking his name after all," she muttered to herself.

She tilted her head side to side as she contemplated my age. "That's a lot of pressure for someone so young," she replied softly, distracting me from her prior comment.

She was right. It wasn't so bad now, I was used to it, and more than that, I just didn't care anymore. If people liked my music, then great... if not, I didn't give a fuck. But back when I started... that shit had threatened to ruin me.

"Yeah." I nodded in agreement. "When I got my big break, I was only twenty-two."

Just a kid.

"I went from performing on the street and working part-time pumping gas, to being number one on the charts virtually overnight. It was a lot to get my head around. I thought about quitting more times than I can remember. It just takes over your life... nothing is your own anymore."

I spoke to her without even realizing that I'd given her the most honest answer I'd ever given anyone. I'd been asked this question, or something similar, in nearly every interview I'd ever done, but I'd never felt compelled to tell anyone the real story, or how it made me feel.

Why her?

Jasper's words about finding the one floated through my mind and I nearly laughed out loud – that bastard sure knew how to mess with my head.

She twirled a strand of dark-red hair around her pale finger as she watched me, a small smile playing on her lips.

"How'd you get here, rock star?"

I frowned. "We took the third exit and—"

She interrupted me with a laugh. "Not *here*, here... here, as in one of the most well-known musicians in the world?"

My ego patted itself on the back at her praise, but I said nothing. I already knew Charlotte wasn't the kind of girl who had a thing for cocky assholes.

"I was playing my guitar and singing down by the shopping centre near my old place... It was the same thing I did every Saturday. I played for hours, and on a good day I could walk away with a couple hundred bucks."

I caught sight of her smile and flashed her one back.

I looked right at her pretty face as I continued. "Long story short, a guy called Trent Black heard me that day. He approached me after I'd finished a set and asked if I was interested in coming down town with him to the studio and singing that song again for the label's producers."

Goosebumps covered my skin as I thought about that day.

"I thought he was messing with me." I chuckled. "But he was dead serious. We got in his car, I played, they loved it, and within five hours of walking away from that street corner, I was signed to the record label."

"That's crazy."

I nodded in agreement. "It just doesn't happen like that, not to anyone."

"It happened to you," she pointed out.

"I got so lucky that day, I owe everything to Trent. He was my manager for three years."

She frowned slightly. "What happened to him?"

"He passed away just over two years ago. I never knew my dad, and Trent was like a father to me. I not only lost a manager that day, but I lost a good friend."

She reached out and took my hand, squeezing it softly and rubbing her small thumb up and down the side.

"That really sucks."

I nodded in agreement. "Me and Jasper get by okay, we're learning as we go."

"So, he's your manager now?" she asked, surprise colouring her voice. "I just thought he was part of your 'posse' or whatever it is you rock stars have."

I barked out a laugh. "Manager is the official term. That way I can give him money and he doesn't fight me on it... and I have someone watching my back that I can trust."

I glanced out the window and realized we'd been parked in the lot for ages.

"Sitting in my car isn't actually the date I planned," I told her quickly. "We should go inside and eat."

"This isn't it?" she asked. "And here I was, all set to update my Facebook status to tell the world what a cheapskate you were."

I chuckled. "I wouldn't do that. You'll have five thousand new friend requests by this evening."

She waved her hand dismissively. "The more the merrier, right?"

I grinned and shook my head in amusement at her quick responses.

"And besides, they'll figure out who I am soon enough anyway... thanks to your little show last night." She narrowed her eyes at me, but I could tell she was playing.

I cringed. "Pictures outside the club?" I asked, not entirely sure I wanted to hear the answer.

I hadn't heard from my publicist at all today, so whatever was being thrown around the internet, it can't have been too bad.

"Oh no, rock star. Not just pictures." She shook her head dramatically. "Video's too. Five million people have probably seen you carrying me across that club by now."

Ah shit.

"It was worth it to get you here." I smirked, playing it down. This was a normal thing for me, but I doubted it was what Charlotte normally woke up to on a Sunday morning.

She rolled her eyes. "You just want what you can't have."

"Who says I can't have you?" I muttered under my breath as I slipped out of the car.

"I heard that," she called as she met me near the back of the car.

"Really though, I am sorry about that... stubborn, arrogant and famous isn't the best mix," I admitted sheepishly.

"Hannah seemed to quite like it," she teased.

I chuckled and reached for her hand. She let me

take it in mine and I mentally fist pumped the air at the small win.

What the hell is happening to me?

I wasn't the kind of guy who did dating and hand holding... I did strip clubs and one-night stands.

You just want what you can't have...

The words bounced around in my head as I led Charlotte towards the door of the diner.

Is that what it is?

Was it the fact that this girl was the first to make me work for her attention? That hadn't happened to me in a really long time. A point I'd made clear to Charlotte in the limo last night.

Idiot.

I bet there was nothing a woman liked more than hearing about how easily I could get my dick wet.

Shit.

Holding her hand, thinking about getting my dick wet, was not a good decision. I held back a groan.

"Do you ever go back to where it all began?" she asked suddenly, dragging my mind from the gutter.

"The street corner?" I asked her, curious as to where she was going with this, and eager for a distraction from the filth running through my head.

"Yeah." She nodded.

"I haven't been back there in years," I admitted, and for some reason, I felt inexplicably guilty about my answer.

"You should," she paused, pulling me to a halt with our joined hands and focusing her big blue eyes on mine. "Everyone should go back to where they started every now and then; it helps you to see how far you've come."

For some reason, her words gave me chills.

I nodded slowly. "You know what? I think I'll do that."

"Good." She smiled, clearly pleased with my answer.

I reached slowly for her chin and grasped it between my thumb and fingers. I leant down and brushed my lips softly against hers.

My pulse sped up and my breathing became a little more laboured at the simple contact.

I was so screwed when it came to this woman.

Charlotte smiled and pushed up onto her tip toes to give me one more, gentle kiss, right on the mouth.

Neither of us said anything. No words were needed.

We walked the last few steps to the door and I let go of her hand so I could hold it open for her.

"After you."

"Such a gentleman," she gushed in a teasing tone. "Who would have thought?"

Just like that we were back to teasing.

"You make a lot of assumptions," I told her light-heartedly as I followed her through the doorway.

"So do you." She winked.

I laughed lightly. She wasn't wrong. I'd assumed she'd jump at the chance to go home with me last night, and I'd assumed I wouldn't have to work for it.

Guess we were both wrong about a few things.

She glanced around the small diner and smiled fondly, before heading towards the 'please wait to be seated sign'.

"Charlotte," I called after her, suddenly desperate to explain myself.

She turned and took a couple of steps back towards me; I met her in the middle, placing my hands on her upper arms and ducking my head slightly to look right into her eyes.

"I just wanted you to know..." I trailed off. "Well, I... this probably sounds stupid..." I struggled to find the right words.

"Well it certainly sounds stupid with you not finishing a sentence and all," she joked with sparkling eyes.

"I just want you to know I'm not here because you turned me down," I told her in a rush. "This isn't about the challenge of getting into your pants... I'm here because you intrigue me. You're different, and I haven't experienced different in a long time."

Her eyes widened slightly and she nodded. "Okay," she replied softly. "Thank you."

I slipped my arm around her and turned her to walk beside to me.

"Well goodness gracious me, if it isn't my boy come home."

I smiled wide at the sound of the familiar voice before I saw the grey-haired, apron-clad woman rushing towards us.

"Nona," I replied with a grin. "You make it sound like I never visit."

I released Charlotte just in time to be enveloped in a bear hug from the only mother I'd ever really known.

"You've got more of this doodling," she scolded me, holding me at arm's length, and gesturing to the sleeve of tattoos I didn't have on my last visit.

I guess it has been too long.

"I know, Nona, but you know how I like letting oversized, sweaty men, permanently draw on me."

She chuckled from deep in her belly and gazed at me affectionately.

It was a running joke between us. I'd told her time and time again that my tattoo artist was a woman, but when Nona got a picture in her head it was a tough job to change it.

I heard Charlotte's soft giggle at the same time as Nona did.

"And who is this?" Nona asked, dropping my arms and reaching for Charlotte.

I smirked at Charlotte's bewildered face as my grandmother pulled her in for a hug.

"Nona, this is Charlotte, Charlotte, this is my grandmother, Nona."

Nona released Charlotte and shook her finger at me. "Shhh, boy, don't be using the g-word in here, one of those old timers will hear ya." She gestured over her shoulder at a group of older men and women playing a game of bingo in the corner.

Charlotte giggled again and I slipped my arm back around her, tucking her into my side.

"Charlotte," Nona crooned, taking Charlotte's hand in hers. "You've no idea how lovely it is to meet you, dear. I've been waiting five years for Parker to finally bring a girl to see me."

"Whaa...what?" Charlotte stuttered, looking up at me. "You've *never* brought a girl out here?" she hissed at me.

Nona answered for me before I even had a chance to open my mouth.

"Well there wasn't no way in hell he was bringing one of those bimbos here to meet me, that's for sure."

I gaped at her as Charlotte tried hard not to laugh.

"Yes, I read all about you, boy, you'd do well to remember that," she told me with her eyes narrowed.

I felt my face heat. No one could embarrass me and bring me back down to earth quite like this woman. It didn't matter how many millions I made, or how many I put into her account, my Nona never changed. I was still just the little shit grandson that she'd raised and loved with her whole heart.

"I like her," Charlotte told me gleefully. "She doesn't put up with any of your shit."

"Of course not, sweetie," Nona gushed at my date.

I rolled my eyes.

Butter wouldn't melt.

"Me either." Charlotte winked at her.

"You picked a good one to bring home," she praised me, reaching for my cheek and giving it a squeeze. "She's got her head on straight this one." Nona nodded in approval.

I shook my head in amusement and shot Charlotte an apologetic glance.

"Do you think we could stay for lunch?" I asked her, eager to finish this conversation.

Nona stepped away and snagged a couple of menus from her station.

"You're in a diner, boy, what else would you do here?"

Charlotte quickly took a menu and laughed behind it.

Damn Nona...

Why did I think this was a good idea?

"You sit wherever you like, honey," she told Charlotte in her sweetest voice.

I couldn't help but smile; she was as smitten with Charlotte as I was after only one glance.

I grabbed Charlotte's free hand and tugged her in the direction of the far side of the restaurant.

"You see that you old geezers." Nona's voice rang out through the room behind us. "My boy there has finally got himself a girlfriend."

I groaned and Charlotte lost it laughing.

CHAPTER 10

Charlotte

PARKER'S GRANDMOTHER was an absolute hoot.

I had no idea what he was thinking when he'd brought me here, she'd embarrassed him for the past hour-and-a-half non-stop – but I was glad he had.

I was getting to see a side to Parker that possibly no one else ever had. It was soft and sweet and a total contradiction to the image he portrayed to the rest of the world.

I was beginning to think that the whole bad-boy persona was nothing but an act.

There wasn't much 'bad-boy' about him when he was getting grilled about wearing clean underwear and socks every day, and certainly not when Nona stood over him and made him eat all the vegetables he'd pushed to the side of his plate... definitely not when she'd scolded him for not getting a haircut more regularly.

I couldn't remember the last time I'd smiled and laughed so much.

We hadn't got to talk as much as I would have liked, every few minutes the grey-haired woman would swoop in and fuss over us, but that was okay. I was learning more about Parker than any conversation could tell me anyway.

It was clear as day that he loved this woman more than life itself. He'd explained to me that when he was born, his dad had taken off, never to be seen again, and his mother had passed away a couple of years after. His Nona was actually his mother's aunty, but she'd raised him as her own.

"Do you miss this? The simplicity of this life?" I asked him as I sipped on my coke.

He glanced around the room and then back to me and sighed. "I miss not being able to take a pretty girl out for a meal without getting hounded by the paps," he admitted, gesturing at me.

"I don't know about the pretty part, but isn't that exactly what's happening now?" I asked. "We're not getting hounded."

He studied me for a moment with a slight smile on his face.

"Not by the paparazzi anyway." He chuckled as he glanced up at his Nona, she was telling an animated story to one of the older women, and pointing in our direction.

I giggled.

"But I should be able to pick you up, walk down the street holding your hand and take you for a milkshake, or a beer, or whatever the fuck you want." He ran a hand through his hair in frustration. "But that'd be suicide," he added in a mutter.

"I guess it just goes with the territory, rock star." I shrugged.

His eyes blazed. "Do you go with the territory, Charlotte?" He reached his hand out and intertwined his fingers in mine.

"I'm not sure," I admitted quietly, right at the same moment his phone rang.

He frowned and pulled it out of his pocket, still holding onto my hand.

"Shit. It's my publicist, I gotta take this."

"Go ahead," I encouraged, letting go of his fingers and missing the warmth immediately.

Ah crap...

The realization hit me like a slap in the face.

I like Parker Sloan... a lot.

This isn't good.

I was intently watching Parker stroll across the room, phone to his ear, so I didn't miss the moment he tensed, his back to me. He slowly turned to look in my direction and I dropped my eyes to fiddle with the napkin in front of me, not wanting to get caught staring.

I peeked up at him after a few beats. He was still on the phone, his mouth moving and his eyes boring holes into me. I couldn't make myself look away from his hard glare.

What the hell is going on?

"Is that rude boy talking on the phone during your date?" Nona appeared out of nowhere, breaking the tense connection between us.

I dragged my eyes from Parker's cold stare. "Oh... um... it's fine," I stuttered. "I don't mind."

Nona slipped into Parker's seat. "I'm glad he brought you here. I worry about him you know," she told me as she patted my hand.

I blushed. "I'm glad he brought me here too," I told her sincerely as I smiled back at her.

I'm not sure he feels the same way anymore...

Parker's hand landed softly on his grandmother's shoulder. I looked up at him but he avoided making eye contact.

"I'm sorry, Nona, we have to go." His voice was curt.

He looked at me for a flash of a second and I got the message loud and clear. We were leaving... *now.* And somehow it was my fault.

He threw a couple of hundred-dollar bills onto the table when his Nona wasn't looking, and the action made me like him a little more.

Even if he looks like he could kill me...

Nona fussed over us all the way to the door,

seemingly oblivious to the tension building between us.

It wasn't until she gave me a hug goodbye that I realised I'd been silly to think she hadn't noticed.

"Don't let him push you away, sweetie. He's a stubborn fool and he could use a woman like you to keep him in line," she whispered in my ear.

"It was so nice to meet you," I replied as Parker ushered me away.

I kept my fake smile plastered on my face as I made my feet move, awkward silence surrounding us as we walked towards Parker's car.

I didn't know what had happened, but I didn't like it. I'd done nothing wrong, but the energy Parker was projecting was nothing like it had been on our way here, or during our lunch.

Not until he took that call...

My gut told me that it wasn't going to be good. I knew I'd done nothing to upset him, but the people in my life seemed to have a bad habit of believing the worst of me.

He held open the door for me, still not looking me in the eye, and waved to his Nona as he shut it with a loud thud.

I took two deep, calming breaths and hoped for the best.

He slid into the car, cool as a cucumber and started the engine.

I let the silence go on for fifteen minutes before I lost my temper.

Fuck this...

If he thought I'd done something to deserve his attitude, then he could damn well tell me what it was.

"Are you gonna tell me what the fuck is going on? Or are you just going to ignore me the whole way home?" I snapped, turning to study him.

He exhaled sharply, and just when I thought he wasn't going to answer, he replied, his voice airily calm. "That was my publicist, Nelly, on the phone. She's been keeping an eye on our little media situation from last night."

"And what?" I snapped again. Clearly there was more to it than that.

"And someone figured out who you were... seems they recognised you from a very public scandal a few years back." His voice was ice cold now.

No, no, no, no, no...

"Okay," I replied quietly, already feeling the familiar ache in my chest as my eyes began to burn with tears.

"Okay?" His voice rose and I shrank back. "What the fuck is *okay* about it, Charlotte?"

I opened my mouth to answer, but no words came out.

None of it is fucking okay!

"Stephen Miles," he hissed under his breath. "You dated Stephen Miles for a year-and-a-half?" he asked it like a question, but it was clear he wasn't looking for an answer.

I cringed at the mention of his name, and I felt my guards snapping firmly into place.

"And then you fucked him over and demanded he give you money to keep quiet." He threw the words at me, his tone laced with disgust.

I shrank further back into myself. I didn't care what he said at this point. This wasn't a conversation, this was a witch hunt.

He's an asshole.

Parker was just like all the others. Hannah and the boys were the only ones I could count on then, and they were the only ones I could count on now.

I didn't reply, and Parker didn't speak again until we were approaching my building.

I sighed in relief as we reached my street, the tears in my eyes barely held back anymore. I wanted to curl up on my couch and cry until my newly opened wounds were closed up tight again.

I'm pathetic and weak.

We rounded the corner and I saw the pavement outside my building – covered in photographers.

"Was that what you planned for me?" Parker choked out.

Oh hell no.

Shock radiated through my body and I snapped.

"Are you fucking kidding me?" I roared at him, all thoughts of being weak forgotten.

Fuck you, Parker Sloan; I'm not that girl anymore.

"Was that *my* plan for *you*?" I gaped at him as he pulled the car to a stop. The photographers started clicking, but we were relatively safe behind the dark tints of his Range Rover.

"Let's not forget that *you* pursued *me*." I jabbed a finger in his direction. "*You* harassed *me*, stole from *me*..." The tears burned my eyes. "You carried me across a bloody dance floor and kissed me in front of a bunch of idiots with cameras for the whole world to see!" I screamed.

His eyes widened.

"*You* never gave *me* a fucking choice!" I continued, still yelling in a fit of rage. "I didn't want this!" I gestured to the vultures that had somehow gotten my address.

He opened his mouth to reply, but I wasn't having it.

It's my turn to talk.

"Yes, I dated Stephen," I admitted, the tears falling now. "And it was the worst eighteen months of my life. He turned me into a shell of my former self, and the day I finally got the courage to walk away from him was the best day of my life."

"But you took his money," he hissed, still holding tightly onto the story he'd been told.

"He put that god damn money into my account without my permission." I scrubbed at the tears falling down my face. "He paid me off to keep quiet about the abuse I endured," I spat the words at him. "That man emotionally abused me for a year."

I reached for my bag. "And I didn't spend a single

cent of that hush money." I turned to open my door, completely done with this conversation.

"Then why didn't you speak up?"

I answered without looking at him. "Why would I? What would be the point? This celebrity bullshit isn't a game to me, rock star. I *hate* the limelight. It turns people into monsters." I shuddered. "And besides, no one would have believed me over him anyway... you didn't."

I opened the door and climbed out into the madness that was now surrounding the vehicle.

"You should have told me!" he yelled after me.

"Fuck you, Parker," I hissed. "You should have asked me first instead of making assumptions and accusing me." I slammed the door and shoved my way through the sea of assholes in my way.

I didn't answer a single one of the calls of my name, not even the one I knew belonged to Parker.

CHAPTER 11

Parker

I PACED THE ROOM, backwards and forwards, getting more and more wild with myself with every step I took.

I'm an idiot.

I've fucked it all up...

Charlotte didn't deserve this shit from me, hell, she didn't deserve this from anyone.

No wonder she tried to avoid me.

"Urrrrggghh!" I screamed as I punched the first thing I saw – a wall.

A fist-sized hole appeared in the plaster in front of me.

I stopped dead in my tracks and let my head fall

forward into the wall, banging it against it a few times as I reminded myself what an asshole I was.

"Wanna talk about it?" J's calm voice came from the living room.

I rolled my head to the side to look at him; I hadn't heard him come in. The guy moved like a ghost in the night.

He was sitting on the couch, where he was apparently content watching the show I was putting on.

I shrugged, not sure what I wanted anymore.

"Sit," he ordered, pointing at the seat opposite him.

I should have known I wouldn't be left alone to deal with this; of course Jasper would be here.

He always is.

I huffed out a breath and pushed myself off the wall, my fist throbbing.

"It's Charlotte," I growled as I dropped myself onto the couch, leaning forward with my elbows resting on my knees and my head hanging low.

He chuckled and I shot him the finger.

"Shut up, asshole. You were right. She's... different," I admitted.

"What'd you do?" he asked straight out – no beating around the bush when it came to Jasp.

"I fucked it up, man," I told him with a resigned sigh.

"What'd you do?" he repeated.

I threw myself back against the back of the seat. "I jumped to conclusions. Let Nelly get in my ear."

"Nelly's a bitch," Jasper replied without missing a beat.

"I know, man, I know."

"So, fire her." He shrugged as though it was as straight forward as that.

"Then what? She's the only woman around here that isn't aiming to get in my pants."

Jasper shook his head. "You're dumber than you look if you think that bitch isn't trying."

I groaned. He was right and I knew it.

"Here's a thought... hire a guy," he suggested. "A straight one."

I nodded and ran my hand through my hair. That would solve some of the issues, but not all of it. Nelly wasn't the only problem here. I was a big part of it too.

"Give it to me from the start, man," Jasper instructed.

So I did. I ran him through the whole date, picking her up, taking her to see Nona... Jasper had made a sound of disbelief at the fact that I'd taken her there. He knew it wasn't a place I'd ever taken a woman before and I had no reasoning as to why I'd changed that now, but the smug look on his face told me that he had his own theories.

"We were just eating and talking when the phone rang."

Jasper nodded, his eyes narrowing slightly.

"Nelly said that she'd been monitoring the situation with the footage from last night. She'd had about a dozen videos pulled, but people were starting to come out with Charlotte's name."

Charlotte Watson...

"She was with fuckin' Stephen Miles, man."

Jasper shrugged, seemingly unfazed with this news.

"The guy's a fuckwit," I hissed at him.

"He is. But you've been snapped with a pretty long line of crazy tramps, man... I don't see how you're in a position to judge."

Valid point.

"You know what that guy's like."

"I do," he agreed. "I know what you think of him, and I'm with you all the way."

"It's not even about him specifically," I muttered. "There was a big drama a couple of years back, around the time I had the misfortune of meeting that bastard. He had a bad scandal go down. Some girl wanted half a mil to keep quiet about what went on... so he paid, and she didn't talk. I actually felt sorry for him, for a fraction of a second, before I laughed my ass off."

Douche bag.

"So, Charlotte's the girl?" he enquired.

"Got it in one," I confirmed.

"She demand the money?" he asked, his eyes narrowing slightly.

"That's what Nelly said." I shrugged.

"You ask her?"

I shook my head, shame creeping in. "Not until

I'd pointed the finger pretty hard in her direction... accused her of planning the same for me."

"You're an asshole, Sloan."

I whipped my head up, the anger in Jasper's voice taking me by surprise – Jasper didn't get mad about anything.

"That's what she said," I muttered.

"A fuckin' blind man could have seen that girl was not after your money or your fame." He pointed a finger at me. "If anything, she was put off by it."

I groaned. "I know that now. Fuck... Nelly got in my ear and filled my head with shit... I was on edge already from being around Charlotte... I didn't think."

Damn it.

"I've swooped in and messed up her life in thirty seconds flat." I groaned again.

"Did you at least shut your mouth long enough to find out her side of the story?"

I grunted. "Not really, but she's got balls, she made me hear it... she said he emotionally abused her."

Bastard... I'll kill him... I've been looking for a good reason.

"When she got out of there he turned it all on her... gave her money she didn't want." I could feel myself getting fired up at that asshole, but more at myself for not having her back. "She said she hasn't touched it."

Jasper shook his head – at my stupidity, if I had to

guess. "Fix it, Parker, man. You'll regret it if you don't."

He's right.

"You fire Nelly," I instructed. "I'm going over there."

I leapt up out of my chair, only to be shoved back down, hard.

"Like fuck you are," he announced. "Fire your own damn publicist and give that poor girl a break."

I frowned, not understanding.

"Fix it tomorrow," he explained. "You've pissed her off, hurt her I bet. And I'd also bet that *somehow* her address got out, which probably caused a bunch of paps to camp out outside her place, am I right?"

Fucking Nelly...

"Yeah..." I admitted quickly, not used to this more aggressive side of Jasper.

He nodded. "Then you leave her the hell alone, dickhead."

Fucker.

But he's right...

I pulled my phone out of my pocket. I may not have been able to go over there, but that didn't mean I couldn't send her something to say I was sorry.

Jasper strolled across the room, back to his usual blasé self.

"Oh hey, Park?" he called from down the hallway. "Don't even think about sending her flowers... she's worth more, and you can do better."

I tossed the phone onto the coffee table in defeat.

God dammit...

I suck at this shit.

CHAPTER 12

Charlotte

"YOU'RE SO FUCKING LAZY, CHARLOTTE."

"Can't you get anything right?"

"I don't know why I waste my time."

"You're nothing to me."

"Another one of my toys..."

I woke up with a strangled scream, my skin covered in a thin layer of sweat, Stephen's words going around and around in my head.

It's just a dream.

Breathe...

It was just a dream.

The only noise in the room was my shaky exhale of breath.

"Damn you, rock star," I grumbled into my pillow.

My heart thumped in my chest at the thought of him.

Parker Sloan had screwed up, big time. But I couldn't seem to find it in myself to hate on him anymore. He'd been an ass, but I couldn't exactly blame him.

He was wealthy, gorgeous, famous and highly sought after.

Crazy is his normal.

He'd no doubt had his reasons for jumping on the defence.

Hannah had pointed out to me, once my tears had died down and her rage had faded, that perhaps Parker had also had his share of being used... and maybe it wasn't so much about me as it was about him, and what *he'd* experienced. She was pissed as hell with him, furious even, but she'd made a good point.

I shook as I thought about the hateful words that had haunted my dreams just now. Parker had brought to the surface everything I'd been keeping bottled up for the past two years.

Stephen Miles...

He'd started out as a dream, and we'd ended as a nightmare.

Our relationship had begun so well. We'd met on a photo shoot – I was doing the models' makeup and he was the new photographer on the scene.

He'd wooed me... completely and utterly swept me off my feet.

I'd thought that he was my happily ever after. I'd spent my days fantasising about becoming Mrs. Miles and having a whole bunch of babies with him. They'd have their father's blond hair and big blue eyes, and we'd live happily ever after.

Now I shuddered at the thought of that animal ever breeding with anyone, let alone me.

Six months into our relationship, Stephen had hit the big time; suddenly he was the hottest photographer in the world. *Everyone* wanted him. The money started streaming in and his ego inflated with every click of the shutter on his camera. He turned into a monster. Fame changed him; it made him condescending, bitter, arrogant and self-righteous.

It also made me his prey.

I found myself living with him, in his penthouse, with nowhere to go and no one to turn to.

I would only see Hannah on the occasional photo shoot, and never in a social setting, not without him – he wouldn't allow it. But he couldn't do much about my job; so thankfully, I still got to see her there.

Hannah and I had worked our way up in the industry and were doing well for ourselves individually. We were both working with some of the most stunning and well-known models, actresses and musicians in the world. I was busy making their faces look even more flawless than they already were, and Han was on fire, showing off the most cutting-edge hair-styles, cuts and colours.

We might not have had much time together, but Han knew me well enough to see I was in real trouble.

From the outside, it looked like I had it all.

Stephen was smart, in public he put on a performance that rivalled some of the actors he was photographing. Everyone commented on how much he adored me... how lucky I was... but at home, he showed his true colours.

He put me down, controlled me, belittled me, he made me feel worthless...

He chipped away at my self-esteem until I felt like I was nothing. He took away the fire in my eyes and left me totally at his mercy.

I endured his abuse for a year before I finally escaped. Hannah had tried to convince me numerous times that I should leave... that I *could* leave him... but I didn't have the guts to do it until that day.

To say he didn't take it well would be an understatement of epic proportions.

He'd broken Hannah's door down trying to get to me, he'd tried to have me admitted to the hospital, stating that he was concerned about my mental state... he'd destroyed the possessions I hadn't been able to take the day that Hannah had helped me run, and he'd made me fear going out in public.

It was all thanks to Hannah and my three older brothers that I'd held strong and stayed free. They were the only people that weren't intimidated by Stephen. At the time, the boys had lived so far away that by the time they'd arrived, most of the damage was done, but I knew they'd played a big part in scaring Stephen enough that he stayed away, physically anyway.

Once he'd finally realised that there was nothing he could say or do to make me come back, he'd put half a million dollars into my account and gone to the media. He'd told the world that he was being blackmailed and that I'd threatened to go public if I wasn't paid off.

He'd ruined my name; virtually blacklisted me from working, and turned the industry against me. And worst of all, he'd done the same to Hannah. He'd diminished our entire careers in one fell swoop.

He was the definition of the devil.

Hannah and I had camped out in her tiny, one-bedroom apartment, worked in bars and took out loans to get by. It weakened our bank accounts, but strengthened our bond. Not once did Han suggest we use the hush money to live off.

That's how I knew she would be my rock forever.

Thankfully, I'd never had to admit to my brothers the extent of the damage, and the scandal had died down a few months later. Hannah and I found that miraculously, there was a small, but essential group of models, actors and actresses that were more loyal to us than they were to him, and we'd slowly but surely been able to rebuild. We worked as a team now. We took on high-end clients, doing photo shoots, film production and their personal looks too, but we also operated a more low-key service from home – we did groups for nights out, weddings, parties... whatever the client wanted. It took us over a year to get out of the red and pay off all our debts, but when we finally got there, business had boomed. I'd purchased the apartment we lived in eight months ago, and Hannah had been investing her money in the stock market.

We'd fought back against the devil and won.

Stephen had moved to Paris and married some model. I'd nearly cried tears of joy when I'd heard the news. That man couldn't be far enough away from me.

Parker obviously didn't know all of this.

I liked to hope that if he did, he would have reacted differently. I'd gotten to see how kind, sweet and caring he could be. I didn't believe that he had accused me of being out to get him, with the intention to hurt me, but the issue was, he'd let someone else make him think a certain way about me, and he hadn't even bothered to get my side of the story before he'd ripped me to shreds.

That was the real problem.

Not that it matters now...

Parker Sloan would be nothing but a fleeting memory.

———

"They're all gone," Hannah grumbled as she swung open the door with more force than was necessary, a dramatic pout on her perfectly painted lips.

"What do you mean they're gone?" I asked, dropping the latest Chloe Walsh romance novel onto the coffee table with a gentle thud.

"I mean they're *gone*. I got all pretty for nothing," she huffed.

I bit my lip and tried to hold back a giggle. Han had spent over an hour styling her hair to perfection, and then forced me to do her makeup so she looked her best when the horde of photographers outside captured her leaving our apartment.

They're gone?

"How can they be gone? There were at least fifty of them out there when I'd tried to go for a run this morning."

I still don't know what I'd been thinking. I didn't run. Ever...

Certainly not on bloody camera.

Yet, something had possessed me, on today of all days, to put on my sneakers and head outside. I'd made it about five metres, gotten completely swamped, burst into tears, and retreated back inside.

"I don't know." Han pouted again as she flopped down onto the couch. "But there's not a single one of them out there anymore."

I rolled my eyes at my friend's deep seated urge to make the pages of the gossip columns.

"Don't sound so disappointed, I'm more than

happy for those vultures to piss off to the hole they crawled out of." I strolled towards the window as I spoke. "Surely their time is better spent watching for Britney Spears or something."

I peered out into the street below, not yet willing to believe that I was free.

Hannah let out a huff. "Britney Spears is old news; do you live under a rock?" she scolded me. "Sometimes I don't even know how we're friends," she grumbled.

I bit down on my lip to stop from laughing; sometimes she just made it too easy to wind her up.

"Why do you think they left?" I asked absently as I searched for any sign of a camera lens.

Hannah's answer was drowned out by a knock at our door.

I froze with panic. "You better have shut the door to the freakin' building, Han," I warned her.

Her eyes widened. "I can't remember," she squeaked.

"Get rid of them," I hissed. "Right now, Hannah Montgomery, or I swear to God—"

"I'm doing it," she interrupted me as she leapt to her feet. "Go hide," she instructed me with a hiss as she approached the door.

I dived behind the couch like some kind of ninja, and peeked out around the side.

She shook out her hair and did a little jiggle to readjust her dress before pulling the door open a fraction.

"Oh shit," she breathed as she saw who'd knocked.

Who the hell is it?

"You shouldn't be here," she told whoever it was with her best authoritative tone.

Hannah darted her eyes back over to me and I gave her a 'who the fuck is it?' look.

She shot me an apologetic stare.

"Can I come in?" the voice behind the door asked.

My skin prickled, and I knew instantly who it was.

Rock star.

What is he doing here?

I didn't know if he was here to apologise, or to try to ensure his reputation was safe... or because he genuinely wanted to see me....

Unlikely...

But I doubted Han had the willpower to keep him out for much longer.

"I don't think that's a good idea. We only just managed, by some small miracle, to get rid of those vultures you caused downstairs," she scolded him, adopting my use of the word.

I had to laugh quietly at that. One minute, Hannah was mourning their disappearance, the next, it was a miracle they were gone.

The girl has got a flair for the dramatic.

"Yeah..." I heard Parker reply. "Sorry it took me so long to get rid of them."

"*You* got rid of them?" Hannah asked, her question mirroring my thoughts.

"Yeah," he replied gruffly. "Had to promise each one of those fuckers an interview... but it worked."

I felt my mouth drop open.

"They won't bother you two again," he reassured her.

"She's really hurt you know?" Hannah blurted out abruptly. "And I'm out of this world pissed off with you for bringing that shit up for her again."

She was. Hannah had ranted and raved until she was red in the face. She'd calmed down, like I had, and seen that it was probably a genuine mistake laced with asshole behaviour, but still, she'd been fuming.

"I know," he replied quietly. "That's why I'm here. Can I come in? I really wanted the first apology to be to Charlotte."

I climbed slowly out of my hiding place and slid over the arm of the couch to sit down. I already knew she wouldn't refuse him his chance to say sorry – I wouldn't want her to either.

I could see Hannah giving Parker the stare down.

She peeked over her shoulder at me and I gave her a small smile to let her know it was okay to let him in.

"Alright..." Hannah told Parker slowly. "But you put a foot wrong, and I'll help her haul your sorry ass right out of here."

Parker chuckled lightly. "Warning heeded."

Hannah stepped aside to let him in.

The minute he laid eyes on me I knew my heart was in trouble.

I sucked in a shallow breath.

He looked like shit. It was clear he hadn't slept and his eyes were all wild and crazy looking. His signature jeans, t-shirt and chucks were in place, but he was missing that sexy confidence he usually wore like a coat of armour.

He looks worse than I feel.

I found myself feeling sorry for *him*. It was fucked up and wrong, but it was there. I cared about him already and seeing him hurt, was hurting me.

He growled deep in his throat as his eyes raked over my face.

"Charlotte," he breathed, his voice husky as he approached me.

I saw Han slip away out of the corner of my eye.

"Rock star," I acknowledged quietly.

He made a choked noise. "Should I just start grovelling now?" he asked, full-blown desperation in his voice. His eyes pleaded with me as he crouched down on the floor in front of me. "Because, fuck, I'm so, so sorry, Charlotte, I don't know if I'll ever forgive myself."

I was the biggest sucker I'd ever encountered. One look into those ice-blue eyes full of sorrow and I'd forgiven him. I wasn't going to tell him that yet... but still.

Total sucker.

"Why are you here?" I asked him cautiously.

"To make it up to you?" he said it like a question as he frowned at me. "I was an asshole."

"You were," I agreed. "But... why do you care? You don't strike me as the kind of guy that goes around begging for forgiveness."

He ran a hand through his messy, dark hair. "I'm not... fuck..." he mumbled, looking at the ground.

I sat silent, waiting for more of an explanation.

He looked back up into my eyes. "It's *you*," he said quietly, placing one of his hands on mine. "I don't know what it is about you, Charlotte, but you've got me hooked."

Me?

I have him hooked?

This conversation was not going in the direction I'd expected. I'd thought he'd apologise and then he'd probably leave. I'd assumed that this was about his reputation, not about *me*.

He must have been able to read the confusion on my face.

"You matter to me," he insisted. "And I know that sounds fucking crazy, since I barely know you, but you do...you're different from anyone I've met in a long time, and I know my life is mental, but I want to find out more about you, if you'll let me?"

I stared hard at him, my mouth forming a surprised 'o'.

Is he...?

What?

"You realise you could walk downtown and take your pick of *anybody* right?" I blurted out.

He snorted in disagreement. "That's not entirely true," he argued.

"It is," I insisted. "I saw it that night in the club."

He slid onto the couch next to me, right in close, so our legs were touching. It gave me goosebumps that I hoped he hadn't noticed.

"Okay... so where were you on Saturday morning?" he asked.

I raised an eyebrow at him. "Getting a coffee at Maurice's."

Same thing I did nearly every morning – visit the coffee shop a few blocks away.

"Alright... so if I'd just strolled into Maurice's, and offered myself up, you'd have said yes?" he asked.

I laughed softly, seeing now where he was going with this. "God no," I answered with a smile. "I would have rolled my eyes and left you to the Cindy's."

"The Cindy's?" he asked, momentarily distracted from his little hypothetical scenario.

I nodded and rolled my eyes. "Yup. They work there, I don't know their real names, but that's what I like to call them... that, or bimbo one and two."

He chuckled. "That's my point, Charlotte; I don't just want some bimbo. I want *you*."

I hated to admit it, but my insides did a flip at his confession.

I sighed. "Well... I forgive you for acting like an ass."

"It won't happen again," he promised, his eyes begging me for forgiveness.

I had to admit, I felt pretty damn powerful right now. I had a bad-boy, tough-guy here who was begging me for another shot.

"I let Nelly get in my ear.... Jasper was right, she's a bitch," Parker tried to explain.

I bit down on my lip, watching his rambling with amusement.

"She spilled your address to the paparazzi." He grimaced. "I fired her, and I'm gonna hire a dude instead... a straight one, like J suggested. These chicks, man, they're too much work," he carried on.

He was adorable when he was sorry.

"I wanted to send you flowers," he mumbled. "But Jasper told me not to. Said you deserved more than that, and he's right..."

I clapped my hand over my mouth to hold in a giggle. He was staring at his hands and was clearly uncomfortable with explaining himself like this.

"I couldn't think of what you deserved, so I pimped myself out to the media to get you your privacy back..."

A giggle slipped out.

"Are you laughing at me?" he asked as he finally stopped talking and looked at me.

"I'm sorry," I choked out between giggles. "You're just kinda cute when you're in trouble."

He let out a deep breath and laughed at himself. "I'm terrible at this shit, babe, just tell me what to do."

"*You're* terrible at it? You remember what happened with the last guy I was involved with, right?" I attempted to joke, even though it was anything but funny.

His eyes turned cold and he grabbed both of my hands in his. "I swear to god, I ever lay eyes on that piece of shit ever again, and I'll kill him for what he did to you." He spat the words, his tone full of venom.

Shivers ran over my skin at the sincerity in his voice.

"But you're too pretty for prison," I told him, my voice all breathy.

"There's nothing pretty about me," he growled as he lifted his body to hover above mine.

He was wrong, *so very wrong*. He was dark and dangerous, and rugged and bad… but he was also pretty and sweet, and kind and genuine.

I was in for one hell of a ride if I decided to keep seeing him. My head was telling me to get out while I still had a choice, but my heart was telling me to just hold on tight and enjoy it.

"You gonna fight me on this, legs?" He licked his lips and my head lost the battle.

I shook my head slowly. "Alright, rock star." I answered, resigned. "But you *ever* believe something about me, without talking to me first, and I'm done," I told him with all the authority I could manage.

"Not gonna happen," he murmured as he lowered himself closer to me.

"I'm not gonna be your play thing," I breathed as his lips lightly brushed mine.

"You're nobody's play thing, Charlotte."

CHAPTER 13

Parker

THE RELIEF I felt from being allowed to kiss her again was insane. I'd never experienced something so satisfying – and she'd barely even touched me yet.

The things this girl does to me...

I'd admitted to myself, her, and even to Jasper, that she was different.

She's something more.

There was something inside of me that had just snapped from the first moment I'd laid eyes on her. I never acted like the crazy bastard I'd been for the last few days, but here I was, begging a woman for forgiveness.

First time for everything.

She was so beautiful, so fragile. She looked like a

little, china doll, and even though she was proving to be anything but breakable, I still felt this overwhelming urge to look after her. My body was always on alert when she was near, as though she might need me to take a bullet, or push her out of the path of a rogue bus or something.

Losing my damn mind.

'Protective instincts' Jasper had told me it was. Well if that's what this feeling was, then my protective instincts for this girl were off the charts.

He'd then proceeded to sing 'Parker and Charlotte, sitting in a tree' and make kissing noises like the five-year-old he was – so I'd taken his advice with a grain of salt.

But sitting here now, with her in my arms, I knew he was right.

I'd give it all to protect this girl.

I was relaxed back against her couch and she was leaning against me, her back to my front. I inhaled deeply against her hair as I played with one of the rings she was wearing.

"What shampoo do you use?" I asked her absently. She smelt so good, but I couldn't put a name to the scent.

"I dunno, rock star, a pink bottle?" she replied, twisting in my arms so she could look at me.

I smiled in reflex to the amused expression she was wearing.

"Why?" she questioned.

"I wanna know."

She shook her head as she laughed at me. "You are the strangest man I've ever met," she informed me as she promptly jumped up to her feet.

I grabbed for her, but missed. "Where are you going?" I demanded.

She turned back and raised an eyebrow at me. "To find out what freakin' shampoo I use, you big weirdo."

Damn right.

I'm gonna buy that shit in bulk.

———

I was one lucky son of a bitch to be here – forgiven by this stunning little firecracker.

Charlotte and I had sat together on her couch and talked it all out for hours and hours. She'd told me all about her relationship with Stephen, from the emotional abuse, to the breakup and his sabotage of her career. She'd told me about how her and Hannah had clawed their way back and were now doing better than ever.

After hearing all of that, I couldn't believe that she'd been so quick to forgive the way I'd acted and how I'd judged her.

She really is something special.

I'd tried to explain why I'd jumped to conclusions and made the wrong assumptions without checking the facts first. I was almost programmed now to believe that people were out to get me – there hadn't been anybody new in a long time that had wanted to get to know me for who I really was and not just to say they knew the 'me' that the world saw.

I'd told her about how, after a little digging, I'd found out that Nelly had inflated most of the information she'd told me – she was hoping to make Charlotte look bad. She'd even fooled Kelvin into telling her the address of her and Hannah's apartment, which she'd promptly made public to anyone with a camera in a ten mile radius.

To say she was manipulative was a fucking understatement.

God knows what else she's been up to.

It was no excuse for my behaviour, but I wanted her to know I didn't go around throwing accusations at people whenever I felt like it. I also wanted to ensure that she wasn't going to set her brothers on me. Those boys sounded like they wouldn't stop short of committing murder if their baby sister asked them to.

I found myself feeling jealous of their relationship. No matter what, they'd always had and would have each other's backs. I had no siblings, but I did have Jasper, and he was the closest thing to a brother I'd ever known.

Charlotte had made a solid point when she'd suggested that I shouldn't have people around me that I didn't trust.

Trust... that was the problem.

Jasper, Nona, Sammy and Kelvin were the only

people I could safely say I trusted one hundred percent these days. I had a feeling that a mere click of her finger would have Charlotte on that list too. I'd misjudged her once, but I knew now that I could trust her.

"What about family? Or people you grew up with?" she suggested as she cut the vegetables for dinner.

I was lurking around, not being of any real help in the food prep, but not wanting to go and sit down either. I just wanted to be near her. Today was a rare, fluke day off for both her and I. I'd had Jasper cancel the meetings and studio plans I had for today, and Charlotte and Hannah had been forced to cancel their clients this morning when their apartment door was still swamped with paparazzi.

I felt guilty, but I wasn't exactly sorry about it. It'd scored me the day with her, and it was damn well worth it.

"I've got some good mates working backstage and doing some of my promotion work," I told her as I snagged a piece of carrot from the chopping board. "And a guy I've known since kindergarten takes care of my social media and all that bullshit."

"That's good." She nodded in approval.

"There's obviously the guys from the band when they're around, and my cousins insisted that they do my shopping for me... clothes and groceries and shit... but I think those girls are just looking for an excuse to go spending up large with my credit cards."

She laughed loudly. "You give them free reign on your credit cards?"

I shrugged. "Yeah, why not? It's only money, right? It's not like I'm short on it."

"What do they buy?"

"Fucked if I know." I chuckled. "But last time I checked, forever twenty-one didn't sell men's clothes."

She laughed again. "You know, it's pretty cute that you let them do that."

I bit the carrot in half. "Don't you go telling the boys about that... it'll screw with my bad-ass reputation."

She rolled her eyes and leant her hip against the bench. "Oh yeah, you're just bad to the bone, aren't you?"

I snaked my hand around her middle and tugged her flush against my body. I dipped my head down to kiss her soft, pouty lips.

She made that little sigh noise that did messed up things to my insides and I knew that this girl was going to be the end of everything I thought I knew.

CHAPTER 14

Charlotte

"I'LL DO THE DISHES," Parker announced as he rose from his chair.

"Damn right you will," I told him, my voice teasing. "It's your fault I've been lumped with them in the first place."

He grabbed my plate and shot me a grin that made my heart leap in my chest.

I watched him stroll into the kitchen, swagger in his step, and sighed at the sight.

Beside me, I heard Hannah make the same noise.

I was finally ready to admit it, the man was *gorgeous*. I was having a hard time figuring out why I hadn't gone for the dark, handsome and covered in tattoos type before.

No one does tall, dark and dangerous like he does.

"*Parker Sloan* is doing *my* dishes," Hannah hissed at me.

I rolled my eyes and carried on watching the show. I hadn't had much of a chance to just stare and appreciate. He was always looking at me.

"Mmmm," Hannah hummed in appreciation. "That is one fine specimen."

"Eyes off my man," I instructed without looking away from his t-shirt-clad torso as he reached up for something from the highest shelf.

His shirt rose, revealing a strip of tanned, tattooed flesh on his back.

Oh god, I am so screwed.

"*Your* man, huh?" Han replied with barely concealed amusement.

Parker bent down to look for something in the cupboard under the sink.

I bit down on my lip, the sight of his fine ass making me want to drag him to the bedroom and have him do dirty things to me.

"Uh huh," I mumbled to her without looking, all of my attention on the man in front of me. "I'm not even sorry," I muttered.

"Where's the brush?" he called over his shoulder.

"Try that top shelf," Hannah called back, knowing full well he wouldn't find it there.

Parker reached up again, and this time I caught a glimpse of not only his sexy back, but a sliver of his toned abdomen too.

Good god.

We both sighed again in appreciation of the view.

"No?" he called back when his search came up empty.

"Maybe under the sink?" I offered.

Hannah and I laughed lightly as he bent down to look again.

The brush was in the drawer right next to him, but I was enjoying the show too much to stop him now.

"Nope," he called back as he spun around to face us.

Hannah was faster than I was and didn't get caught making eyes at him, I wasn't as quick off the mark.

He smirked at me in that bad-boy way he had down pat. "Like what you see, legs?"

Fuck it... I'm owning it.

I nodded slowly and licked my lips in an attempt to tease him.

He stayed where he was, but the tense of the muscles in his arms and shoulders gave him away.

I affect him too.

"It's in the top drawer.," I admitted sheepishly.

He grinned and muttered under his breath something that sounded a lot like 'you'll be the death of me, woman'.

———

"I'm not gonna rush this," I told him firmly as we said goodbye at the door. "I need to spend some more time figuring out what kind of guy you are before I go giving it up."

"Giving what up?" he asked, frown lines appearing on his brow. He was leaning against the door frame, towering over me in that sexy way men did in the movies.

"You know..." I insisted with a blush.

"I don't know what you're talking about?" He shook his head in confusion.

"My... you know..." I mumbled.

"Her vagina!" Hannah called loudly from the kitchen.

Jesus.

Parker spat out a laugh and shot me a knowing smirk, his poker face slipping.

Bastard knew exactly what I meant.

"Thanks for that, Han!" I yelled back, now thoroughly embarrassed.

Parker dipped his head to look into my eyes. He lightly gripped my chin between his thumb and fingers and tilted my head up.

"I would never rush you," he promised. "I'll do my best to jump through any hoop to prove what kind of guy I really am."

"Why'd you have to go and turn all sweet?" I breathed.

He grinned wickedly.

"You were so much easier to turn down when you

were a cocky prick," I complained, my eyes still locked on his.

His pupils dilated slightly.

"Oh, babe, I'm still that cocky prick, but there's no way you're getting away from me now."

His voice held authority and promise, but not the kind to be feared... the kind to be anticipated.

I felt myself shudder under his intense gaze.

He was doing that thing again where he just oozed sex appeal. I liked to think of myself as a capable woman who was in control of her emotions, but there was something about this man that was slowly turning me into putty in his hands.

"I think you'd better go," I whispered. I was hanging onto my last shred of self-control.

"Judging by those eyes you're giving me, I think I should stay." He smirked, knowing exactly how quickly my resolve was crumbling.

I shoved him lightly, further out the door. "Not gonna happen, rock star." I grinned.

"Call me Parker," he growled at me.

"I don't believe I've ever met a Parker?" I pretended to ponder the thought. "I just met some egotistical rock star in a club." I shrugged innocently at him.

"You serious?" He huffed out a breath.

I shot him a 'deadly serious' look.

Lesson one for Parker Sloan: being famous wasn't gonna cut it.

Not even close.

CHAPTER 15

Parker

I TUGGED her into me and grumbled into her ear. "All this 'rock star' bullshit... it's all because I didn't introduce myself to you properly?"

I saw goosebumps forming on her creamy skin, and I gave myself a mental high five for gaining that kind of reaction from her.

"Mmm hmm," she murmured against my chest, and I felt some goosebumps of my own rising. "You're rude."

I chuckled. I wasn't going to get away with a thing when it came to this girl. She wasn't going to put up with a single ounce of my bullshit.

Guess this is my first hoop to jump.

"Charlotte?" I asked as I leant back to look at her.

She raised a perfect eyebrow at me.

"I'm Parker. It's nice to meet you."

Her eyes softened, and even though I thought this was a fuckin' waste of time, it was worth it to see that look on her face.

"Parker." She smiled and my name rolled off her tongue, sweet as honey. "It's nice to finally meet you too."

Jesus.

I'm so far gone.

———

I went home that night the most full of inspiration I could remember being. I headed straight for my in-home studio and grabbed my acoustic guitar.

Normally, I had to make notes on paper, work them and re-work them, over and over, just to get any resemblance of flow or structure.

But not today.

Today the words just flew out of me. The entire drive home, my brain had been filled with chords, melodies and lyrics and I strummed the tune effort-lessly now.

It was about her.

"Captured my attention... can't think straight..."

"Got me walking in circles... always handing out questions that I can't take."

"Can't explain what she's doing to me."

"Her eyes see more than what I give... cut through my facade..."

I belted out all of the words I had running through my mind.

It could be good.

Fuck it... it would be great.

I strummed the final chord on the guitar and sat there silently, breathing hard.

"Where the hell'd that come from?" Jasper drawled from the doorway.

I just about dropped my guitar in shock – I'd made the mistake of thinking I was alone.

"Shit, man. Sneak up on a guy why don't ya?" I huffed.

He ignored me. "Well? I haven't heard that before."

"Just came to me," I mumbled as I reached for my lyric book to write it all down while it was fresh – even though I knew it was all recorded.

My studio had this innovative tech system installed. It began recording the minute someone walked in the door. I was well known for having moments of brilliance and then forgetting how it went two minutes later. The idea had been Jasper's. It was the best investment I'd made for my music.

"Hell of a song," he acknowledged.

The silence stretched between us, me writing, him watching.

I was normally like a little kid on Christmas morning

when I'd written a new song. I couldn't wait to play it for J – he was both my biggest fan and my harshest critic. But this felt too private... too intimate to share with him yet.

"I take it she didn't kick your sorry ass to the curb then?" he finally asked.

I shook my head as I scrawled the words across the page. "Nah, I got a break I didn't deserve... she's something else that girl."

"You are one lucky son of a bitch," Jasper replied in agreement.

I dropped the pen into the spine of my song book and looked up at him. He had more to say – I could tell.

"Say what you wanna say," I offered.

Jasper didn't need to be told twice. "Don't fuck it up this time. You might not know it yet, but that girl is gonna be the start of something good for you, man. She's a game changer."

My throat felt suddenly dry, and I tried to swallow deeply without much luck. Jasper's words were making me feel all kinds of freaked out.

Because he's right.

"How do you know?" I asked him quietly.

"I've never seen you act like this," he said simply.

That's because I have never acted like this... ever...

"You took a girl to see Nona? That's huge... you were going to bring her home after knowing her five minutes... and not a hotel, but here... *home.* I think you can figure it out, man." J turned and began to saunter away. "She's good for you, Park... that's gonna be the best song you've written in years," he called back over his shoulder.

He was right about that too. I had a knack for knowing when I was onto a winner, and right now, I was. But this was Charlotte's song. I didn't care how many millions it might make me, it was for her – and I decided right then and there that I'd only record and release it if she wanted me to.

No matter what happens between us.

CHAPTER 16

Charlotte

"SO, I heard something about you yesterday," Kenleigh stated, totally out of the blue as I put the finishing touches on her makeup.

She looked flawless, as always, although it had little to do with the products that I'd just applied to her face, or the well-practised skill I'd used to do it. Kenleigh was just one of those women who always looked perfect. I'd seen her right out of a gym session, and she was still stunning. I guess that was why she was one of the highest paid fashion models in the country.

"Did you now?" I deadpanned. I glanced across the room at Hannah, but she was too busy creating some interesting-looking up-do on Harriet's head to notice my impending interrogation.

"Now you know I'm not one to listen to idol gossip..."

I refrained from rolling my eyes. Kenleigh was a sweet girl, but she was the undisputed queen of gossip. If there was something going on in the world, then Kenleigh knew about it.

"But word on the street is that Parker Sloan has bagged himself a sweet little red-headed makeup artist." She waggled her brows at me.

She was watching me like a hawk through the mirror as I busied myself touching up her already perfectly styled brows.

"Can I give no comment?" I answered with a grimace. The last thing I needed was Kenleigh Houston all up in my business.

She giggled lightly in that cute girly way she had completely nailed. "I knew it was going to be true," she replied gleefully. "One look at you and I could just tell."

"You're not going to warn me off him, are you?" I asked her cautiously. Kenleigh might have been a gossip, but she'd always been pretty good to me and she'd looked out for me when I'd needed it. She was actually one of the few who had stuck by me and Hannah through the whole Stephen debacle.

"Warn you off Sloan?" She waved her perfectly manicured hand at me like the idea was ludicrous. "Hell no, honey, that boy is damn fine."

I blushed.

"I heard he's crazy about you, Lotte."

I laughed. He'd certainly displayed some crazy tendencies. My mind wandered back to that first night in the club. He wasn't just crazy, he was bat-shit crazy. But I was quickly learning that I loved that about him.

"You really like him, don't you?" she mused, and I realized she was still watching me closely.

I sighed.

May as well give her something to talk about.

"I do... but we had a fight," I confessed.

"I heard, saw the pictures... watched the videos." she replied without missing a beat.

My jaw dropped. Nothing was private in this business.

"You've obviously resolved things," she prompted.

I nodded and couldn't help the smile that spread across my face. "Fine. He's won me over, is that what you want to hear? That already I'm falling in love with a man who happens to be the most famous musician in the world right now?"

She giggled again and squeezed my hand as she stood up, seemingly impressed with herself for getting the answer she wanted. "I'm off to hair," she answered with a cheeky smile. "It's good to see you smiling, babe."

I shook my head in disbelief as Kenleigh strolled over to Hannah, and took Harriet's spot on the chair.

Harriet came and took up residence in the seat in front of me. "So..." She smirked. "Parker Sloan, huh?"

I groaned.

It was going to be a long day.

———

"Lover boy is here again!" Hannah bellowed from the living room. "I'm going out, you two make me sick."

I caught sight of her grin as I hurried out to get the door.

I swung it open and there he was. *Again.* The exact same as the last four nights.

The male sex god in front of me smiled his best panty-dropping smile, the one with the dimple, and I let out a breath I didn't realise I'd been holding.

"Hey, legs," he said simply, but his eyes said so much more...

It's good to see you.

I've missed you.

That's what my eyes would have been saying if they could talk.

He turned me to total mush. I couldn't seem to remember what I used to do with my spare time before I met this man.

What did I think about before I had his ice-blue eyes and sexy smile to daydream about?

I couldn't remember that either.

Parker had only been in my world for a few short days, but he was making his presence firmly known.

I surprised him by reaching forward and wrapping my arms around his neck, landing a kiss on his perfect, cocky mouth.

His hands found my waist and wrapped me up tight like he was afraid I'd run away.

"Hey," I breathed.

He ran the tip of his nose slowly up and down mine, before lowering his mouth to kiss me again, deeper this time and until we were both gasping for air.

Oh wow.

My head was spinning, all thoughts of Parker.

His soft lips... his addictive scent...

"I missed you," he murmured quietly.

"I can tell," I whispered back.

"See? Making me sick." Han's voice came from behind me, ruining the moment.

"I'm not even sorry," Parker replied as Hannah wriggled past us.

"See you lovers later," she called over her shoulder. "Don't wait up!"

I peered around Parker's side. Hannah was sneaking off down the hallway looking like an absolute sex kitten in a black slinky dress and stiletto heels.

"Where are *you* going?" I demanded.

"Out..." she replied with a wave of her hand as she disappeared around the corner.

Parker and I had never been completely alone together. Just the thought of having no buffer between this man and me made me nervous as hell.

It wasn't that I didn't want alone time with him... I did.

God, I do.

But I was nervous. It wasn't any great secret that Parker had been with his fair share of women. One quick Google search would probably have shown me a stream of them – not that I'd ever look. Just the thought of Parker being with someone else caused a lump to form in my stomach and my throat to go dry.

I'd never been a jealous girlfriend type, but that very thought alone had made me want to punch something.

"You're nervous," Parker observed.

I wasn't aware he'd been watching me. My eyes were still fixed firmly on the spot where Hannah had disappeared from.

I tried to play it off with a nonchalant huff, but it came out as a very unladylike snort instead.

Parker chuckled and I felt the vibration through our touching bodies.

"Shut up," I grumbled into his chest.

"It's okay, baby, I won't bite," he taunted as I tried to escape his hold, my face flaming red. "Well... not hard anyway." He added the cliché statement with a smirk, still holding me tight.

I don't know why the hell I was freaking out over this.

I'd had sex before. Plenty of times... and there

was nothing to say that tonight would be the night for Parker and me anyway.

But there was this... *energy*... simmering between us that I couldn't deny any longer.

I knew it.

He knew it.

Hannah obviously knew it.

Maybe it's time to do something about it.

———

"You've never told me about your parents?" Parker asked casually as he sat his beer down on the coffee table.

We'd made dinner together, well, I'd made dinner and he'd distracted me the entire time. We'd eaten, cleaned up and now we were on the couch, listening to music and having a drink.

"Haven't I?" I murmured as I sipped on my cider.

I knew damn well I hadn't. I'd told him all about my older brothers, but I'd deliberately left my parents out of the conversation.

"You know you haven't," Parker replied softly. He was getting too good at reading me already, I don't know how he knew, but he seemed to have a sense for when something was hitting a nerve for me.

"There's not much to tell." I shrugged.

He nudged my knee with his hand, wanting me to look at him.

His ice-blue eyes were probing when I did meet them. "I'd like to hear it anyway."

"Okay..." I agreed reluctantly. "But I was being serious – there really isn't much to tell... I barely saw them growing up. My dad's a really successful businessman and my mum is like one of those Beverly Hills housewives, all glitz and glam but she's got no real substance."

All about appearances.

"They had Tyler when they were really young, and the twins when they were in their mid-twenties. I have no doubt that they planned never to have any more kids. Mum had a tummy tuck and all that nonsense. Anyway, I came along six years later, a total surprise. The boys were already being raised by nannies, so I just got added to the pile."

"That's really sad," he replied softly.

I shrugged again. "It's all good. I got a lot of love from Floyd, Louis and Tyler... we didn't need them. Mum and Dad were always more concerned with jet setting, meetings and money than they were with us."

"When did you last talk to them?" he asked. He was playing with my fingers, which he had intertwined with his as I talked.

"Ummm..." I thought about it. "I think it was when all the Stephen drama went down..." I nodded, acknowledging to myself that I hadn't heard from them since. "Yeah, Mum called to tell me that I was tarnishing their reputation and that they were both disappointed in me."

Parker gaped in disbelief and I nodded.

Yes, my parents are that awful.

"Yep. That was it. Ty snatched the phone from me, told Mum to go fuck herself and instructed Dad to go help her."

I let out a giggle. I may have had shitty parents, but I had the best brothers.

Parker laughed at that too.

"They made sure we had nice clothes and fancy electronics, but all we ever really needed was the one thing we never got... money and status can't replace love."

"They sound like dicks," Parker stated.

"They are." I grinned in agreement.

"How'd you turn out so good, legs?" He nudged me again.

I rolled my eyes at the nickname he'd dubbed me with. "You know, I do have to thank my mother for my love of cosmetics. She had the *best* makeup collection. And sometimes, not very often, but sometimes, she would show me how to use some of her stuff. I can still remember it, back when I was about eight years old, perched on the side of her bed, watching her apply her makeup with such skill. I think that was when I first fell in love with it."

Now it's my life.

"So, I guess I do owe that to her," I acknowledged.

"I wish she could have given you more, babe."

"Me too." I sighed. "But I had three oversized men-children to look out for me instead. I did okay."

Parker chuckled. "I'm intrigued to meet these guys one day."

My stomach fluttered at the mention of the future. I don't think Parker even realized what he was doing when he said things like that. It was always, 'one day I'll take you to this great little place' or 'we'll go there when the weather warms up' or 'I can't wait to teach you this'.

He was making hints at a future between us left, right and centre. And I liked it, more than was probably wise.

This wasn't reality – having every evening together wasn't how a relationship between the two of us would work. I was so busy with the business and he was an international best-selling musician who probably had tours and concerts coming up all over the world.

Shit. Tours...

That reality hit me like a slap to the face. I hadn't even considered Parker going on tour before this moment... some musicians spent months and months on the road.

Where would that leave us?

"You're panicking." Parker tightened his grip on my hand. "Do you not want me to meet your family?"

His voice sounded more hurt than I would have expected.

"No, of course you can meet them," I reassured

him quickly. "It's not that... I was just thinking about you going away on tour." I blushed. "I was thinking that I'll miss you."

His features relaxed, the tension between his eyes easing immediately and a wide easy smile graced his lips.

"Well, babe, you are in luck." He grinned in that cocky way that made him look sexy as hell. "I don't have any tours on the cards. Just some local shows and a few to fly out to, but those are only a couple of nights max... I'm over touring – it's a lonely life."

"Well... good," I answered lamely, having inadvertently revealed more about my feelings than I intended to with my previous statement.

He grinned like the cat that got the cream, and I knew I was about to get a hard time.

"You'd miss me," he boasted, sitting his beer down and leaning forward like he was ready to pounce.

"You make a big deal about this and it's the last compliment I'll ever give you," I warned him, scrambling back away from him until my back hit the arm of the couch.

"You'd *really* miss me," he carried on, seemingly oblivious to my threat.

I squeaked as he lunged, closing the gap between us. He landed with a soft thud on top of me, his toned arms holding the majority of his weight off of me.

"Admit it," he demanded, rubbing the tip of his nose up and down mine in that way I already loved.

"I'd miss you," I admitted, my voice husky.

God, I would miss you...

"It's okay, legs..." he murmured. "I'd miss you too."

———

"Arms up," he instructed softy.

I lifted my arms up in the air and he grasped the hem of my t-shirt before lifting it slowly over my head and arms, breaking the tense connection our eyes had made.

He sucked in a deep breath and I felt myself blush.

I was so god damn nervous.

It'd never been this way with a man for me. I'd never felt this... *bond* that I felt with Parker.

We connected on a level I hadn't even known existed.

"You are so beautiful," he murmured as he stepped into my body, giving me my first real taste of his skin against mine.

His shirt had been the first thing to go the minute we'd set foot inside my bedroom, and I could safely say that I'd never seen a sight so faultless in real life.

It was pure heaven. He was warm and soft, yet rock hard at the same time.

My whole body tingled at the contact and I shuddered.

"God, Charlotte." He huffed out a breath. "I

haven't even touched you yet and I'm already losing my mind."

I nodded in agreement. I don't think either one of us had ever stood a chance at resisting this.

I reached down for his belt and undid the buckle. His button and zip were the next to be undone, revealing the top of his black boxer briefs.

"Give me a minute," he mumbled, clasping my hands in his and halting my progress.

I looked up at him and nodded. I didn't know why he wanted me to wait, but I didn't care. I knew I'd wait forever if he told me to.

"Stay here, legs." He waited for me to nod in acknowledgement.

I wasn't going anywhere.

No way.

I was too far gone.

He strolled over to the docking station on my cabinet and slid his phone into it.

He hit play and turned slowly around. A beautiful, soft acoustic melody floated through the room from behind him. The sight of him walking towards me with his jeans undone and low on his hips was enough to make even the most innocent of girls have dirty thoughts.

He stopped right in front of me, eyes blazing and it was as though he was baring his soul to me.

"Is this your sex playlist?" I asked as I reached up to wrap my arms around his neck.

He shook his head softly. "No." His voice was rough.

I tilted my head back to look up at him in question.

"It's my *Charlotte* playlist," he whispered. "These are your songs."

Oh my...

I'm totally and utterly gone.

His fingers, calloused from years of playing the guitar, skimmed lightly over my skin, and suddenly I felt like an instrument. The look in his eyes told me that he knew exactly how to play me.

"Parker..." I whispered, unsure of what else I could say. He was so unexpectedly sweet and thoughtful.

And so damn sexy...

He tugged my hands from around his neck and placed them on the band of his jeans, instructing me without words to pick back up from where I left off.

I gripped the rough fabric in my hands and tugged down, his black jeans skimmed down his legs and he worked his way out of them, kicking them free. He stood before me in nothing more than his black boxer briefs and I'd never felt more aroused.

My body was shaking with desire and I wasn't even out of my clothes yet.

Parker obviously felt that it was time to remedy that situation; he reached for the band of my yoga pants and crouched down in front of me, tugging them down with him.

He placed soft kisses to my thighs as he went, sending shivers up and down my spine.

The music in the background was building slowly, making the moment feel more intimate and intense.

Nothing in my life had ever felt so erotic.

He tapped lightly on the top of my foot and I lifted it, stepping out of my pants. He repeated the action on the other foot and I complied. It was as though my body had forgotten how to function without his instruction.

I almost felt like I was his puppet – he pulled a string and I moved. Just the idea of that should have repulsed me – given my history, but I knew I could trust Parker. He wasn't Stephen – he was nothing like him and he'd never, ever take advantage of me.

Parker skimmed his fingers lightly up the sides of my legs and stomach as he stood up tall. I shuddered; just the lightest touch from him was enough to set my whole body on fire.

"You've got no idea, do you?" he murmured as he cupped the side of my face in one of his hands – the other finding its way to the curve of my back.

I leant into his touch and hummed deep in my throat.

"You've got no idea just how tempting you are, do you, legs?" His voice was low and raspy as he moved in near; he was so close I could feel the warmth of his breath on my skin.

"Me?" I murmured, more focused on his lips than his words.

"Tantalising..." he breathed.

His lips made contact with my neck and I barely managed to hold back a groan of satisfaction.

"Desirable." His lips brushed my skin again, just below my ear.

"Irresistible," he muttered before drawing the lobe of my ear into his mouth and sucking it gently.

"Parker..." I groaned. I didn't know how much more I could take. He was building me into a frenzy with little more than a few whispered words and gentle touches – I was going to physically combust when he really got down to it.

"Hold on around my neck," he instructed, his voice a murmur against my skin.

I did exactly as I was told – I gripped my hands around his neck and clung on.

His rough hands grabbed hold of my thighs and hoisted me effortlessly into his arms, pressing my core against the very noticeable bulge that had formed beneath the fabric of his boxers.

I bit down on my lip and ground myself against him – unable to hold back any longer.

"That's it, baby, just like that," he moaned.

He walked the few steps to the bed and bent down, lowering me onto the mattress.

I lay back, looking up at him. "Take them off," I ordered, gesturing to his underwear.

His eyes never left mine as he slipped his thumbs

into the waistband of his underwear and slid them down his legs.

His dick stood hard and proud, pointing up towards his belly button. I'd be lying if I didn't say the sight scared the shit out of me. I was a little woman – and there was no way in hell that third leg was going to fit inside me easily.

He's like a god damn tripod.

"Now mine?" I told him, but I was so nervous, it came out like a question.

He chuckled. "You asking or telling, babe?"

I didn't even know anymore, I just wanted him inside me – even if it was going to hurt like hell.

He must have read my mind because he reached for my underwear and tugged them down roughly – throwing them over his shoulder.

Right now, he looked exactly like the bad-boy the world thought he was.

And it's hot as hell.

He could be my bad-boy any day of the week.

He gripped my ankles and pushed my feet up towards my butt, so my knees were bent.

He crawled into the space between my legs and my heart thumped in anticipation. I expected him to press his weight against me, but he didn't – not yet. He stayed up, looking down at me with a look of pure appreciation on his face.

I felt myself blush as he took his fill of my body.

"I might have to change your nickname," he

mumbled as he pulled the cups of my bra down exposing my breasts.

"Why?" I panted as his thumbs rolled over the hard peaks of my nipples.

"I thought those sexy damn legs were my favourite... but after seeing these..."

He lowered his head down and sucked one of my nipples into his mouth before releasing it with a pop.

I whimpered from the pleasure that took a direct path to my core.

"After seeing these beauties..." he carried on. "I might have to rethink how I address you from now on." He chuckled.

I might have been all but writhing under the heat of his touch, but I wasn't about to let the idea of naming me after my rack slip by without comment.

"Hell no..." I murmured as he began his sweet torture on my other breast. "There's no way you're calling me, boobs." The words came out all breathy and unsure – not at all authoritative.

He chuckled deep in his throat. "We'll see."

He rolled me over slightly, unhooked the clasps of my bra and tugged it off over my arms before throwing it in the same direction my underwear had gone.

"But the only thing I want to see right now, legs, is me buried so deep inside you, you can't remember your own name."

Oh god yes.

I lifted my hips off the bed and pressed against him – a not so subtle hint to take me.

He gripped his hard length in his fist and gave it a few fast pumps before lining up to enter me.

I sucked in a deep breath and waited for the burn.

He froze. "Condom." He shook his head at himself. "Sorry, babe."

I released the breath I was holding with an uneasy giggle.

He leaned over me, his bulging bicep hovering right above my head as he reached for the top drawer of my bedside cabinet. He rummaged around until he came out with a box of condoms.

"How'd you know where they were?" I asked in-between placing soft kisses to the skin on his arm.

He chuckled as he nestled back in between my legs and ripped open the foil packet with his teeth. "Does anyone keep the rubbers anywhere other than the top drawer?"

Valid point, well made, rock star.

He slid the condom on and lined himself up again.

I inhaled another sharp breath.

"Relax, baby... this won't work if you don't relax." He told me gently.

"Okay," I whispered.

He leant down so his weight was pressed against me. He kissed my lips tenderly at first and then more passionately until I was gasping for air.

I felt him press against me before he pushed inside.

It was a damn tight fit.

God was it tight...

I could feel him stretching me as he slowly pushed in further.

It hurt like hell.

He let out a hiss right as I was about to tell him to stop. "That's it, baby, are you okay?"

I nodded and bit down on my lip and tears prickled my eyes.

"Charlotte?" he whispered.

I looked up to meet his eyes.

"We can stop..."

I shook my head quickly. "Just give me a second."

The burn was fading now into a much less intense ache. "Can you move?" I asked timidly. "Slowly," I added.

He nodded and kissed me hastily on the lips before lifting his hips and slowly drawing out, before pushing slowly back in again.

I let out a whimper. This was right on the cusp of pleasure and pain and I couldn't even decide if I wanted him to stop or carry on.

"You okay?" He repeated the movement again and this time it was definitely more pleasure than pain.

I nodded. "Keep going."

He did.

Parker dropped his head to my neck and nipped gently at my skin.

"Mmmmm," I moaned. That was the sweet spot.

He lifted his hips again and this time I came up to meet him.

"Legs," he groaned. "Damn, baby..."

He moved in and out of me, me meeting each of his slow thrusts, until we both came totally undone, one after the other.

———

I traced my fingertip lightly over the guitar he had tattooed on his upper arm. It was surrounded by a variety of other colourful images, but this one stood out the most to me – it had from day one.

"I like this one," I told him as I touched it again.

He turned his head to glance at it. "You like all of them." He smirked.

One hundred percent.

"I don't know... I'm not overly fond of that skull you've got on the other arm," I teased.

"Oh, c'mon, it's an old favourite."

I screwed up my nose in disapproval. "Doesn't do it for me."

He laughed lightly. "You and I both know, legs, one look at my ink and you go all mushy inside."

I placed a kiss on the guitar. "What can I say? I'm a convert."

"I knew from the start I'd sway you to the dark side," he replied, his voice cocky and sure.

I lightly punched his arm. "You damn well did not!"

He chuckled and kissed the top of my head. "Nah, you're right. I had no clue... all I know is that I've never wanted anything as badly as I want you, legs."

Oh. My. God.

"The moment I saw you, something broke inside of me, and I've got a pretty good idea that the only way I can be whole again... is if I've got you by my side."

"Parker..." I whispered. I was lost for words.

There was a damn good reason this man had won awards for his songwriting talents – he was an abso-lute master with words.

I didn't know how I felt about his confession, or what I wanted moving forward, but I knew I was in no way able to resist him. The universe had plans for the two of us – that much was obvious... and what-ever those plans might have been, I doubted I had the willpower, or the desire to stop them.

It wasn't fair really, Parker was beautiful, he could sing like an angel, he was sweet and an absolute god in the sack. The day the big man was handing out things, he got a bit heavy handed with Parker.

He smiled and my heart fluttered.

I knew what was happening here.

I'm falling in love.

CHAPTER 17

Parker

"WHAT THE FUCK is your deal today, man?" Jasper finally snapped as he roughly dropped a ten-thousand-dollar speaker to the floor.

I scowled at him.

Truthfully, I was surprised it'd taken this long for him to ask. He'd endured me acting like a prick all day.

A whole ton of shit had been grating on me today; I couldn't get a verse of a new song quite right... the media had been up my ass when I'd left home this morning... and then I'd been mobbed by a group of fans when I'd made the stupid decision to go and buy myself a coffee... but mainly, it was Charlotte that had me in this mood.

That first week with her had been like a dream. I'd promised her I'd be there every night to do the dishes, since it was my fault. And I was. If scrubbing a few pots and pans gave me an excuse to see her, then it was worth it.

By some small miracle, we'd both had clear schedules in the evenings, and we'd been free to eat, hang out and watch movies together. Well, actually it wasn't entirely true... I never had a free schedule, but I'd lived up to the 'bad-boy' rep I'd unjustifiably earned, and skipped out on any prior commitments I had. I'd brought takeout a couple of times, and other nights Charlotte had cooked for us. She wasn't as good as my Nona, but she certainly wasn't bad.

I'd relished the time I'd spent with her. It was the first time in the past five years that I'd felt somewhat normal. I was just a guy, courting a girl that he was interested in. We'd talked and talked, I'd made her blush on more than one occasion, and she'd kept me in line with her quick wit and smart mouth.

I knew things about that girl that she didn't even know about herself.

We'd spent so much time together that I'd easily slipped into a routine that consisted of seeing Charlotte, talking to Charlotte, and thinking about when I could see Charlotte again.

By Monday night I'd done my time with the dish brush and I couldn't help but feel disappointed that I'd have to give her and Hannah some space.

Tuesday I'd been fine – I was still high on seeing Charlotte.

I could picture her perfect body sprawled out on the sheets beneath me, and even though I was dying to have her again, that memory alone could have lasted me a lifetime.

I'd pumped out more lyrics for her song and perfected a section that had been sitting flat. That was the first day since I'd first laid eyes on her, that I hadn't gotten to see her in person.

Wednesday, I'd finished the song entirely and recorded an acoustic demo in the studio to give to her.

It was still in my pocket.

That was the real problem.

Seeing Charlotte.

Or lack thereof...

We'd talked for hours on the phone Tuesday night and messaged most of the day Wednesday and Thursday, but I'd quickly realised it wasn't enough.

I'd spent those days in and out of meetings and interviews. Charlotte was working. I couldn't find the time to see her, and she assured me that she didn't have the time either. As much as I wanted to sulk, Jasper had given me the hard word – or as much of a hard word as he was capable of, and told me to get on with my work. So, we'd made dinner plans for the end of the week.

Today was Friday and I'd been carrying around this damn USB stick for too long. It was burning a hole in my pocket, and the deep-seated desire I had to see her was overwhelming me more and more with each passing hour.

I was dying to give this song to her. I wanted to see her face as she listened to the words. My plan had been to give it to her after I took her out tonight.

But now I can't.

Charlotte and Hannah had been called in at the last minute to do a big shoot that they couldn't turn down. It was three hours' drive away and they'd had to drop everything and run. They wouldn't be back until tomorrow afternoon and I had a sold-out gig here in town to play tomorrow night.

That's what was up my ass.

I miss my girl.

I couldn't pinpoint the exact moment I'd started referring to her as 'my girl'. I hadn't said it out loud yet, and I certainly hadn't earned the right to claim her... but I'd thought it. And we'd be having that talk... real soon.

I growled at Jasper, but didn't give him an answer.

"You sound like a wolf when you do that." He chuckled.

I shot him a 'don't push me' look.

"Women trouble?" he offered.

"*Woman*. Singular," I corrected him.

"Oh, man." He whistled low. "She's under your skin real good," he stated, and for once his tone wasn't mocking.

"Yeah," I grumbled as I messed around with the guitar in my lap.

I felt Jasper sit down next to me but I still didn't look up. I was embarrassed for snapping at him all day and I really didn't appreciate feeling like a precious little pussy.

"Is everything all good with you two?" he asked, seeming genuinely concerned. I knew he liked Charlotte, and I also knew he really didn't want me to fuck this up.

"Yeah…" I nodded. "No… fuck… I dunno, man." I ran my hand through my hair in frustration. "I'm all messed up… this isn't me, J. I don't get all worked up over shit. I don't care if I have to go three weeks without a woman, let alone three days."

"She's not just any woman," Jasper pointed out.

"I don't even know if we have something yet. We've only had one real fucking date, and I'm over here obsessing about her… dying to see her again… writing songs about her…"

"Songs, as in plural?" he asked in surprise.

I nodded. "Drafted three more. But none as good as that first one."

"Shit, Park." He blew out a breath. "That's some serious inspo."

He was right. There had never been anything in my life that had been as inspiring as Charlotte was proving to be.

"You think I've lost it over this girl?" I blurted out without thinking. I wasn't really one for heart to hearts, but here I was, growing a vagina and sharing my feelings...

"Judging by that bottle of raspberry shampoo in your shower, I'd say yeah... maybe."

My head snapped up at his statement. "Jesus," I muttered. "What the fuck has a guy gotta do to get some damn privacy around here?"

Jasper shrugged, not in the least bit sorry; in fact, his gold eyes were amused. "My plumbing was out."

"Dude, you know I've got a guest bathroom, right?"

He shrugged again, still not giving a single fuck. "Your shower has that big double jet." He gave an appreciative moan.

I mumbled a string of curse words that had him grinning like a loon.

Jasper lived in the house next door. When we weren't touring, we needed to be able to meet without the inconvenience of press, media and fans hounding us. We'd tried living together, but I needed the space. J had rented a place across town, but it was just a pain in the ass. In the end, I'd brought the house next to mine, and told him it was a perk of the job. It made it easier for security too. These days, Jasper was nearly as much of a hot commodity as I was. He had his own stream of loyal followers that were as bat-shit crazy and unpredictable as mine. Sammy lived downstairs in my house – I'd had it set up as a self-contained unit, and he was able to keep a pretty good eye on Jasper's property too.

Jasper wasn't exactly known for his self-preservation skills, and he'd refused to have live-in security – so having Sammy close and monitoring his security system was the best I could do.

Jasper had tried to buy his place from me numerous times, but I'd ignored him. It wasn't that he couldn't afford it; I just had more money than I could spend and he was the closest thing to a brother that I had; I didn't want his money.

We'd had a gate put in between the houses, and it was perfect – except when Jasper decided to use my shower.

"So, do you jerk off with that shit or what?" he asked so casually you'd think he was asking about the weather.

Christ.

I'd be lying if I said I hadn't thought about it.

I stood up and sat my guitar in its stand with a little more force than was necessary. "I'm done with this conversation." I announced.

Jasper just chuckled.

"Get me two side stage, V.I.P. passes, J," I called over my shoulder, my plan spurring into life in my head again.

If I couldn't go to Charlotte, I was gonna bring her to me.

"Too easy," he drawled.

"And call a fucking plumber," I added with a growl.

CHAPTER 18

Charlotte

WE'D BEEN HOME all of thirty seconds when the buzzer sounded.

Hannah was the closest to the intercom.

"Hello?" she answered through the speaker on the wall.

"Yes, hello, I have a delivery here for a Miss Watson?"

"Come on up," Hannah replied, holding down the release buzzer for the front door of the building.

She looked expectantly at me.

I shrugged. "I got that last shipment of makeup... I haven't ordered anything else."

My phone dinged in my bag at the same time the knock came at the door.

"Be me," I told Hannah as I rummaged in my oversized bag for my phone.

I heard Hannah making small talk with the delivery guy and then the door shut.

I finally located my phone along with the kitchen sink and hurriedly checked it.

The message was from Parker, and just the sight of his name made my heart flutter.

"Going in for sound check... I've been thinking about you all day. Please come? I'm going crazy without you, legs."

I frowned at the screen. "Come to what?" I thought aloud.

Hannah's squeal stole my attention. "His fucking concert, baby!" she shrieked.

I spun around to face her. She'd ripped open the box and was bouncing up and down holding some sort of pass on a long cord.

"You're shitting me." I gaped as I made a beeline for her and what she was holding.

"Nope!" she shrieked again, cuddling the piece of plastic to her chest like it was her most prized possession. "Side stage... V.I.P. passes." She swooned.

I reached for the pass that Hannah didn't have in a death grip and stroked the silky plastic.

Oh, he's good.

I grinned to myself. "Very slick, Mr. Sloan," I muttered under my breath as I caught sight of a note that Hannah had obviously overlooked in her excitement.

I unfolded it and the sight of the manly script did strange things to my belly. I could almost imagine Parker, leaning over, pad resting on his knee, his calloused hands scrawling away.

"Charlotte,

I'm sorry I couldn't get these to you myself, but you have them now.

I want you to come and watch me perform, babe... hell; I'm dying to see you standing on the side of that stage.

J will look out for you.

There's a car coming for you at six.

– P"

My mouth fell open and I thrust the note towards Han.

I rushed across the room and swiped my phone off the hall table.

I messaged him as fast as I could.

"I can't believe you did that... thank you, I can't wait to see you sing."

His reply was almost instantaneous.

"It's nothing. But I do have a few surprises for you tonight..."

I grinned like crazy reading his reply. The little dots appeared at the bottom of the screen and I waited to see what else he might say.

"Fuck... I gotta go. See you at the show, legs x"

I was elated. At the risk of sounding a bit like a fan girl, I was so pumped to see Parker perform live. He was an amazing singer, and I knew the magnetism he possessed would make for an electric performance.

"I don't think I've ever loved you as much as I love you right now." Hannah's voice pulled me from thoughts of Parker on stage.

I laughed at her, she was practically radiating delight.

"A *Parker Sloan* concert," she squeaked.

"Down girl," I warned her. "We can't have you humping anyone's leg."

She threw a wadded-up bit of paper at me. "I make no promises."

I shook my head and laughed. Thanks to Parker, this was definitely going to be a night to remember.

———

"You ladies can watch from right here." Jasper gestured to the most prime location this place had. We were side of stage and the view of Parker would be completely unobstructed.

"Thanks, Jasper, we really appreciate the tour," I told him with a smile. Hannah had appreciated the tour a little more than me, but still, I'd loved every minute of seeing where the magic happened.

The only place we didn't go was into Parker or the band's dressing rooms. Part of me was disappointed, but the other part of me was content with the slow burn of desire building within me. I had a feeling that seeing him up on that stage was going to send me into overdrive.

"Pleasure," Jasper drawled in a thick, fake southern accent and tipped an invisible hat in our direction. "And Park would kick my ass if I didn't give you two the royal treatment," he added with a cheeky smirk.

He was dead on about the royal treatment.

Parker hadn't been kidding when he said a car would pick us up at six. Six on the dot, the buzzer had sounded and a dapper-looking gentleman had appeared at our door.

A glossy black limo had been waiting for us outside and Hannah had nearly lost her shit, she was so excited.

I'd assumed we were going straight to the venue, but I'd been mistaken. A note from Parker sat inside the car, a single red rose with it.

"Hey baby,

I'm impressed you got in this car willingly, wasn't so easy the last time.

Dinner's on me.

Eat, drink, relax...

I'll see you soon.

– P"

I'd snorted out a very unladylike laugh at the memory he was referring to.

We were treated to a dinner at the most exclusive and expensive restaurant in town. We had wait staff at our beck and call, and nothing was off limits. Our waiter had even been instructed by Mr. Sloan himself that we were to have nothing but the very best.

I felt like a princess.

Two bodyguards had escorted us from the car, into the back entrance of the venue, and we'd been informed that they would be our shadows for the night.

I'd let out a disbelieving laugh, but Jasper hadn't thought it was too funny.

"I swear to god, Charlotte, I can't deal with him right now, I know damn well you don't need a shadow to go take a piss, but try telling him that," Jasper had told me, utter exasperation on his face.

I'd held up my fingers in scouts honour and promised not to give hulk one and two the slip.

Parker must have been one scary bastard when he wanted to be, because the look of relief on Jasper's face was palpable.

And then, here we were. In a position hundreds of thousands of women, and probably a hell of a lot of men, would kill to be in.

The noise of the crowd drew me in and I couldn't resist any longer. I peeked out of the alcove and gasped at the sight in front of me. There were more people out there than I'd ever seen in one place. My eyes bulged.

How the hell does he deal with that?

"What happens now?" Hannah asked Jasper excitedly.

I pulled back away from the madness in front of me.

Jasper flicked his wrist to check the time. "In about... two minutes, I'll go out there and introduce your boy." He winked at me as he said the last part and I felt myself blush slightly.

Parker's not mine... is he?

My mind spun with the possibilities.

Jasper carried on, oblivious to my brain explosion. "He's got the band up there with him tonight, so he'll work the crowd, introduce the guys, and then smash the shit out of those tunes we all love so much."

I giggled. Jasper was a funny guy. A bit quirky... incredibly chilled... I liked him. I could see us being friends, given the chance. I could also see him and Hannah being a problem. I didn't miss the little looks he was shooting her every few minutes.

I got it.

Totally got it.

Hannah was a knockout. She'd taken my advice and calmed the hell down with her outfit choices. Tonight, she'd gone with a pair of black skinny jeans that were so tight they looked like they were painted on, sky-high black heels and a white spaghetti-strap camisole. Her hair was styled into a sleek bob, and her makeup was smoky and seductive.

She looked smoking hot. Jasper would have to be blind not to notice.

I already had the two of them pinned as a one-night stand ending in disaster.

But hell, what do I know...

I glanced around the stage again. There were crew members, dressed all in black, darting around all over the place. They moved like a well-oiled machine.

"Mikey!" Jasper called to one of them. "Sort that fuckin' loose cable out man, you break Park's neck and I'll have to kill you."

The man quickly complied. I hadn't even noticed the hazard. Jasper was obviously not as blasé and oblivious as he liked to make out. He barked out a few more orders about things I never would have even considered an issue.

I was impressed.

I was about to tell him as much, when I felt eyes on me.

Parker...

I turned to search for him, but came up empty. Parker was there somewhere though, I just knew it.

Jasper clapped his hands together loudly, causing me to jump slightly. "Show time, ladies."

And just like that, he sauntered out onto the stage, the light following him as though it was some perfectly synchronized routine.

I guess it is...

The noise that followed was deafening. I couldn't even imagine how loud it would be when the crowd caught sight of Parker.

"Good evening, beautiful people," Jasper drawled

into the mic in the centre of the stage. "How we all doing tonight?"

The crowd screamed and yelled until they all blended into one.

"Holy hell," Hannah muttered in my ear.

I nodded in agreement.

"I'm gonna get me a piece of that fine ass, if it's the last thing I do," she half yelled, so I could hear over the roar of the crowd – her eyes fixed firmly on Jasper.

Called it.... totally called it.

I shot her a look of indifference.

If Han wanted to get it on with Jasper, chances are, she would. Hannah was a girl who got what she wanted ninety percent of the time.

The crowd had begun chanting Parker's name, at the request of Jasper.

"Alright, alright." Jasper chuckled. "Here he is... ladies and gents... Paaarrrrkeeeerr Slllloooooaaannn." He drew out his name like a boxing announcer does and I couldn't help the goosebumps that broke out over my skin.

Parker stepped out onto the stage, black jeans, white singlet and his guitar slung over his back. His hair was dishevelled, like he'd been running his hand through it, and I'd never seen someone look so utterly appealing. It took everything I had in me not to run out onto that stage and lick him all over.

"Parker!" a woman screamed so loud it made me cringe.

"Parker Sloan." Hannah shook her head with a look of disbelief.

"Rock star," I breathed.

He turned as though he'd heard me, and shot me the most breath-taking smile I'd ever received.

I nearly staggered backwards.

He's so beautiful.

I don't know how I hadn't seen it before. This man was perfection. Pure sex and sin rolled into a delicious package.

I must have been doing a terrible job of keeping my thoughts off my face, because he shot me a knowing smirk before turning his attention back to the crowd, bumping fists with Jasper and stepping up to the mic.

The rest was a blur. I had no clue what song he sang first, or what the drummer's name was. I couldn't tell you if I sang along, or just stood with my mouth hanging open.

Watching that man sing was like foreplay. I wanted him so badly I couldn't even focus.

But even I didn't miss when he switched things up.

CHAPTER 19

Parker

I HAVE THIS TRADITION... at all of my shows; I
get a girl up on stage and sing her a song – 'Blue Eyed
Girl'. I've done it from day one, my very first show,
and continued to do it, even when that little punk
Justin Bieber started asking if anyone wanted to be
his baby.

Douche.

Every show, this part was the same. Someone,
usually J, would pluck a girl out of the crowd, bring
her up on the stage, and I'd sing her the song about
the blue-eyed girl. It didn't matter what colour eyes
she had, that girl *always* turned to mush.

Tonight, was the first time in five years, and over
four hundred shows, that I wouldn't be pulling a

random girl from the crowd. It was also the first time I wouldn't sing 'Blue Eyed Girl', which was ironic really, because I knew the girl I'd be singing to had the most beautiful blue eyes.

I gave Jasper the nod. He was side stage, keeping an eye on Charlotte and Hannah for me.

He nodded back with a grin.

I knew I could count on J.

I'd given him strict instructions, and so far, he'd complied.

Number one: They weren't to go anywhere without protection – if Charlotte went *anywhere* then one of Sammy's guys went with her. No exceptions. I don't think I would have been able to concentrate on the music if I'd been worrying about her getting caught up in any of this madness.

Number two: He was the only person to get them drinks. I didn't trust anyone working those bars, and I'd brought in a selection of drinks, just for the girls.

Number three: He had to help me get Charlotte on stage, even if it meant throwing her over his shoulder and carrying her out here to me.

I was seriously hoping it wouldn't come to that. I wasn't sure I had it in me to watch his hands on her tight body without causing a scene.

I sat down on the front of the stage, my legs dangling over the edge. "Now I know there's something I usually do about now..." I trailed off as the crowd started screaming for me to pick them.

The beast was in full force this evening.

"But I'm not gonna do that tonight." I broke it to them with a grimace.

The crowd went eerily silent for a moment, before the groans of disappointment rang out.

I chuckled. "You all want me to be happy, right?" I winked at the mass of bodies.

A chorus of suggestions like 'I'll make you happy' and 'you'll be happy with me, baby', were thrown my way.

"Thing is, ladies, I've got someone right here who makes me very happy."

I don't know how, over the noise of the crowd, but somehow, I heard Charlotte gasp. Maybe it's because I was hyper aware of her. I'd watched from the corner of my eye as her body swayed back and forth to the music through my whole set, I'd watched as she sang when she felt like it, and I certainly hadn't missed the way she'd made eyes at me like I was some kind of god.

Fuck… I've missed her.

Every move I'd made, every chord I'd played had been on another level, the fact that she was here, watching, just heightened my awareness and put my senses on high alert.

It was a tough freakin' gig staying here in the middle of this stage when she was over there looking as appealing as she was. Those over-the-knee, high-heeled boots and loose-fit denim shirt dress she had on had given me a hard-on the minute I'd laid eyes on her. I was glad I didn't wear a mic, because the strangled groan I'd let slip as I walked out left very little to the imagination.

I turned to look at her and couldn't help the deep chuckle that reverberated from deep in my chest.

"She looks terrified," I told the crowd.

Some of them laughed, some let out a big 'awwwww'... some grumbled and moaned.

Charlotte pointed at herself as if to say 'me?'.

I nodded in response.

She shook her head furiously and took a couple of steps backwards.

"I'll do it if she won't!" Hannah called out with a shit-eating grin.

I chuckled again.

"J, mind giving me a hand, man?" I spoke into the mic.

Jasper appeared behind Charlotte and gave her a not so subtle push forward.

"All yours, Park," I heard Brock say behind me. I'd requested two chairs to be set up centre stage, facing one another, and that the lights were dropped on the band. I jumped to my feet and handed him my electric guitar, instead, taking the acoustic guitar he had ready for me.

"Thanks, man."

I glanced back over to Charlotte who was being forced out onto the stage by Jasper.

Shit... she's nervous as hell.

I sauntered over and stopped directly in front of her. "Hey, babe," I murmured as I tucked a stray strand of hair behind her ear. "You mind doing me a solid and sitting that sexy little ass down on that chair over there?" I gestured behind me.

She was looking up at me, her eyes as wide as saucers. She gaped, but seemed unable to form any words.

"Thanks, J, I got it from here," I told Jasper with a smirk.

He looked as though he didn't quite share my opinion, but backed off to stand with Hannah.

I took her hand and tugged her out further. The crowd went wild the moment they caught sight of her. As jealous as some of those fans might have been, this was unheard of for me... this crowd was getting to see something special, and they knew it.

I led her to the chair and sat her down.

Her body was rigid and tense.

I stood behind her and leant down to whisper in her ear. "It's just me and you, legs, forget about the beast." I tipped my head in the direction of the screaming crowd.

I heard her soft giggle and saw her shoulders relax slightly.

I moved around and sat down opposite her, looking right at her gorgeous face.

"Now I know I usually sing 'Blue Eyed Girl'..." I told the crowd through the mic sitting on the stand in front of me, my eyes never leaving Charlotte's. "But tonight, I'm gonna ask this pretty girl if I can do something different."

Charlotte gave me a confused look.

"I wrote a song," I carried on. "Inspired by the beauty in front of me."

The crowd let out a series of cat calls and 'ohhhs' and 'ahhhhs'.

"And if she doesn't mind, I want to sing it for her."

Charlotte looked like she might be going to pass out.

I swung the mic around so the crowd couldn't hear. "That okay with you, babe?"

She nodded numbly, but her eyes were alight with fire.

I took it as a yes.

"Well alright then," I drawled as I put the mic back in its place. "This here is called 'Captured'."

CHAPTER 20

Charlotte

HOLY... sweet...

Woah...

I couldn't even form coherent thoughts with Parker sitting across from me like this. His rough fingers were plucking and strumming at the guitar like it was an extension of his body. His toned arms were flexing as he strummed, and a vein was standing out in his neck as he tensed, his body tight and in control.

The way he played was hypnotic, and I worried for a moment that he was putting me into some kind of trance – that was exactly what Parker did when he sung, he pulled people in and held them there, like gravity.

When his mouth opened and the most heartfelt lyrics spilled out, I'd known I was a complete goner.

He wrote this... about me.

I couldn't believe it. The words... they were beautiful. My heart skipped a beat at the realisation that he felt this way about me. It wasn't even just about the words, his voice was perfect – he could have thrown out some half-assd lyrics about whatever kind of nonsense, and I still would have fallen under his spell.

I knew I was crying like a baby – something that was totally out of character for me, but I didn't care. This moment was worth it.

I also knew somewhere in the back of my mind that thousands of people were witnessing this moment right along with me, but he'd been right, it didn't matter... it was just me and him now.

His voice turned husky as he finished the song and stilled in front of me, his blue eyes staring straight into mine.

There was a moment, just a fraction of a second, of pure, absolute silence. It's like the crowd was waiting for a reaction from me.

A hiccupped sob broke free and I laughed.

Parker gave me a heart-stopping smile.

The crowd went wild.

Parker Sloan, ladies and gentleman.

————

I watched the last of the show in a daze. The need to claim this man was more than I could handle right now.

Passion, heat and desire was still building between us. Even now, as he bid farewell to the crowd, I knew his focus was entirely on me. They screamed and yelled, the same way they'd been doing all night, but it was like Parker couldn't even hear them anymore.

His eyes sought out mine and locked on like his life depended on it.

He handed off his guitar to a crew member without even looking at the guy.

I wanted to scream at him to keep it on. That guitar in his hands was one hell of a turn on. But there would be time for that later, and there was no way I could form words now even if I wanted to.

He sauntered over to me, more sex and sin than I'd ever been privy to witness.

As he approached I opened my mouth to speak, not even sure myself of what would come out, but I didn't get the chance.

Parker lifted me into his arms and backed me against a sectional wall with a thud. My legs clamped around his waist like an iron vice, but still I didn't feel close enough. The pressure of his hips held me firmly in place, and I locked my arms around his neck, clinging on even though he more than had me.

He slanted his mouth over mine in a kiss that was as rough as it was urgent. He tasted of the coke I'd seen him sipping on stage. His tongue thrust into my mouth, persistent and dominating. All I could do was hold on for the ride.

I hummed deep in my throat.

He kisses like a God.

I would have needed to be five kinds of naive not to notice the hard bulge in his pants, I didn't care if it was me or the thrill of the crowd that had him throbbing, either way, it was mine now.

"Come to every show," he growled as he broke away, gasping for air.

I nodded. "Only if you sing to me," I breathed.

"Deal," he murmured against my neck.

"Release that song, Parker," I whispered as he nibbled and teased the skin under my ear.

He pulled back to look me in the eyes. "You sure? That's your song, legs."

My eyes watered and my heart rate accelerated into overtime. I tucked my face into the crook of his neck and murmured into his skin. "Release the damn song, rock star, the world needs to hear it."

CHAPTER 21

Parker

"THAT'S JIM AND PETE." I pointed out the guys, who were still on stage grabbing some of their gear.

"And this here..." I clapped down on the big man's shoulder as he approached us. "Is Ricky."

Charlotte gave him a warm smile.

"Ricky, Charlotte, Charlotte, Ricky," I introduced them with a wave of my hand.

Ricky shot Charlotte what I'd started to call his 'full beam' smile. I'd seen the guy literally charm the pants off women with that thing.

"Hey, Little Red," he quipped, teasing her.

I tensed slightly, expecting Charlotte to chew him out with some of that spit and fire she'd thrown my way when we first met, but she just let out a half snort, half laugh.

"Like I haven't heard that one before," she deadpanned. "If you're gonna give me a nickname, at least attempt to be original," she added with an amused gleam in her eye.

He clutched his chest in a dramatic fashion. "Urgh, you wound me, Little Red."

"That's gonna stick, isn't it?" she demanded, her hands finding residency on her hips.

He grinned and nodded enthusiastically. "Like shit to a blanket."

"Well, I'd call you 'Big Rick'..." she drawled. "But we both know how that's gonna play out."

Ricky let out a loud, booming laugh.

I couldn't help but join in and laugh at the two of them, ribbing each other like old mates.

That was Charlotte for you; the girl wasn't intimidated by anyone. Not even a six-foot, two-hundred-and-forty-pound drummer, with more tattoos than brain cells.

Ricky let out a big, rumbling laugh. "Cool chick, Park. I'll have some fun with her."

I didn't even get time to answer before Ricky was calling out to Pete and Jimmy.

"Petey, Jim-Bob, come meet Little Red."

"Motherfucker," Charlotte muttered, giving Ricky a playful jab in the ribs.

And just like that, she was part of the family.

Right where I want her to be.

____

"C'mon, Parker, *rock* my world." Charlotte giggled from her spot in the booth.

She'd been going with the rock puns for a solid half hour. It shouldn't have been funny anymore, but my brain was so far gone on this girl, I couldn't help but egg her on and join in her silly game.

"Oh, I've got something *rock* hard for you, babe." I smirked.

Her mouth formed a small 'o' as her eyes darted between my face and my crotch.

"Tease," she muttered under her breath when she realised I was messing with her.

She snuggled back into my side and eyed up the club scene surrounding us. The boys were all milling around, some of them picking up chicks, some just drinking and watching. This is what happened after every show, for some of the guys, the after party was the highlight of the whole night.

Charlotte didn't seem the least bit phased by the hordes of groupies that were hanging around – not that I'd spared any of them a second glance. She seemed totally comfortable here with me, even if we'd barely moved out of our cosy booth.

I was more than happy to be antisocial tonight.

Got everything I need right here.

"I want to play a game with you," she whispered in my ear, her breath was warm and smelt of vodka and lemon. I let my gaze travel down the length of her body. She was pure seduction right now and she didn't even know it. Her dress had ridden up slightly, revealing another inch of her creamy thighs... and those boots.

God-freakin'-damn.

Those fuck-me boots would be the death of me.

"I'm in," I answered without hesitation.

She ran a finger down my arm. "It's called..." She paused dramatically, and a giggle slipped out. "Paper, scissors, *rock.*"

I chuckled loudly, shaking my head at myself. "I should have seen it coming."

"But yet, you didn't." She laughed, thoroughly impressed with herself.

I must have been ten kinds of messed up over this girl – I was still laughing. It wasn't necessarily her joke, but hearing her laugh that made me smile.

"You know I don't actually play rock music, right?"

She nodded. "But 'pop star' just doesn't have the same ring to it." She smirked.

"I wouldn't call it pop either, smart-ass."

"Hip hop?" she prompted.

I shook my head.

"No," she agreed, shaking her head along with me. "You just don't fit in any of the boxes." She feigned disappointment with a pout.

I grinned. "Well I sure do my best to fit in your box, babe."

She laughed long and hard at that. "Touché, Mr. Sloan, touché."

She tossed back the rest of her drink and I grinned. Charlotte was well on her way to being drunk. I doubted it was something she did very often, and I was enjoying watching her let her hair down.

I'll keep her safe.

I'd even stopped drinking a couple of hours ago; I was having way more fun watching my girl let loose anyway.

———

"Do you think they'd play 'We Will Rock You' if I asked?" Charlotte pondered aloud, a shit-eating grin on her face at her latest rock star pun.

"Okay... time to go you little smart-ass." I chuckled.

"No, no, no," she insisted, her hands flying around in overly large gestures. "Let's dance," she slurred, nodding enthusiastically at her own suggestion.

I chuckled to myself. At this point, I doubted Charlotte could even stand up straight.

"This club is jumpin' jumpin'," she added with a lazy smile.

"Did you just reference Destiny's Child?" I asked with a grin.

Her eyes widened. "Oh my god." She grabbed my

bicep in a death grip, her eyes wide. "Do you know Destiny's Child?"

Sweet Jesus.

"Annnnd, we're out of here," I announced.

"Noooo," she whined.

"Yessss," I replied.

I won the argument.

Charlotte was so drunk, she protested with the power of a wet kitten.

I hoisted her up and slipped my arm around her middle, supporting her weight. It would have been easier to carry her, but I didn't think Charlotte would have appreciated the whole club witnessing that.

"Let's get you home," I murmured in her ear.

"Your place," she demanded.

The thought of Charlotte in my bed, even just for sleeping – and possibly throwing up, if her current state was anything to go by, gave me a thrill that rivalled playing live.

"Yeah, babe, my place," I reassured her as I placed a kiss on the top of her head.

She gave me a dazzling smile.

I caught Jasper's eye across the room. Hannah was standing next to him; something I'd noticed had become a reoccurring theme throughout the night. I gave him a subtle chin lift, and looked at Hannah.

Get Hannah home safe.

Jasper responded with a chin lift of his own.

On it, man.

We didn't need words to communicate.

I could count on J to keep Hannah out of trouble. Although if that look on his face was anything to go by, the two of them would be making trouble together.

At home...

In between the sheets.

"They..." Charlotte pointed lazily in their direction. "Are *totally*... going to bang."

I laughed loudly. Wasted Charlotte was oddly insightful.

"Wait!" She came to a screaming stop, pulling my arm back with her. "We haven't got the hulk." She attempted to swing around and look for Sammy, she was so wobbly on her feet I had to physically catch her to stop her from falling.

"He's here, legs, we're good." I chuckled at her sudden concern for my burly bodyguard.

"No, no, no," she insisted in her drunken slur. "We can't just leave him here." Her eyes widened.

"Legs, he's right here," I insisted.

I didn't even have to look around to know that Sammy wouldn't be far behind me. He was the best of the best. He kept a low profile, didn't miss a single thing, and moved whenever I did. If I asked him to – he stayed behind, but the closest I'd ever gotten to an out-of-control situation, since having Sammy on staff, was the night I met Charlotte. And that was all my own doing – even given my crazy state that night, Sammy and his team had kept things under control.

"But h—"

I stifled a laugh. Apparently, Charlotte lost the ability to let things go when she got drunk.

Sammy chose that moment to make his presence known. "I'm right here, Miss. Now, how about we get you home?"

"Sammy!" Charlotte crooned, apparently over-joyed that he was in fact very much present and okay.

She reached out for him and looped her arm through his, much to his surprise. "I was so worried...." she rambled.

Sammy shot me a 'what the fuck do I do?' look, but I just shrugged and laughed.

Drunken Charlotte had him now.

———

Damn...

Turned out I'd been right about the vomiting.

We were on round three now, and if I hadn't seen it for myself, I wouldn't have believed that Charlotte could hold that much liquid in her tiny body.

"Do you feel better yet, babe?" I asked as I wiped her face with a cool cloth.

She nodded. "I'm never drinking again." She groaned.

"I'll second that motion."

"I'm so sorry," she mumbled as she tried to push the damp hair off her face.

I lightly moved her hand away and completed the

action for her. "Honestly, Charlotte, as disgusting as this is, I still like taking care of you."

She made a noise of disbelief.

I didn't blame her. Cleaning up someone else's vomit wasn't exactly the top of my to-do list, but I was in over my head with this girl – nothing was off limits.

"It's fine, babe," I reassured her. "You sure you're feeling better?"

She nodded in response.

"Good." I kissed the top of her head. "Bed." I lifted her into my arms, her hands lightly holding onto my bare shoulders, her big blue eyes looking up at me with gratitude.

"I could walk," she commented quietly.

I knew she could. I just liked holding her.

I sat her on the side of the bed. "Strip off," I instructed as I moved towards my drawers. I found a Guns N' Roses t-shirt and tossed it back in her direction. "Put that on, legs, I'll just take a shower."

"You should wear no shirt more often," she replied, her eyes glued firmly to my body as she licked her lips.

Jesus...

Keep it together, Sloan.

The only reason I wasn't wearing a shirt right now, was because she'd thrown up all down the front of it.

I shot her a smirk in an attempt to cover my reaction and strode to the bathroom quickly. There was no way in hell I was going to watch her undress. And

I couldn't take much more of her ogling me like that without reacting.

Not tonight.

Charlotte wasn't up to it, and I knew myself well enough to know that my self-control would snap if I saw what she had on under that dress.

Even if we both smell like puke... I still want her.

I showered quickly and slipped back into the room wearing only my boxer briefs.

Charlotte's light snores filled the room.

She was curled up in my bed, her red hair a dark, wild mass against my white pillows.

My heart tightened in my chest at the sight. I'd imagined Charlotte in my bed, in a variety of different scenarios, but no matter how hot or heavy my fantasies got, nothing even came close to this.

I slipped under the covers, being careful not to wake her and curled myself around her body.

"Goodnight, beautiful, this is only the beginning," I whispered to her.

CHAPTER 22

Charlotte

I WOKE UP WITH A GROAN.

Where the hell am I?

I froze as I realized I was pressed up against a warm body.

Not just any body.

A hard as rock, toasty warm, *very male* body if the stone length nudging against my ass was anything to go by...

I lifted the covers slowly and relaxed as soon as I recognized Parker's tattoos.

And this is why I don't drink.

I couldn't remember much past arriving at the club for the after party. I could remember teasing

Parker with rock puns... something about Destiny's Child...

Oh hell.

I groaned again.

This was not good. There was a high chance I'd made a total fool of myself in front of a whole room of people, Parker included.

A deep chuckle took me by surprise.

I turned slowly so I could look at him, he slid over a fraction to give me room to turn, but he didn't let go of me.

I groaned yet again as my eyes took in the sight before me.

That is not fair.

He looked like he'd had a stylist come over, muss him up to sexy perfection and then leave again.

I was willing to bet money on the fact that I looked like something the cat had dragged in.

I was that wasted last night, I knew there wasn't a chance I would have cleaned my face and I was willing to bet my hair would be doing some crazy morning-after business too.

I didn't have a clue what I was wearing and I was too scared to look down and check.

"If you look that good every morning, we're seriously gonna have to rethink this thing," I grumbled as I snuggled into the pillow, trying to hide as much of my face as possible.

He shook his head. "No can do, you threw up on me, there's no backing out now."

My eyes widened and I froze.

"I did what now?"

He smirked. "Puked." He grinned. "*Everywhere.*"

I closed my eyes and took a couple of deep breaths.

Making a fool of myself, level one hundred.

"All down my front," he carried on. "My fault really, I wasn't quick enough."

I could feel my cheeks staining bright red and I turned to bury my face in his pillow again.

"Then you and the toilet went a couple of rounds, and Bob's your uncle," he finished. I could hear the amusement in his voice.

"Fuck my life," I muttered back. "I'll clean it up, the bathroom and your clothes," I promised. "I'm so sorry."

"It's all good, I took care of it already."

I didn't know what to say to that. It would appear that he'd taken care of everything, me included.

I turned so I could see him – haggard appearance be damned. He was looking at me with warm eyes and a wide smile. He didn't look pissed off or disgusted in the slightest.

"You should have just stuck me in a cab and sent me home."

His eyes narrowed and turned hard. "There is no way in hell that I'd ever leave you alone in that state," he half growled at me. "Not a chance in fucking hell."

My pulse raced. "Why not?" I asked timidly.

This conversation was veering into new territory

for us. We both knew it, but it was time we talked about what this thing going on between us was.

I was falling for this man, hard. And not because he was a famous singer who'd wooed me on a world stage... although that certainly didn't hurt, but because he was kind and sweet, and caring and protective.

And sexy as hell.

I noticed for the first time that he was shirtless. I'd missed this view of Parker. I hadn't seen all of him since the time we'd shared at my place.

Well, not that I can remember anyway.

He was magnificent. He really was a work of art. The tattoos covering nearly every inch of his flesh made him more defined and masculine. He would have been glorious to look at without them, but with all that ink, he was on a whole other level.

I licked my lips absently as I trailed my eyes over the designs and pictures.

"Why not?" he demanded, repeating my question and pulling me back to our conversation.

I nodded my head slowly and forced my eyes back up to his face.

"Because you're my girl," he replied, exasperated. "And I'll take care of you no matter what, Charlotte. Even if that means holding your hair back while you puke."

My heart thumped in my chest.

"And I will never, and you better fuckin' hear me when I say *never*, leave you when you're vulnerable."

His eyes had softened despite the warning tone in his voice.

"Hell, I have enough trouble being away from you when I know you're tucked up safe in your bed."

"I'm your girl?" I breathed, so shocked I could barely speak.

"You wrecked my favourite Rolling Stones shirt, so you damn well better be."

Holy shit.

I could have sprung up off the bed and happy danced the day away at this news.

Wow.

"Quarter of the population is in love with my boyfriend... I'm not sure how I feel about that," I teased.

"Pffft," he scoffed. "More like half."

His reply was light hearted, but I didn't miss the heat that flashed through his eyes at the mention of being my boyfriend.

I wanted him more than I'd ever wanted a man in my entire life. And I wanted him right now.

"I want to kiss you," he murmured, stroking a soft path down the side of my face with the tip of his finger.

Read my mind.

But there was no way I was doing this without a shower and some stolen toothpaste and he obviously knew that as well as I did.

I grimaced.

He gestured to the door off to the side of his

bedroom. "Take all the time you need," he replied with a smirk.

CHAPTER 23

Parker

THE WATER SHUT off and my heart rate sped up in anticipation. I knew she wouldn't be long now – she had nothing clean in there to put on.

I shifted uncomfortably, getting harder just at the mere thought of it.

Charlotte had the body of my dream girl.

Who am I kidding? She is *my dream girl...*

The series of events that had led me to her were nothing short of coincidental. I could have easily gone to a different club that night, but I didn't... I could have gone to a hotel with a groupie, but I didn't... I could have stayed in V.I.P. and never laid eyes on her, but I didn't.

Fate handed me an opportunity when it brought Charlotte onto my radar, and I wasn't giving her up without one hell of a fight.

The door from my bathroom creaked and I sat up straighter against my solid wood head board.

God damn.

Charlotte stepped out, the light from the bathroom pooling around her in the still-dim room.

She was wearing nothing but a white towel. Her hair was a damp mass, pulled to the side, and her face was clean from any makeup. Charlotte may have been a talented makeup artist, but she didn't need any of it – she was a natural beauty.

So damn gorgeous.

The scent of her raspberry shampoo wafted towards me.

Pure heaven.

"You have my shampoo," she stated with a hint of question in her tone.

I shrugged. "I told you I liked the way you smelt."

She laughed softly and shook her head. "You are so lucky I'm not put off by all of your crazy."

I'm lucky alright.

"You just gonna stand there all day or are you bringing that sweet little ass of yours over here?"

"You gonna say please, or do I need to teach you some manners, rock star?" She smirked.

She didn't move an inch.

"*Please* bring that sexy little ass over here," I amended.

"See, was that so hard?" she teased as she strolled towards the bed.

"I can tell you something that *is* hard."

"Always so crass, Mr. Sloan, what would the world think if they knew you had such a filthy mouth?"

I expected her to stop short of the bed, or sit timidly on the side. But no, not Charlotte, she came straight up to me, straddled my hips and sat right down in my lap.

That action alone nearly had me losing my mind.

"I don't think anyone would be too surprised by that," I murmured as I got more and more distracted by the sight in front of me.

The swell of her breasts peeking out of the top of her towel was so damn sexy. Her skin was warm and flushed as I traced the outline with my fingertip.

"That tickles," she whispered.

"What about this?" I asked as I leaned forward and kissed along her collarbone.

She sighed. "That feels good," she replied, her voice soft and breathy.

"And this?" I asked against her soft skin as I moved higher to the spot just below her ear.

She moaned and I took it as a sign I should carry on.

I swept her hair back out of the way, and continued kissing, nibbling and sucking every patch of skin I came across, taking my time worshipping every inch of her.

"Parker," she moaned.

I got even harder at the sound of my name falling from her lips.

I trailed my way back down towards her towel. I looked back up at her, waiting for her approval to remove it.

She held my gaze and reached down to loosen it off before letting it drop to pool around her hips.

God damn.

I couldn't imagine ever becoming immune to the sight in front of me. She was perfect in my eyes. There was just something about this little woman that drove me past the point of insanity.

I could feel my dick straining against my boxer briefs – I was so hard it was becoming uncomfortable.

I shuffled her back and before I got the chance to pull down the waistband, Charlotte's hands were there, doing it for me.

I'd been so careful with her last time – she was so small and fragile, I'd barely even moved inside her.

I wasn't one to brag, but I knew I had a big dick – it wasn't like I was inexperienced with women, and I'd had more than a few comments about the size of my junk.

But looking at Charlotte and her tiny little body, I found myself wishing for the first time ever that I wasn't so well endowed.

I wanted to be able to take her however I felt like taking her. I wasn't exactly known for my restraint... as a general rule, I liked sex rough, hard and fast.

None of those three things had been on the menu last time, but surprisingly, I came harder and faster than I could ever remember doing.

I looked at Charlotte in wonder.

There is just something about you, woman.

I hissed as she grasped my hard length in her tiny hand and worked it up and down. My head fell back in pleasure as I let her take charge.

She made a little moan of satisfaction and I couldn't keep my hands off her any longer.

Her perfect breasts were bouncing with her movements and proving why they were one of my favourite parts of her body.

I dipped my head to kiss her creamy skin before sucking on one of her nipples.

"That feels so good." Her voice was breathy and soft as she arched her back, giving me easier access.

I cupped her breasts, one in each hand and kissed, sucked and nibbled at anything my mouth came into contact with.

She worked my dick faster and began grinding herself against my thighs, looking to gain some friction. I knew I was doing a damn fine job of whipping Charlotte into a frenzy.

I wonder if I could make her come like this...

"Could you come like this, legs?" I murmured to her.

Her eyes were closed now, as though she was in deep concentration. "Mmmm hmmm," she moaned.

I'll take that as a yes.

I went back to my work until she was writhing on top of me. She was right there on the edge, but just couldn't fall off the cliff.

"So close..." she whispered.

I reached down between us and slipped my hand between her legs. She was so ready for me. My dick throbbed at the thought of being inside her but I was going to make him wait his turn. This was about Charlotte right now, not me.

I found her sensitive nub and rubbed my calloused thumb against it.

That small amount of contact was all it took for her to come apart entirely.

She let out a moan that made my dick jump.

"Parker," she breathed as her head fell forward onto my shoulder.

I need in.

Right now.

I gently lay her on her back on the bed and reached for a condom from the drawer. I sheathed myself as fast as I could before flipping Charlotte onto her stomach and slipping in between her legs.

"You okay, baby?" I asked. I lifted her hips up so she was on all fours and lined up to push inside her.

She made some kind of incoherent mumble and I couldn't help but grin to myself.

Charlotte was still firmly in pleasure town.

I ran my hand over her smooth back and pushed in, in one firm stroke.

Charlotte cried out and I stilled inside her.

Fuck... is she hurt?

"Oh. My. God," she panted. "That feels *so* good."

I grunted my approval before dragging my dick nearly all the way out and slamming back into her.

I knew I was being too rough, but Charlotte wasn't complaining and I wasn't sure I would be able to stop for any other reason.

Shit that feels so incredible.

I picked up speed, chasing my release already. She had me so damn wound up I wasn't going to need long.

"Rock star..." she panted. "Oh god..."

Apparently, I wasn't the only one losing control. I thrust into her again and came with a growl, spurting hot and hard into the condom.

She cried out as she reached climax for a second time and slumped forward onto the bed.

I followed her, falling to the side and tugging her against my body. We lay together silently for a few minutes, our laboured breathing the only sound.

"That was... that was..." she stuttered. "I don't even know what the hell that was." She finally decided.

"You told me to 'rock your world'..." I chuckled as I tried to catch my breath.

She covered her face with her hands. "Oh no... I'm never drinking again."

"You said that already."

"I mean it!" she insisted.

I kissed her temple. "Don't say that, you're a real entertainer with a few vodkas under your belt."

She groaned again and buried her face in my chest. "I hope no photographers caught sight of me last night."

"Nope." I chuckled. "Sammy had you covered, legs."

I waited to see if she remembered her concern for my burly security guard or the way she'd smothered him half to death with her excessive talking and affection.

"Oh nooooo," she groaned.

There it is.

I laughed long and loud, shaking her small frame with the action.

"Oh yes," I confirmed.

"You're going to have to fire him," she announced. "I'll never be able to look him in the eye again."

"Don't sweat it, Little Red, next time maybe just a few less vodkas." I chuckled.

———

"And down there is where Sammy lives." I pointed to the staircase that led downstairs.

She tilted her head to the side. "He lives with you?" she asked in surprise.

"Sure does," I confirmed as we arrived back in the living area.

I'd shown her my whole place, top to bottom. It was a nerve-wracking thing for me – this was not at all the norm for me, but much to my relief, Charlotte had loved it. She was especially intrigued and impressed with my studio.

"So, he's here right now?" She winced, obviously remembering her antics from last night.

I smirked and nodded. "He's got a whole self-contained flat down there. Everything he needs... but him and I, we mainly keep to ourselves." I chuckled.

"Good," she mumbled, her face flushed red.

"I didn't think I'd ever need live-in security, but I'll tell you, one crazy-ass fan scaling the side of the house and climbing in through a second storey window is enough to make you re-evaluate things," I mused.

Charlotte chortled. "I suppose she was naked, waiting on the bed for you, was she?" She joked, her voice thick with sarcasm.

Exactly right.

I shot her a 'hit the nail on the head' look.

She burst out laughing. "Oh, you're kidding me? That's hilarious."

I chuckled and ran my hand through my hair. "I had to call Sammy to come and sort her out... we started the remodel downstairs the next day."

She shook her head and laughed.

I smiled as I watched her. Her long red hair

moved around as she giggled and her cheeks flushed with colour.

She's so beautiful.

Her laughter had quickly become one of my favourite sounds, and I cursed myself for not being a funnier guy – if I was, I could have listened to her laugh all day long.

"So..." She glanced around and shrugged nervously. "How many women have you given this tour to?"

"Not counting my break-in stalker?" I joked.

She smirked. "Not counting."

"One," I answered honestly. "Well, two now." I winked at her.

Charlotte cocked a surprised brow and waited for me to explain.

I decided to let her squirm for a moment.

"So, who was the lucky lady?" she prompted when I didn't answer.

I could tell she was dying to know.

"Nona," I replied with a smirk.

She smiled fondly at the mention of my grandmother before surprise took over her face again. "Seriously? You've never brought a girlfriend or whatever here?"

I shook my head. "Hell no, you ever heard of clingers?"

Rule one. No crazies in the house.

"Where did you take them then?" she asked as she tilted her head to the side. She was still twirling a long strand of dark-red hair around and around her finger.

I knew she was letting her curiosity get the better of her, and I doubted she actually wanted to hear the answer, but I couldn't just ignore her question.

"Hotels," I answered.

She flinched.

I felt like an ass, but it was the truth. "Sorry, legs, but you shouldn't ask questions that you don't want to know the answers to... I won't lie to spare your feelings – you'll always get the truth from me."

She nodded in acknowledgement of what I was telling her.

"But then why am I here?" she asked quietly as she looked around my home again with a slight rise and fall of her shoulders.

I took her hand in mine. "Because you're not like any other girl I've ever met. You're different, Charlotte... you don't belong in some seedy hotel room... you belong here with me."

She giggled nervously and stepped forward into me so she could bury her face in my chest.

"Damn you, Parker Sloan... you certainly know how to make a girl feel special," she murmured against my shirt.

Nailed it.

"It's only for you, legs."

She tipped her head back and smiled up at me. "I'm already swooning, okay, you can stop."

I chuckled and swept the loose strands of hair

away from her pretty face. "Sorry." I placed a kiss to her forehead. "It's hard, ya know? Sometimes I forget just how charming I really am."

She laughed and I felt that beautiful sound right down to my bones.

CHAPTER 24

Charlotte

I GLANCED over at Parker as he drove us across town, back to my place.

"Have you had a proper girlfriend since you, you know... got famous?" I asked cautiously. I wanted to know, but at the same time, I wasn't sure how I would handle hearing about an ex of Parkers, especially if I found he wasn't really over her or something stupid like that. He'd made it clear that he'd always give me the truth, so it was up to me to decide if I could handle the truth.

"One," he answered curtly, not saying anymore.

He obviously didn't know me as well as he thought, if he thought I'd be content to leave it at that.

"And..." I prompted.

He groaned and shook his head. "I knew I wouldn't get away with that one."

So, he does know me after all.

He sighed in defeat. "Her name was Katie, I knew her from before I hit the big time, we'd sort of grown up together. At school she was the pretty, popular girl that I'd secretly been in love with for years. She'd never shown any interest in me back then, so I don't know what possessed me to think she was genuinely interested in me all of a sudden."

I was surprised by this. Parker was gorgeous, talented and kind. I couldn't imagine that he ever would have gone unnoticed by the opposite sex – rock star status or not. But I did know one thing for sure, I was definitely searching Google for this Katie chick the minute I was alone.

"Anyway, we got together, she lapped up the attention and I made myself believe she really cared about me... long story short, I broke it off after six months and it was messy... real messy."

He sighed and ran a hand through his hair.

"I caught her fucking around with another guy. Literally caught the two of them red handed... and she had the nerve to look me in the eye and tell me it wasn't how it looked." He rolled his eyes. "He was balls-deep inside her, so I'm pretty confident it *was* how it looked."

I'd felt like I might have been going to cry, right

up until he used the phrase 'balls-deep'. Now the tears forming in my eyes were tears of laughter.

"I'm so sorry." I choked out, trying to keep the giggles at bay. 'But *balls-deep*?" I lost it. Laughter exploded out of me.

"He *was* balls-deep," he insisted before laughing himself.

"Sorry." I giggled. "It's terrible really."

He nodded. "It should have been, but I didn't even give a fuck when I found them backstage, ya know? She'd shown me her true colours on more than one occasion by this point, and that's why I knew I had to end it, it was almost a relief."

"Did you know the guy?"

He nodded. "My publicist. I was more gutted to lose him than I was to lose her."

Shit.

"I've really had a bad run with those," he joked "I'll have to remind Jasper that the last 'straight dude' I hired for the job ending up fucking my girlfriend."

I probably shouldn't have been teasing him, but it was obvious he wasn't actually in the least bit phased by the ending of that relationship, so I figured there was no real harm done.

"Well I've suddenly got a thing for men with tattoos, so if you could take that into account when hiring the new guy, I'd really appreciate it."

"I knew that you were a sucker for my ink." He grinned triumphantly.

I rolled my eyes at him. "That would be the stand out piece of information for you, wouldn't it?"

"Damn straight." He winked. "And besides, you're at least one thousand times smarter and more real than Katie ever was. You're not going to go banging the minions when you've got the king waiting at home." He had a shit-eating grin on his face, and I knew he was intentionally acting like a cocky bastard.

I made a fake gagging motion and he laughed loudly.

"All hail the King," I deadpanned.

Parker flicked the radio on as he chuckled at my reaction.

"Speak of the devil..." I giggled as one of my very own rock star's songs came on.

"Oh my god!" I swooned like a fan girl. "I loooove this song."

He groaned.

"Sing it for me?" I pleaded, batting my eyelashes at him.

"Nope," he replied without missing a beat. "I'll pass."

I reached for the dial and turned it up louder.

Parker shook his head in amusement as I belted out the chorus of his hit song 'Touched'.

His hand snaked out in an attempt to turn it down, or maybe even off, but I caught it and clasped it in mine.

"You're a terrible singer," he yelled over the music.

He wasn't wrong – I was awful. But I didn't care.

"You sing it for me then," I yelled back with a wink.

"Anything to make you stop," he teased before launching into the verse with all of his vocal perfection.

I sighed as I leaned my head back against the leather seat of his Range Rover and watched him.

I don't know what it was about that husky voice of his, but it got under my skin like nothing ever had before.

There was something special about watching Parker sing... he felt it deep down in his bones, and it was obvious for everyone to see that he was doing exactly what he was put on this earth to do.

His talent was incredible.

And sexy as hell...

"Is that you Han?" I called as I heard the clatter of keys on the hall table.

"Who else would it be, you little nut bar?" she called back from the living room.

I pulled my hair up into a bun as I strolled out to give her an interrogation about her whereabouts, just like any good friend would.

"You didn't sleep here last night." I pointed an

accusatory finger at her the moment I laid eyes on her – still in last night's clothes.

"Neither did you." She pointed right back at me.

"You know where I was." I winked at her. "Question is... where were you?"

She narrowed her eyes at me. "You're awfully chipper for someone who drank their body weight in vodka last night."

"That..." I pointed at her again. "Would be thanks to all the vomiting." I grimaced. "And you're changing the subject."

"You vomited in front of Parker?" She gaped, apparently outraged with my behaviour.

"Not just in front of him." I shrugged.

Hannah's eyes bulged.

"On him too," I added with a grin.

She let out a small whimper. "Well... it was good while it lasted." She sighed.

I tilted my head to the side and watched her with amusement. "He's in my room right now, Han."

She gaped again. "You threw up on a freakin' millionaire, celebrity rock star and he didn't run a mile?"

I shook my head and smirked. "He even rubbed my back and held my hair for me," I bragged.

"Some kind of sorcery," she muttered in an accusatory tone as she headed for the kitchen. "At least that explains the flash-ass car out front and the bulky dude dressed in the 'I blend right in' suit," she called out sarcastically.

I'd forgotten Sammy had followed us over here. I absently wondered just how long he would stay out the front of my building for.

He's committed.

I flopped down on the couch. "Han?" I called after her. "You *will* tell me where you were."

"I think we all know the answer to that question," she called back after a few beats.

No way.

I leapt up out of my seat and followed after her into the kitchen.

"Hannah Montgomery," I hissed. "Did you, or did you not, bone a certain rock star's manager?"

She winced.

"Well?" I demanded.

"Technically *he* boned me," she offered with a grimace.

I happy danced for a few moments. Hannah didn't join me.

"Was he bad in the sack?" I asked when I noticed the subdued look on her face.

She swirled the cup of coffee she'd made and shook her head slowly.

"Was he a prick to you?" I demanded, suddenly feeling like I needed to kick Jasper Jones' ass.

She shook her head again. "No. He was a gentleman." She sighed in a dreamy way. "He was... perfect."

What the hell is the problem then?

I raised my brows at her in question.

"I guess I'm kinda sad to see it end. We both agreed it was a one-time thing," she explained with a quiet, longing tone that I wasn't accustomed to hearing from her.

I was about to start giving her a hard time about the stupid agreement they'd made when I got distracted by the sight of Parker.

He was still pulling his black t-shirt over his head, giving me a perfect view of his toned chest and abdomen. His tan chinos were slung low on his hips, and his hair was damp like mine from our shared shower.

The thought of that shower had me squirming.

"Tell him to put it away. It's hurting my eyes." Hannah groaned dramatically.

I laughed at her teasing. "We'll talk about you and Mr. Jones later," I hissed as I headed for the sex on a stick that was wandering around my living room.

"I wasn't expecting an audience." He chuckled as he pulled his shirt the rest of the way down. "I hope she hasn't been here long." He winked at me.

I blushed. Thankfully Hannah had only just arrived home; things had gotten a little heated... and loud.

Very, very loud...

Parker's performance in the car had got me all hot and bothered and I hadn't been able to hold back when we'd walked through the door and found ourselves alone.

Not that Parker was complaining.

"I only just arrived," Hannah called from the kitchen where she was apparently eavesdropping on our conversation. "But the 'I just took an after sex shower' look doesn't leave much to the imagination to be honest with you."

CHAPTER 25

Parker

"I WANT to tell you something that you already know."

Charlotte tipped her head to the side and looked at me in slight confusion. "Why would I need you to tell me something that I already know?"

"Because I need to say it out loud... and to be honest, not knowing what you think about it is killing me."

It wasn't just this that I wanted to tell her – it was everything. I wanted to share every little detail of my life with her.

What I had for lunch... how many children I want...

Everything.

"Alright, rock star, I'm listening – let me have it." She smiled as she sat the book she was reading down onto the coffee table and looked up at me with her beautiful bright eyes.

I shrugged. "I love you."

Plain and simple.

I told her the words without an ounce of hesitation. I'd rehearsed it in my head a thousand times, from full-on and cheesy, to short and sweet. In the end, I'd decided to just come out with it – I knew what I wanted to say, I knew what I wanted her to feel, and if the tears forming in her eyes were anything to go by, I'd achieved what I set out to do.

She nodded and bit down on her lip in what I knew as an attempt to stop her tears overflowing.

I chuckled. "What, no witty remark today, legs?"

She shook her head.

I reached for her hands and tugged her up to her feet. She buried her face in my chest and wrapped her arms tightly around my middle.

"Do you feel like giving me any kind of feedback...?" I asked nervously.

She giggled.

Say something... anything...

"You were right."

I was right?

"About...?" I prompted.

She sniffed and swiped at the tears on her cheeks. "I already knew." She smiled in her beautiful, cheeky way.

Of course you did... you can read me like a book...

I huffed out a laugh. "And is it okay with you?"

Do you love me too?

She tipped her head back to look up at me, and I felt the familiar sensation that could only be compared to the cliché of a swarm of butterflies fluttering around in my stomach.

"I mean, I guess so." She shrugged nonchalantly. "Since I love you too, it's probably pretty convenient."

Fuck yes!

Warmth spread through my veins. I knew she was in love with me. We were only saying aloud the words that our actions had been showing all along. But even though I felt like I already knew, hearing it felt like nothing I'd ever experienced.

I'd told girls I loved them before – but I'd never meant it as much as I did when I said it to Charlotte.

I lifted her off the ground and slung her over my shoulder.

She shrieked. "Put me down you brute!"

I slapped her ass. "You think you're so funny, don't you, smart-ass? Holding out on me."

She giggled hysterically. "I was joking!"

I slapped her ass again.

"Put me down!" she begged between giggles.

I slid her down my body and groaned at the feel of her against me.

She looked up at me like she knew exactly what I was thinking – and she felt the same way.

"You love me?" I questioned.

She bit down on her lip and nodded at me shyly.

"Say it again." I tugged on a lock of her beautiful, long red hair.

"I love you." She giggled.

"Again."

"I love you." She lightly slapped my chest.

"Once more," I pleaded.

"You'll never stop."

Not if I have my way.

I begged her with my eyes.

She rolled her eyes and then smiled sweetly. "I love you so much more than you know," she told me, her eyes reflecting that love like nothing I'd ever seen.

I shook my head in disagreement. "I know just how much," I told her before meeting her lips with mine.

———

"C'mon, legs, I've got someone you're gonna meet today," I told her as I bustled her out the door of her apartment. I hadn't seen her since Sunday when I'd first told her I loved her, so today I'd managed to book out some much-needed free time to work in with her schedule.

"Alright, alright, bossy." She rolled her eyes. "At least let me put my coat on."

I glanced at my watch, we had plenty of time to get over there, but with my luck, we'd get mobbed by paparazzi or fans the minute we entered the centre of town.

"Is it another family member?" she asked with a cheeky smile, and I knew she was thinking about my Nona.

"No." I chuckled. "I think you've had about enough crazy for now."

I tugged her back when she reached the door before I did. I'd swapped cars and done a few laps before heading over here, but there was no guarantee that I hadn't been followed. I peered up and down the street, and when I was satisfied with what I saw, or more to the point, didn't see, I took her hand and led her out to my car.

I was just opening the door for Charlotte when I saw a guy with a camera around his neck jogging towards me.

"You were almost too late," I called out to him, a grin on my face.

"I know." He sucked in a deep breath. "I was right across town when I got your message and I only had my bike." He panted again, nearly doubled over.

I glanced at Charlotte and she looked utterly perplexed by the unfolding situation.

Introductions...

"Charlotte, this is Snitch," I told her, letting her know it was okay. "He grew up in the same town I did," I explained. "I help him out with some exclusive shots when I can, and in return, he puts the others off my trail when he can."

Charlotte smiled and crinkled up her nose. "Well that's a bit cute," she mused.

She held out her hand to him. "It's nice to meet you."

Snitch shook her hand. "You too, miss."

I glanced at my watch. "We really gotta hit it, man."

"No problem" He raised his camera and backed up a few steps.

Charlotte shot me a devilish look as I gestured for her to get into the car. I could hear Snitch snapping a few shots from behind me.

"He biked all the way over here, just to get a photo of you opening my door for me?" she asked in disbelief.

I chuckled. I knew Charlotte, and I knew she wasn't willing to let this go just yet.

"He'll get good money for these shots," I reassured her. "I don't drive women around very often, actually make that ever. Now get in, we'll be late."

"He'll get better money for these."

I opened my mouth to ask her what she meant, but I didn't get the chance.

She pushed up on her toes and kissed me, taking my hands in hers while she did.

She broke off the kiss and looked up at me. She placed my hands and hers, right on her belly, over her coat.

I held back a laugh. I knew what she was doing.

In a few hours' time, the entire world was going to think I'd knocked her up.

"Just so you know, I'm not actually pregnant," she called out to Snitch with a grin.

"Oh, this is gold," he called back. "I like her, Sloan."

"Everybody does," I replied without taking my eyes off the little shit stirrer in front of me.

She giggled and jumped into the car, done with her little show for now at least.

"What's next, huh?" I smirked at her after I climbed in and Kelvin started the car "A fake wedding? Pushing a doll around in a pushchair pretending it's a baby?"

She giggled. "You have to admit, it's pretty funny."

"You can ring my Nona and tell her it was all a ruse." I shook my head in amusement. "She'd probably get a real kick out of that actually."

It was no secret that Nona was a fan of Charlotte. *Huge fan.*

All of a sudden, she was calling me twice as much as she had before, but she didn't use the extra calls to ask about me, she usually just wanted to ask how Charlotte was. She always made sure to check that I was treating her right, spoiling her... but not just by using my money. That was Nona's advice. 'Money comes and goes' she said, 'but knowing how to treat a woman right stays forever'.

Looking over at the beautiful woman in the car next to me, knowing that I'd do everything in my power to keep her safe and happy, I knew Nona was right.

"Where are we?" Charlotte whispered as we navigated the twists and turns of the quiet back hallways and staircases. She suddenly stopped dead in her tracks and tugged me back by our intertwined hands. "Is this the part where you hold me captive in some abandoned building?" she hissed. "I saw the preview of that movie too you know."

Is she serious?

"Are you serious?" My jaw dropped and I flicked my eyes to her face – she was grinning like an idiot.

Smart-ass.

"You won't be laughing when I tie you up to a bed and keep you there for the day." I chuckled.

"Oh yeah?" She raised her brows at me. "And who says I wouldn't enjoy something like that?" Her voice was thick with attitude.

I held back a groan, all that sass was driving me wild.

As it was, I was having a hard time keeping my hands off her, and until we went through that door up ahead, we were all alone – a dangerous position for our modesty.

"You push me up against that filthy wall and

there *will* be trouble," she warned me, already two steps ahead of my thoughts.

There goes that idea.

It was like she could read my mind.

I laughed. "Who says I was going to?"

She pointed an accusatory finger at me. "That stupid look on your face, that's who."

"Alright, Sherlock, just up here." I chuckled as I placed my hand on the small of her back and guided her forward.

We approached the unmarked door and I tapped on it twice.

"Come on in," a female voice called from behind the door.

I took Charlotte's hand in mine and turned the handle.

CHAPTER 26

Charlotte

"THIS IS SO COOL," I repeated for the one hundredth time.

Parker laughed.

"How naïve am I that I've never actually set foot inside one of these places?" I mused as I looked at the hundreds and hundreds of photos that lined the walls of the tattoo artist's studio.

This woman had done more tattoo jobs than I'd had hot dinners.

She was the best in the country – or so Parker told me. And I was inclined to believe him. There were a ton of well-known celebrities and sports people on these walls... the kind of people who wouldn't trust just anyone to ink them – people like

Parker. Every single one of these tattoos was flawless, done with absolute precision and skill.

It was obvious this wasn't the kind of place just anybody could walk into. This joint was exclusive. Even Sammy trusted it – he was hardly ever content to stay home when Parker went somewhere public, but Parker had told me that he hadn't even complained about it once.

"What are you getting this time?" I called over my shoulder to Parker.

He'd removed his shirt, and Asha, his tattoo artist, was busy drawing something freehand onto his left pectoral. The front of his torso was some of the only clean skin he had left. His abdomen was more or less bare, but his arms, some of his sides, parts of his chest, most of his back and even some of his legs were all covered in ink. He even had a couple of tattoos on his hands... and his neck, while not entirely covered, wasn't left untouched either.

"You'll see," he answered. "But not until it's done."

This piqued my interest.

I turned to face him. "Are you worried I'll talk you out of it?" I teased him.

I peeked my head around further and he shot me a 'stay where you are' look.

I was just messing with him. I couldn't see a thing from where I was standing, but I couldn't deny that I was curious – his reluctance to let me see was only making me want to know more.

"Why can't I see?" I asked more genuinely this time.

"Because, woman, it's a surprise, just let me surprise you for once."

"Ha! For once? You're obviously forgetting the time you pulled me out on stage and serenaded me in front of thousands and thousands of people." I pointed my finger at him.

"She's not wrong," Asha mumbled as she drew a few more sweeping lines onto my boyfriend's chest.

"Oh, I see how this is gonna go down, you girls stick together, huh?" Parker grinned with a shake of his head.

Asha winked at me before going back to her work.

———

"Does that hurt?" I asked curiously. I was fairly certain it would have – having a needle scratching a picture into your flesh and all. But it can't have been too bad... Parker certainly hadn't been put off coming back again and again.

He tilted his head in the direction of where I was sitting, on the other side of the room, far enough away that I couldn't see what was happening.

Asha had been working on him for two hours solid now, and I didn't know how the hell she managed to concentrate for that long.

"Nah, not really," he answered. "I mean, it's not

like it's enjoyable, but I wouldn't say it's too painful either."

I watched carefully as Asha grabbed the little pot of red ink she had sitting on the small table next to her.

Black, white and red.

Those were the only colours she had set out.

I was dying to see what was going on that chest of his.

"About another hour and we should be done." Asha spoke to no one in particular.

One more hour and I get to see.

———

"Oh my god," I breathed.

It was Little Red Riding Hood. Well, a version of her. The picture was of a scene, with a figure in the middle, her back facing the viewer.

She had on a Little Red Riding Hood style cape, but it was black and the hood was down. She had long, dark-red hair flowing down her back and over her shoulders. The background was all in black and white, and was kind of blurry, like it didn't really matter where she was, but she was clearly surrounded by people.

It was beautiful.

It was me.

"I don't understand," I whispered as I reached my

hand out towards the picture, stopping short of actually touching his reddened skin.

"It's you," he replied softly. "I know you're not thrilled about being called 'Little Red' but it's not a bad representation."

My heart thumped so loud in my chest that I could hear it pounding in my ears.

"Why?" I asked, bewildered by the fact that he wanted a permanent depiction of me etched into his skin.

"Because no matter where I am, no matter who's around, all I see is you," he told me.

Holy. Shit.

"And I got it over my heart, because my heart belongs to you, legs."

"Oh my god," I repeated. "It's... it's..." I stuttered. "I can't believe you did this for me," I finally managed.

His eyes blazed. "Of all the things I'd do for you, this here is *nothing*."

I felt like I was going to pass out. He was so intense, and I was so in love with him. It was overwhelming.

"I love you," I whispered. "God, I love you."

"I love you more, legs."

Normally I would have argued that point with him, but seeing him standing here, proudly displaying a symbol of me over his heart, I decided to let him have it this time.

"So, what do you think?" Asha asked me as she came back into the studio.

"It's *incredible*," I praised her. "Your work is amazing."

She smiled as she wiped down the small table she'd sat the ink on. "You know where to come if you ever decide you want some ink then."

I gaped at her in disbelief. "Are you serious?"

She laughed. "Why wouldn't I be?"

"You thinking of getting some ink, legs?" Parker asked curiously as he shrugged his shirt back on.

I blushed. "Oh, no... I mean, I don't know... I haven't really thought about it. I'm just surprised you'd let me in to this place." I gestured around the space.

Asha laughed again. "Why wouldn't I?"

"I'm not famous or anything... I'm totally not a big deal."

She raised her eyebrows at me. "Hun, Parker Sloan just got a picture of you tattooed right onto his chest... you're a bigger deal than you think, at least in his eyes." She winked at me as she went back to her cleaning.

I was stunned into silence. I'd obviously never been one to fall into the trap that fame and fortune created, and this wasn't about that at all, but the fact that my man was willing to make a gesture this grand, told me that I was about as high as it got on his list of priorities.

And damn it feels good...

CHAPTER 27

Parker

"NONA WON'T BE happy you've got more draw-
ings," Charlotte teased me.

"She'll survive." I smirked.

I don't think Nona actually minded the tattoos; I
was under the impression she just liked to have something to lecture me about.

"When did you get your first one?" she asked
curiously.

That was Charlotte for you. She was like a
curious kitten. She had to know everything about me
and I'd be a damn liar if I said I didn't feel proud of
myself for it.

"Sixteen." I smiled at the memory. "Me and
Jasper lied about how old we were and got a tattoo

each." I chuckled at the memory. "Nona was fuming."

Charlotte giggled. "What did you get?"

I laughed and shook my head. "You won't believe it..."

"It's that damn skull, isn't it?" she demanded.

I didn't answer, but laughed in confirmation of her suspicions.

She swatted my arm. "*That* is what you went with for your first tattoo?" She shook her head in disbelief.

"The guy didn't exactly have a lot to choose from..." I grinned at the memory. "And I still think that out of the two of us, I got a better deal."

Her eyes bulged. "What the hell did Jasper get that could be worse than that skull?"

I laughed loudly. "A rose, with a tribute to his mother underneath."

"Oh, he didn't!" she cried out with a laugh. "Is it done any better than yours?"

I chuckled again. "It's worse... I think the guy was getting tired." I sniggered. "That, or he knew we were underage and that we wouldn't be coming back to complain about the shitty job."

Charlotte half groaned, half laughed. "You're joking... you know you're rich now, right? Asha could fix that."

I'd thought about it several times, but that was as far as I knew I'd ever get with it.

"Nah." I shrugged. "I don't think I'd ever get any

of my tattoos re-done... they tell a story, ya know... it might be a terrible tattoo, but for two sixteen-year-old boys, it was literally the best day ever, and that's all I think about when I look at it."

She smiled sweetly at me and my insides warmed.

"You should tell Nona that story; she might change her opinion of your scribbles." She winked at me.

"I just might do that."

"She seems more worried about you having clean underwear on anyway." She giggled. "I don't even want to know what that's all about."

I shrugged and shot her a grin. "I'm pleading the fifth."

I grabbed for her but she skirted out of my reach. "What, were you like some skiddy undie little punk or something?" she teased me in mock disgust.

I chuckled loudly and shrugged again. "Maybe I still am."

She screwed her nose up. "I'm going to have to keep an eye on you... that is so feral."

I grabbed for her again and she moved just in the nick of time.

"Well maybe you should just move in with me then."

Her step faltered and I got hold of her this time. I tugged her into my lap.

She didn't say a word, but just looked back at me with big, wide, blue eyes.

I nuzzled into my favourite spot on her neck and breathed her in.

This right here is where I should be.

"I mean it, legs, I want you here with me. Will you think about it?" I pleaded, utterly terrified of her turning me down.

She nodded, but didn't say a word.

My lips landed on her skin and she trembled.

"I'll show you what I'm prepared to offer, shall I?" I whispered against her throat.

She tipped her head back further and made a breathy moaning sound that had my dick instantly hard.

So sexy...

"Yes please," she breathed.

I'd show her alright. I'd show her exactly what she could have, *anytime* she wanted if she moved in here with me.

I don't care if it takes all night....

I'm selfless like that.

CHAPTER 28

Charlotte

"CHARLOTTE!" Hannah bellowed through the house. "Charlotte, I need you. *Right now!*"

I flung open my door. "Calm it down, woman, I'm right here."

Han appeared at the end of the hallway, her laptop in her hands. "Fuck, babe, it's not good. But I don't want you to jump to conclusions, okay?"

Ice filled my veins as I took in the look of pure terror on my best friend's face. All of a sudden, I wanted Parker. I wanted him to hold me tight and tell me that whatever was on that laptop wasn't going to hurt me. But he couldn't – he was away playing a sold-out gig... and I had a sinking feeling that whatever was going on, it was about him.

"What is it?" I demanded, holding my hands out for the laptop.

Hannah shook her head. "Sit down and I'll show you."

I rushed back into my room and sat down on my bed. "Give me it," I demanded.

Han looked torn for a moment before sitting next to me and turning the laptop so I could see the picture on the screen.

My heart pounded in my chest.

"It's fake, it's gotta be fake," Hannah insisted.

Her voice echoed in my ears and I felt light headed, my eyes almost going blurry.

The image looking back at me was a selfie, it was posted to a Facebook gossip page three hours ago and had already accumulated half a million reactions and had been shared over thirty thousand times.

It was titled... 'When the baby momma is away, Parker will play'.

I wasn't actually pregnant, but that little stunt I'd pulled a few weeks ago had come back to bite me in the ass big time, so I knew they were referring to me – that and the inset picture of me in the corner made that pretty clear. Also, I wasn't away – Parker was, but that was beside the point.

Their lack of ability to perform research, doesn't change that picture...

Parker's smiling face looked back at me and I felt sick to my stomach.

"It's not real, babe. It's gotta be fake," Han repeated.

I looked over at the blonde-haired, brown-eyed girl that Parker was wrapped around.

Katie.

"I know that girl, Hannah, this photo is as real as they get."

CHAPTER 29

Parker

"PARK, MAN, WE NEED TO TALK," Jasper whispered in my ear.

Fear shot through me. He'd just interrupted a conversation I was having with the label executives after my show finished. I knew that there was no way that Jasper would bust in like that unless it was important.

Really fucking important.

I nodded at him and turned back to the suits. "I just need a minute with my manager, something's come up."

They all gave me their nods of approval and I looked back to Jasper.

He inclined his head in the direction of my dressing room, indicating that we should talk in there, rather than out here, and I swore under my breath.

This was bad news.

If we needed privacy, it meant I was going to hit the god damn roof.

The minute the door was shut behind me I let out a loud string of curse words. "What the hell is it, J?"

"It's bad news, man. You're not gonna like it," he warned.

"Just fucking give it to me, I can't take this suspense bullshit... you know that."

He sighed and reached into his pocket for his phone. He pushed a few buttons, looked at me in compassion and handed it over.

I shook my head at the photo in front of me and frowned. "Katie?" I asked in confusion. "What the hell has this got to do with anything?"

"Look at when it was posted, and check out the caption."

I skimmed over the details.

What the hell?

Posted today?

What the fuck is going on?

"That fuckin' bitch!" I roared when I realized what was going on.

She was trying to ruin me and Charlotte. She may not have posted the image herself, but it didn't take a fuckin' rocket scientist to figure out how

Shelley Corbett, the gossip queen, had gotten her hands on it.

"I'm gonna end her for this." I paced the room, wanting to throw the phone across the room, only holding back because it wasn't my own.

"I think you've got bigger problems right now," Jasper told me quietly.

I froze and felt the colour drain from my face.

Charlotte...

"She doesn't think it's true, does she?" I stalked across the room to get in J's face. "Holy shit, man, have you talked to her, or to Han?"

He clamped his hands down on my shoulders. "Calm the fuck down," he instructed. "I spoke to Hannah."

I let out a relieved breath.

He grimaced and I felt my stomach nose dive again.

"It wasn't good. She told me to tell you she was going to cut your balls off and feed them to you with a knife and fork, and then I heard Charlotte yelling at her in the background to get off the phone."

I stared at him.

"I didn't get a word in before she hung up, and now I can't get hold of either of them."

I felt my world crumbling down around me.

"Get me on the next plane home, J, please."

"Already booked," he told me.

I closed my eyes in relief. I'd never been happier

to have my best friend by my side than I was right now.

"Get your shit, Park, these suits will have to manage without you... we gotta go, right now."

———

I couldn't get Charlotte or Hannah the whole drive to the airport. It had rung the first few times, but not now.

Straight to voicemail.

Every. Single. Time.

I'd stood on a stage, all alone, in front of more people than I could possibly imagine, but I'd never felt as nervous as I did during this two-hour plane ride. I would have taken the private jet, but we weren't scheduled to leave until tomorrow and it wasn't here, even with the wait time to board, flying commercial had still been our fastest option.

"She's not like other girls, man, she'll believe you," J told me quietly from the seat next to mine.

I nodded my head in agreement. Charlotte wasn't like the other girls that had passed through my life. She was so far from it.

That was why I was so scared.

She has to believe me.

Charlotte was the game changer for me. She was sweet, forgiving, loyal and she wasn't easily fooled either.

That's what I'm counting on.

She was also fierce, and she wasn't going to take this shit lying down once she found out it was fake.

IF... if she finds out it's fake...

I jiggled my knee up and down nervously. I just had to hope I got the chance to make her believe me.

CHAPTER 30

Charlotte

"SHUT THAT GOD DAMN PHONE OFF," I snapped at Hannah. If it wasn't her phone ringing, it was mine. If it wasn't Jasper calling, it was Parker.

I just need a minute to think.

"Show me it again," I demanded, holding my hand out for the laptop again.

"Lotte, don't torture yourself, babe," Hannah pleaded with me.

I rolled my eyes. "What happened to 'it's fake'?"

She shot me an apologetic glance. "That was before I found out that you recognised this bitch."

"It's Parker's ex-girlfriend. I searched her on Google one time," I explained. "So, I don't think it's fake, but..."

"Doesn't mean it's not old..." Han thought aloud.

"Exactly," I agreed. "So, hand me that damn computer and let me look at the picture of my boyfriend with another fucking woman."

Hannah grabbed it without further argument and loaded the image back up on the screen.

"I really hope he's not a cheating bastard... he's just *so* easy on the eye." She sighed as she stared at the picture before handing it over to me. "It'd be a shame to have to get rid of him."

I studied the photo hard and my stomach turned at the sight.

I'd never really been a jealous type, but I undoubtedly was now. Just one look at this girl touching my man made me want to scratch her eyes out.

"Do you think he's cheated?" Hannah asked me quietly.

I thought hard before answering her. I thought about every moment I'd spent with Parker and how much he adored me, the way he looked at me...

I knew he loved me.

I loved him.

I trusted him.

I believed in him... I believed in us.

"No." I shook my head. "Parker wouldn't do that to me," I answered with certainty.

Hannah let out a relieved breath. "So, what do we do now?"

"I'm not sure." I shook my head. "There has to be something..."

I stared at the picture for what felt like forever, but got nowhere. He looked younger, but that wasn't enough. I needed one hundred percent proof so I could make this right.

"My turn..." Hannah took the laptop from me again. "God, there is just something sexy about a man with tattoos." She swooned as she ogled Parker.

The light bulb flickered to life above my head.

"Gimme," I demanded as I snatched the computer back.

Hannah scowled at me.

There wasn't much of Parker's chest showing, but there was enough... enough to see that my tattoo was missing from his body.

I nearly cried tears of relief.

"Oh, thank god," I breathed. "It's old... I can prove that it's old."

Hannah was looking at me like I owed her an explanation.

"Let me show you something." I reached for my phone and powered it back on.

I flicked through the camera roll until I found the photo I'd taken of Parker and I, only a few days ago. He was shirtless and I was tucked against the right side of his body, so his new ink was on full display. It was a cheesy photo, I was pointing at the tattoo of me and also at myself, a surprised look on my face. It was completely staged on my behalf, but I loved it. The look on Parker's face was gorgeous, he was smiling at the camera, and I could tell he was looking at me via the image on the screen, his smile was wide and his sexy dimple was in full force.

I turned the screen around to show Han. I hadn't gotten around to telling her what Parker had surprised me with.

"Is that..." She gaped. "Holy shit! He got a tattoo of you?"

I nodded shyly.

"Oh, score, baby." She held her hand up for a high-five.

I laughed and smacked my hand against hers.

"He only got it on Tuesday," I prompted her, hoping she'd be able to make the connection.

She studied my phone for a few beats before grabbing her laptop and looking at that picture again.

"Oh snap." She grinned triumphantly. "That silly bitch! We've got the perfect way to prove this pic is old."

I nodded in agreement. "And I've got a plan for the how," I announced.

CHAPTER 31

Parker

I WASN'T AN OVERLY patient man at the best of times, and even less so when I was under this kind of stress.

We'd sat on the tarmac for about fifteen minutes longer than we needed to, due to a 'scheduling issue' that was preventing us from getting off this damn plane.

Now, the baggage was taking *forever* and I was starting to lose my shit.

Maybe I should have waited for my plane after all.

I stalked over to the 'help here' sign and gave the chick behind the desk my best 'I'm trying to be charming' smile. "Hey there, is there any way we could speed this up? I kinda have some place I need to be."

She blushed and fidgeted with a stack of papers on her desk. "I'm so sorry, Park-, err Mr. Sloan." She blushed an even deeper shade of red. "There's nothing I can do... but it really shouldn't be long now."

I grumbled under my breath, gave her a half-hearted smile and looked around for Jasper. He'd gone to the bathroom about ten minutes ago and I hadn't seen him since.

Great timing to take a shit, man...

I put my head down and tried to avoid making eye contact with the other passengers as I walked across the room. I knew they all knew who I was, but not one of them had approached me. I was giving off a loud and clear 'fuck off' vibe, and I was happy to know it was being received accurately. I slunk down in a seat and reached into my pocket for my phone. I hadn't even turned it back on yet.

Jasper appeared next to me, startling me. I didn't know how the hell the guy did that, but for a reasonably tall guy, he was awfully stealthy.

"You bomb that toilet, man?" I asked absently.

I need to get the hell out of here.

I'd seriously considered just leaving my bag here and figuring that shit out later, but the present I'd bought for Charlotte yesterday was in there, and if I ever got the chance to talk to her again, I wanted to be able to give it to her.

J surprised me by laughing loudly, like something was the funniest thing he'd heard in a long while.

I glanced over at him and he was looking at something on his phone. "Park, man, I think I just might love that girl of yours." He shook his head in disbelief... or amusement, I wasn't sure.

What now?

"What the hell are you talking about?" I demanded, grabbing the phone from his hands.

A huge grin spread across my face as I took in the post on the screen in front of me.

Charlotte had updated her Facebook page.

She'd posted the photo of the two of us that she'd taken right after we'd gotten home from the tattoo studio. She was being a complete goof and I loved it. Her red hair was wild and wavy, just like in the drawing over my heart and her eyes were bright and alive.

She looked like a woman in love.

God she's beautiful.

She had captioned the photo. "Missing this guy right now, but at least I know he's taking a piece of me with him wherever he goes. Shelley Corbett, let's play a game of spot the difference shall we? (And I'm not talking about the blonde piece of ancient history) #Don'tLetTheTruthGetInTheWayOfAGoodStory #FreshInk #LookingForTrouble #NiceTry #PSI'm-NotActuallyPregnant"

She'd tagged me in the photo, and even gone as

far as to tag that pain in the ass Shelley in her caption too.

"It's a shame she couldn't tag Katie." Jasper chuckled. "She's got sass that girl, and hell... I like it."

I didn't know what to say. This thing was blowing up. I had no idea how many views the image of Katie and I had gotten, but I doubted it was more popular than the two million reactions this post had hit in the past two hours.

People were sharing it left, right and centre and the comments ranged from praise for Charlotte for standing up for her man, to people hating on Katie, to people telling me that they knew I wasn't that kind of guy in the first place.

Charlotte was such a private person, and for her to put herself out there like this, was a massive deal. She hated the spotlight, but she'd jumped in, full force... for me.

No woman had ever defended me like this before.

"Well damn," I stated, still smiling like a fool.

"Yeah, man," J agreed. "That's epic."

I felt someone approach me and realised too late that I'd let my 'do not approach' barrier drop. I glanced up and saw it was a young guy hovering around, which was surprising; I was normally approached by women.

"Hey," he said nervously. "I just wanted to check you'd seen it..." He gestured to the phone in my hand.

"Your girl... she's awesome, bro. I've just seen what she put online."

I grinned up at him. "Fuck yeah she is."

He laughed and held out his hand. "I'm Jacob, I'm a big fan."

I looked at his hand and smiled as I remembered Charlotte lecturing me about introducing myself properly.

Just because you're famous, doesn't excuse you being a rude asshole...

"I'm Parker. It's good to meet you." I shook his hand firmly.

He gestured to my shirt-covered chest. "The Little Red Riding Hood reference, I like it." He nodded in approval as he turned to walk away, obviously having made the connection of what the image represented for me. "I hope you two get a chance to live your lives without all this bullshit."

I huffed out a laugh. "Me too, Jacob," I called after him.

God, me too.

As I knew it would, talking to one fan made all the rest feel confident to come out of the woodwork. I spent the next thirty minutes talking and signing shit for half the airport. I actually regretted ditching Sammy back at the arena – not that I was planning on telling him that.

When our bags arrived, we made a run for it. I still hadn't got around to turning my phone on, but I decided I wouldn't bother. It'd be blowing up from all this drama, and the only person I really wanted to talk to was Charlotte anyway.

I know exactly where I'm heading.

CHAPTER 32

Charlotte

"WHY HASN'T he called me back?" I asked Han nervously as I chewed on my bottom lip.

I'd called Parker right after I uploaded the photo, but it had gone to voicemail, so then I'd text and apologised for ignoring his calls earlier and to tell him I loved and missed him. But I hadn't heard back... not one single word.

I was beginning to get worried.

What if I did the wrong thing?

Parker probably had a team of people employed by him to handle this kind of stuff, and he may not have had a publicist right now, but I'm sure he had someone more qualified than I was to sort this mess out.

"He will call," Hannah tried to soothe me.

"He might not, Han, what if he's pissed I turned my phone off and didn't talk about it with him before I took matters into my own hands?"

"The only person here that should be pissed off is *you*. His crazy ex is the one stirring up trouble. That's not on you, girl. You just stood up for yourself and your man. I think Parker will be proud."

"Then why won't he call me?" I whined. I'd caved after about an hour of waiting and called him twice more, and Hannah had taken my phone away before I got the chance to hit redial again.

"For the love of god, woman, it's late. He had a show tonight so my guess is he's either at his appearances, or he's called it a night. Maybe you should just go to bed and worry about it tomorrow."

I laughed humourlessly. "You really think I'd be able to sleep right now?"

"A girl can dream," she muttered. "I could certainly go for some sleep right about now; all this revenge posting has taken the life right out of me." She yawned.

"Go to bed then," I encouraged.

"And leave you out here to get all worked up? Uh, uh. I don't think so." She shook her head. "Not happening, Little Red."

"Urgh," I groaned. "Don't you start calling me that too."

She winked at me like a smart-ass. "You don't like the new ink?" she questioned.

It was actually quite the opposite. Just the thought of him getting marked with a representation of me made me hot, not to mention the fact that it was beautifully done.

I shook my head. "I *love* the tattoo... it's the nickname I could take or leave."

She sighed. "God that's hot. I wish I had a guy that'd get a shrine to me tattooed into his flesh."

I snorted.

A shrine.

She's so damn dramatic.

"Why don't we watch a movie in bed? There's no point in just sitting around waiting for a call that probably isn't coming."

She had a point. There was every chance that Parker and Jasper were busy and that we wouldn't hear from them until tomorrow. If I was going to sit here all night, I may as well try to take my mind off him.

"Fine," I begrudgingly agreed.

I forced myself to get up out of my seat and trudge towards the hallway. It was after one in the morning and I knew I needed to sleep, but I just couldn't seem to turn my mind off.

Hannah grabbed a DVD from the cabinet and switched off the lights as she followed after me.

We both froze as we heard a key turning in a lock.

Our lock.

"Did you just hear—"

"Shhhh," Hannah interrupted my whisper. "Grab a weapon," she hissed.

"I don't have a fucking weapon," I hissed back. "I'm a makeup artist, not a ninja."

"We're both going to die," she whispered.

"The bathroom," I whispered back. "Get to the bathroom, right now!"

The sound of the door handle turning spurred us into action and we dashed for the hallway.

"They've got a key... we're gonna die!" Hannah cried, in full hysteria mode now.

I tugged her into the bathroom and shut the door quietly behind us before securing the lock.

"Call someone," she pleaded, pointing to the phone in my hand.

Who the hell do I call?

I knew who I wanted to call, but Parker hadn't been answering. Even still, my thumb scrolled down to his name on its own accord and hit the green call button.

I heard a loud bang in the living room followed by a string of curse words.

I winced and Hannah looked like she was going to pass out.

"It's ringing," I whispered to her.

We both scrambled away from the door as a sliver of light came underneath it. Whoever was in our apartment had made their way into our living room.

"Oh fuck," I breathed. I squeezed my eyes shut tight.

That was when I heard it, 'Life In The Fast Lane' by the Eagles.

It was a great song, and it also happened to be Parker's ringtone.

He's here.

I exhaled a relieved breath and reached for the lock on the door.

"What the hell are you doing?" Hannah hissed, swatting my hand away.

"It's Parker," I hissed back.

"You are bat-shit crazy, woman, he's not even in town... are you trying to get us killed?"

"It's Parker for fuck's sake," I told her more loudly.

"Shhhhhh."

"I bet you two grand that it's Parker," I told her, as I held her arm back and turned the lock with my free hand.

"I can't use two grand if I'm dead," she cried dramatically.

I shoved her to the side and swung the door open.

"Parker?" I called and crept into the hallway. I knew it was him, but my crazy best friend had me on edge.

Hannah slammed the bathroom door shut behind me and I heard the lock turn.

He appeared in the doorway and my god, was he a sight for sore eyes.

"Legs," he choked out. "I didn't mean to wake you."

I heard a sobbing noise and it took me a moment to figure out it came from me.

I was crying. Big fat, ugly tears streamed down my face as all the pent-up emotions from the day, and the stress of thinking we had an intruder overflowed from within me.

"Charlotte," Parker whispered as he jogged over to me. He scooped me up in his arms as my legs gave way beneath me.

"I... I... could... couldn't... g... g...get you... on... on the phone," I stuttered in between sobs.

"It's okay, baby, I'm here, it's okay."

"I hear crying!" Hannah yelled from behind the bathroom door. "Are you being killed?"

I let out a laugh against Parker's chest that came out sounding like a half sob, half hiccup.

"I told you it was Parker, you fool," I snivelled.

"How'd he get a key?" Hannah demanded – still in hiding and refusing to believe I wasn't being murdered.

That was a damn good question.

I tipped my head back to look at him.

He shot me a sheepish look and rubbed at the back of his neck. "Would you be mad if I told you I'd asked Jasper to make a copy of your key one night when you stayed over?"

"Forced Jasper to make a copy you mean," Jasper called from the living room.

I jumped, startled by his voice, I hadn't realized he was here too.

"Jasper?" Hannah called timidly from inside the still locked bathroom.

"Yeah, barbie?" Jasper called back as he strolled into the hallway, casual as anything, as though it wasn't well after midnight on the most exhausting day I could remember having in a long, long time.

I heard the lock on the bathroom door unlatch before it opened slowly and Hannah appeared.

"I'm not giving you two grand," she told me as she breezed past, heading towards Jasper.

I giggled and shook my head.

"I think I need a hug too," Han teased as though she wasn't bothered in the least. She wasn't fooling me though. She'd been more rattled than I had.

"Bring it in, you little fruit cake," he told her as he opened his arms for her to cuddle in to him.

I couldn't help but notice how comfortable they were together, and I hadn't missed the fact that Hannah had only deemed the situation safe once she'd heard Jasper's voice... I made a mental note to talk to Hannah *again* about the 'one time only' situation these two idiots had agreed to – it was obvious they still both meant something to one another.

Jasper rested his cheek on the top of Hannah's head and took a deep breath almost as though he was as relieved to have her in his arms as I was to be in Parker's.

I looked away.

That was another mystery to be solved another day.

"God, I missed you," Parker whispered as he held me tight, rocking me gently side to side, kind of like you would do to soothe a baby.

"I missed you more," I whispered back.

"I'm so, so sorry this happened, legs... the thought of you being hurt by something like this cuts me so damn deep." He looked down into my eyes as he spoke, and I could tell just how distraught he was by the situation.

I didn't blame him for this – not at all. All he'd done was be his famous self... the madness just followed him.

"I'm just *so* tired," I told him as tears pooled in the corners of my eyes for no real reason at all. I tried my best to hold them back. "Could we talk about this after a few hours sleep?"

Parker nodded at me quickly. "Of course, baby, whatever you need."

I snuggled into his chest. "I just need you."

I closed my eyes and breathed in the familiar scent of the man I loved.

Nothing has ever smelt this good...

I could feel the exhaustion taking over as my eyelids got heavier. I took another deep breath.

Not even bacon smells this good...

I was vaguely aware of Parker lifting me off the floor and into his arms – much the same as he had on that first night in the club. I heard the conversation Parker and Jasper had about them both spending the night, but it was like I was listening to it from the other side of a hotel wall... I couldn't make out the exact words.

Parker carried me into my room and somehow managed to hold me up with one arm as he stripped back the covers from my bed and placed me gently down onto the sheets.

"Charlotte?" he murmured quietly as he brushed my mane of hair to the side.

"Mmm hmm?" I answered sleepily.

"Thank you for believing in me," he said, his voice betraying his emotions.

My eyes flickered open so I could look at his gorgeous face. "Thank you for being someone I can believe in," I replied simply.

He placed a soft kiss to my lips before stripping off and crawling in next to me and holding me tight like he couldn't get close enough.

I'd never felt so safe or loved in my entire life.

CHAPTER 33

Parker

THE PHONE RANG ALOUD in the room. Charlotte had asked me to put it on speaker phone and I'd agreed, on the condition that she stayed quiet. I didn't want her losing her shit and giving Katie the satisfaction of knowing that this little stunt had hurt her. And I knew it had hurt her – no matter how strong or level headed she had been, seeing me with another woman, even if it were in the past, had hurt her.

"Hello?" a frazzled-sounding voice answered.

"Hello." I frowned. "Is this Katie?"

"Speaking," she replied.

"It's—"

"Don't you dare throw that in the house!" she

yelled, obviously holding her hand over the mic and speaking to someone on her end of the phone.

I shot Charlotte a 'what the fuck' look and she shrugged in return.

There was a series of bangs and then she spoke again.

"Sorry, I didn't catch that, who is this?"

"It's Parker," I told her quickly.

"Parker?" she asked, confusion colouring her voice. "As in Parker Sloan?"

"Yes, Katie, it's Parker Sloan."

"Parker? Really? Um... hey?" she replied. She seemed distracted, like she had something important going on in the background.

I had no idea what the hell was going on here, but this conversation wasn't going as I'd expected it to. I'd been expecting a smug, ego-filled reply. But that wasn't what was happening.

"We need to talk," I told her sharply.

"Can you give me two seconds?" she asked, and I heard her put the phone down before I could give her an answer.

Unbelievable...

There was some yelling, some crying and the sound of footsteps before the line went quiet.

"Are you still there?" she asked.

"I'm here."

"So... hi..." She sounded confused. "What can I do for you, Parker? I haven't heard from you in a really long time. Is something wrong?"

I felt my anger rising, I wasn't in the mood for playing games. Charlotte must have sensed I was running out of patience, because she reached out and took my hand in hers, stroking the side gently with her small thumb.

I took a deep breath, her touch calming me. "I think you can figure out what we need to talk about, Katie. I don't have time for this shit."

I heard her suck in a breath. "What the hell are you talking about?" she demanded.

Even Charlotte couldn't placate me now. "Cut the shit, Katie. You and I both know that you released that photo to fuck with me and Charlotte."

"What?" she screeched. "I don't have god damn clue what you're talking about... Parker, I don't even know who the hell Charlotte is, let alone why I'd want to 'fuck with' you both."

"It's all over Facebook, you can't pretend—"

"I don't have a Facebook account," she interrupted me, her voice rising with agitation now too. "I don't even have internet in the house."

What?

Now I was confused.

"I don't understand," I stated dumbly.

"No, Parker, *I* don't understand. You call me, totally out of the blue, when I'm busy with my husband and my children, and then you start throwing accusations around that are totally outrageous."

I felt like a scolded child.

"You have children?" I asked, unsure of why I was surprised.

"Yes, I have a nearly two-year-old and an eight-week-old with my husband, Jack," she replied, sounding tired.

Shit, shit, shit.

I knew from the tone in her voice that she was telling the truth. She wasn't responsible for this.

"I think I should explain," I offered.

"I think that would be a good idea, Parker."

"Well... that was... interesting?" Charlotte said it like a question.

I was more confused now than I was when I'd gotten on the phone in the first place. I'd let myself believe that it was Katie being a shit-stirring bitch, even though I hadn't heard from her in years. Now that it was clear she'd played no part in it, I didn't know what to think.

Katie was not only completely in the dark about the whole situation, but now she was fuming mad too. She had as much, actually more to lose than I did. Charlotte and I had even spoken briefly to her husband, Jack, who happened to be a lawyer, about what could be done about this image being posted without our permission. I had my own lawyer, or course, but the guy was a douche and I didn't like to ring him unless I had no other option.

I'd gotten off the phone after promising to do what I could to find out who was responsible. I didn't like Katie much after what she'd done to me, but it was obvious she'd turned her life around and was doing her best to be a good wife and mother.

So, what now?

I couldn't even figure out where that photo had come from, or how someone had gotten their hands on it. It had been on social media once, but that was years ago, and I'd pulled it down after we'd broken up.

That had to mean that someone had kept that image, all this time.

And for what purpose? Just to fuck with me?

I'd given J the job of calling every social media site that had posted it, and threatening to sue if it wasn't pulled. There was no way it was ever going to disappear now, but at least we could try and minimise the exposure.

Jasper was one hundred percent convinced that Nelly was responsible for this, but I had my doubts. She had nothing to achieve by being a bitch, she had already been fired and there was no way in hell I would ever offer her a job working for me again. There was nothing for her to gain by doing this – and if I knew one thing about Nelly, it was that she was only out for what she could get for herself.

The last thing she'd want was me coming after her with a lawsuit.

None of this made much sense... but I was

famous – I got it. Weird shit happened to famous people. But it wasn't as though I had some scorned ex-lover, or some feud with some other musician. There was no genuine reason for somebody to want to mess with me and Charlotte. She had her own demons from the past, but from what I understood, Stephen was married, on the other side of the world, and hadn't bothered her for years.

We were right back to square one, and I was well out of my depth playing detective.

———

We spent the better part of the day trying to figure out what the hell had happened, and the longer we took, the more the view, like and share count grew on both Charlotte's post, and also on Shelley's.

This thing was blowing up big time.

Being without a publicist currently was terrible timing, I'd probably never required damage control quite as much as I did right now. Jasper was doing his best, he'd spoken to what seemed like hundreds of people, and I'd heard him making some pretty creative threats.

I think he's enjoying himself a little too much.

The one person we really wanted to speak to – that silly bitch, Shelley – wasn't available to talk, or so her assistant told us. She was the only person that was going to be able to offer any real insight into where the photo had come from... and she wasn't talking. Chances are, she would never reveal her sources anyway.

I did know one thing, if she didn't call back soon, I was going to get my asshole lawyer on the phone and have him sue her for defamation.

She might have been a big deal in the world of reporting, but she would not want to go head to head with me over this thing – I had more money than sense, and I wasn't afraid to use it.

CHAPTER 34

Charlotte

I WOKE up covered in sweat, mid-scream – something that had never happened with Parker asleep in the bed next to me.

Images of Stephen flooded my mind and I felt a tear slide down my face and fall onto the pillow.

"Legs?" Parker asked drowsily, reaching around for me.

I let out a deep breath and realised I was shaking from the intensity of the dream.

"Baby?" he asked again, his voice slightly panicked now.

"I'm okay," I choked out.

Parker sat up straight at the sound of my voice. "Oh, Charlotte, what's wrong?"

He reached around until he found me and pulled me in tight against his chest.

I let out another shaky breath, feeling better for being in his arms already.

"It was just a bad dream," I whispered.

He stroked my back slowly. "Tell me about it."

I shook my head. "I don't remember."

"Don't lie to me, legs," he replied quickly, his voice turning hard. "It was about that bastard, wasn't it?"

I nodded into his chest, embarrassed by the fact that Stephen still had a hold over me.

"About the way he treated you?" he pushed.

I nodded again.

"Are you okay?" he asked, his tone gentler now.

I shook my head.

No.

Stephen's words were still weighing me down – doing their best to make me feel worthless.

I don't know why he was making a reappearance now of all times. I was happy... I had Parker, I had a good job, I had so much more than I did when I walked away from him, yet the memories of him had chosen now to come back with full force.

It was almost as though my subconscious was trying to get a message to me. What that message might have been, I had no idea.

"I've got you," Parker soothed as he held me tight, nestling us back down under the covers. "I'll have you every night if you let me." He tucked his body around mine, my back to his front, and hummed into my ear. I recognised the song as 'Only You' by Aaron Krause. He began to softly sing, and I felt my body relaxing into his, his voice a soothing rhythm that eventually lulled me to sleep.

———

"I'm going to have to call Ty," I groaned.

We were having no luck finding out what this photo was all about, and honestly, I didn't really care anymore, but Parker was pissed, and he wanted to find out whose life he needed to ruin.

I'd really been hoping it wouldn't have come to this. I really, *really* didn't want to involve my brother in my drama… in fact; I'd been hoping he was off on vacation in some faraway land where there was no Wi-Fi…

I already knew that I'd be shit-out-of-luck with that idea.

Ty would never go anywhere without Wi-Fi.

"Your brother?" Parker asked with a frown. "What's he gonna do about it?"

I sighed, and Hannah smacked me lightly on the arm. "I didn't even think of that. We should have just called him in the first place." Her eyes danced with excitement.

"I was specifically trying *not* to involve him," I groaned again.

Hannah snorted. "That's cute. He's probably

already figured it out and is just waiting for your call." She rolled her eyes.

She's probably right.

"Is anyone going to explain what the hell you're both talking about?" Parker interrupted us.

Hannah bit into an apple. "Her brother, Ty, is one of those hacker geeks," she explained between chomps.

"He's a qualified computer programmer," I corrected her.

Who am I kidding... he's a hacker...

She snorted out a laugh. "Yeah, that might be the 'official term'." She waved her hand. "But he's totally a hacker," she insisted to Parker, who was watching us with a look of amusement on his face. "And he's good too."

I grimaced. Hannah had been known to flirt with the oldest of my brothers from time to time. She batted her eyelids and he gave her whatever she wanted. One time, she'd managed to have him hack into a well-known online store and lower the price of a designer purse she wanted, to cost price. She'd paid a fraction of the retail price and had it shipped out to her. I couldn't tell you exactly what Ty had done on that keyboard – but the store was absolutely none the wiser.

He'd even offered to just get it for her for free, but she'd insisted she wasn't a thief, she just didn't see the sense in paying a four-thousand-dollar mark-up.

I rolled my eyes at the memory.

"I could do with a new purse actually." Hannah smiled, obviously thinking about the same thing I was. "Let me call him," she offered as she reached for the phone.

I snatched the phone away from her. "No. No freakin' way. You two are going to get yourselves arrested one of these days," I hissed.

She rolled her eyes. "That's an insult to your brother," she accused. "He's too good to get caught."

I pointed a finger at her in warning. "For God's sake, Han, just behave yourself for two minutes would you?"

"Come watch a movie with me, barbie," Jasper called. "Let the adults deal with the boring shit."

I'd forgotten Jasper was even still here. He could be as quiet as a mouse sometimes and these past two nights had been no exception. There was a neatly folded pile of blankets and a pillow on the couch each morning, from where he'd supposedly slept, but I was doubtful that he'd even used them. I made yet another mental note to find out from Hannah what was going on between them.

Hannah pouted, but went and sat next to Jasper on the couch – it was an interesting dynamic to watch, he seemed to be able to tame her when nobody else could.

"You've got a kooky-sounding family, legs," Parker teased.

"You're telling me?" I rolled my eyes as I scrolled through my contacts looking for Tyler's number.

"You think he'll be able to help trace where it came from?" Parker asked, his voice sounding hopeful.

I sighed in defeat that I was giving in and calling him for help. "He hasn't come across something he couldn't hack yet, so yeah, I'd say the chances are pretty good."

Parker looked impressed.

I dialled the number and waited for the telling off I was sure to be getting.

The phone rang only twice and I held back a groan, knowing that Hannah had been right when she said he was probably waiting for my call.

"I was wondering how long it was going to take for you to call me," he drawled.

I pinched the bridge of my nose and cursed under my breath. "Sorry, Ty, just don't be a dick... just this once, okay? We need your help," I pleaded.

"*We* huh? I take it from your use of the word, and that sassy little post on your Facebook page, that lover boy isn't a cheating bastard after all?" he scoffed, and this time I did groan.

Nothing was ever simple with my brothers. Nothing ever stopped short of a full-blown interrogation.

When all that shit had gone down with Stephen, I'd had to force each of my brothers to swear on their lives that they wouldn't get involved. I needed their support emotionally – what I did not require, was the specific set of skills that they each possessed. Not every girl had a hacker, a boxer and a race car/stunt driver for brothers. The three of them together screamed trouble. The celebrity status of Stephen Miles wouldn't have protected him for even a fraction of a second against those three.

I took a deep breath and braced myself. "Yes, *we*," I confirmed. "My boyfriend, Parker – as I'm sure you're already aware, and I have been having some problems that I need your help with, and yes, you're correct in your assumption that he is *not* a cheating bastard."

He chuckled down the line. "Oh, I'm aware of the situation alright, short-stuff. The only reason I wasn't onto it sooner was because I had a date last night."

"Ooooh, and who was the lucky lady?" I asked sarcastically.

"Her name was Billie, and to be honest she was a little dull."

I laughed at his frankness.

"Anyway... she's only just left, so I'm kinda late to the game."

"She only just left?" I cried. "You *just* told me she was dull?"

"She was," he agreed. "But surprisingly, I was okay with her being dull... in my bed... all night long... we didn't do much talking to be fair."

"You're disgusting."

"You love me," he boasted.

"Out of obligation," I mumbled.

I heard him tapping away on his keyboard, our banter clearly not getting in the way of his work.

"Are you going to tell me what the hell you're doing?" I demanded.

He chuckled. "Calm your tits."

I took another deep breath and rolled my neck. I glanced at Parker who was listening to my end of our exchange with delight. Siblings ribbing one another was funny if you weren't stuck in the middle of it.

"Put him on speaker, babe?" Parker asked.

I hit the speaker button. "You're on speaker with me and Parker," I informed Tyler.

"What? No Hannah banana?"

"I got banished to the couch!" Han hollered out to him, obviously still within ear shot. "They think we're bad news together."

Ty chuckled. "They're not wrong there, princess."

Parker shot me a 'what's that about?' look at Ty's use of the term 'princess', but I just laughed and shook my head. It wasn't meant as a term of endearment – if anything, it was a dig at Hannah's diva tendencies.

"So, I'm on the line with 'I'm a Teen' magazine's sexiest bachelor am I?" Tyler prompted.

Parker laughed loudly. "If the shoe fits..."

"So, what's the deal with this cosy little picture? Because if you're screwing my sister around, I'll end you," Ty threatened.

Well that went from zero to one hundred reeeeaaaal quick.

"Whhhhyyy?" I moaned as I covered my eyes, my face blushing scarlet. "Why couldn't I have had sisters?"

Why do brothers have to be so embarrassing?

I peeked over at Parker, expecting him to look shocked, or surprised, or pissed off... or anything other than thoroughly amused like he was right now.

He grinned a massive, genuine grin at me – obviously enjoying my embarrassment.

"Trust me, man, I'd never intentionally do anything to hurt her," he reassured my brother, with his eyes firmly locked on mine. "But regardless, I respect the warning; you wouldn't be a very good protector if I didn't feel the threat loud and clear."

The line went silent for a moment.

"He sounds alright, Lotte."

"*He* can still hear you," I replied.

"I know," Ty answered, and I could hear the smile in his voice.

Parker chuckled – not at all fazed by Tyler's attempt at being the staunch guardian.

I rubbed my temples. When I woke up this morning, I had not been expecting a family meet and greet. "Can we just get back to it?" I begged.

"Already on it," Ty promised. "So, I assumed you would want to know where it came from?"

"Yes," I breathed. "That would be great."

"So, I've tracked its path through social media,

and the first person to post it was a… Shelley Corbett from HDN news, but I can see you've already figured that much out yourself…"

"Yeah." I nodded as I listened. We had.

"Can you hack her emails?" I asked, before laughing at the ludicrous question I'd just asked. "Who am I kidding? You're already doing it, aren't you?"

He chuckled. "So, I hacked into her work account – which might I add, needs a serious firewall update."

"Ty…"

He was so easily distracted when it came to all that computer mumbo jumbo.

"Sorry… so she received the image about a half hour before she posted it online. The server's scrambled from the sender's end, so I'm just tracing it back to the original source through a series of channels. But don't worry, whoever sent this doesn't have anywhere near enough of a clue to keep me out."

He tapped away a few more times.

"And there we go," he announced triumphantly, even though this was nothing more than child's play to him.

"Who was it?" I demanded.

"You'll have to give me a minute to look around, but the I.P. address is located in… Paris?" He sounded confused. "Do you even know anyone in Paris?"

"I know a few… but none with a death wish,"

Parker chimed in. It didn't matter who he knew – I already had my answer.

My blood boiled. "I only know one person that would do this," I ground out.

"And there it is," he confirmed. "The image came in, and went out again... we're in the right place."

"Hack him," I demanded, full-blown rage taking over.

"Ah 'hack' his what?" he asked, his voice excited at the prospect, even though he obviously didn't approve of my use of the term 'hack'.

"Everything," I hissed. "His whole damn life."

"Consider it done," he replied as he hit his keys a few more times.

"God this guy watches a lot of porn." He chuckled.

I was seething, Parker approached me and tugged gently on my arm in question, but I was too mad to speak. I just shook my head at him.

"Woah... it looks like the wifey likes to pose in the nude..." He whistled low. "Or is this one the wife?"

"Ty!" I snapped.

"Sorry," he replied quickly. "Maybe if you'd just tell me whose fucking computer I was in, I could spend less time snooping around, and more time destroying his life."

He made a valid point.

"Stephen Miles," I announced, my tone laced with venom. "So, I really hope you're not exaggerating when you say you can ruin him."

Parker growled deep in his throat from behind me, and I spun around to face him. He looked wild. There was this feral look in his eyes that I'd never seen before, and I knew that if we were to set him and Stephen loose in a cage right now, there would be absolutely no contest – Parker would rip him limb from limb.

"Motherfucker!" He slammed his fist down on the dining table. "I'll kill him," he ground out.

"Consider it done," Ty replied in an airily calm voice. The darkness in his tone caused my skin to break out in goose bumps. "He can kiss his career goodbye." He chuckled humourlessly. "His bank accounts are now frozen, the nude pictures of his side pieces have been made public..."

I'd never been more grateful for my brother's skills and efficiency than I was in this moment.

He tapped away on his keyboard. "Every fucking last thing he has, I'll take it from him, Charlotte," he promised me.

This was why I loved my brothers. They might have been a total pain the ass most of the time, but they'd do anything for me –Tyler especially.

"Thank you," I whispered.

There wasn't one ounce of guilt in me for doing this right now. I should have let my brothers take care of him when he'd messed with me the first time, but I hadn't.

I'd thought of myself as the bigger person, and I'd done things the noble way as Hannah and I had slogged our way back. The boys didn't know how hard it had been for us. I hated the thought of them giving up anything to help me – so I simply didn't tell them how rough things had gotten.

"Put lover boy on the phone and go take a minute," Tyler instructed me, and for once in my life I was happy to do what I was told.

Parker held his hand out for the phone and I gladly passed it to him.

I was exhausted.

I'd thought that Stephen was out of my life forever, yet, here he was, making some kind of last ditch attempt to fuck with me. But worse than that, he'd fucked with Parker, and that shit wasn't okay with me.

"That god damn prick," Hannah cussed as I joined her and Jasper in the living room.

"If that brother of yours doesn't ruin him thoroughly enough, Park will finish the job, you know that, right?" Jasper stated as he watched his friend talking with the phone up to his ear now. "He's been looking for an excuse to bring the pain to that bastard, and fucking with you is about the worst thing he could have done."

I nodded in acknowledgement at the truth in Jasper's words. I had no doubt that Parker was the kind of man that protected what was his. And luckily enough for me, I was his now.

Parker spoke down the phone to Ty for a few minutes and then handed it back to me; he sat down next to me in the seat and pulled me into his lap.

"All good, Ty?" I asked with my eyes closed.

I was bone tired. I breathed in Parker's scent and felt myself start to relax.

He placed soft kisses to the top of my head.

"Oh, I'm good alright," Tyler replied enthusiastically. "I've been dying to take this prick down for years."

I had to laugh a little at that. Now I just had to let Louis give him the beat down and Floyd drive the getaway vehicle, and I'd have three very happy brothers.

"Just make sure you don't get caught," I told him, unable to switch off my sisterly worrying.

Now it was his turn to laugh. "I appreciate your concern, short-stuff, but I'm already out, and he could spend the rest of his life trying to figure out who hit him, and he still wouldn't come close."

"Thank you, Ty."

"No problem, sweetheart," he replied genuinely.

There was still something bugging me about this whole situation.

"Where'd he get that picture, Ty?"

I was assuming that he'd discovered I'd finally met someone new, and this was his attempt to hurt me... but it still didn't explain where he'd gotten that photo from in the first place.

"I haven't looked into it yet, I'll let you know

when I have the name, shouldn't be more than half an hour, okay?"

I breathed out deeply.

"Are you alright?" he asked softly.

"I'll be fine. You've taken care of the karma, and I've got Parker and Hannah here to look after me."

"And me," Jasper chimed in, pretending to be offended by his exclusion.

I laughed. "And Jasper," I amended.

"I'm glad you're not alone."

Parker had started raking his fingers through my hair now, and I hummed appreciatively.

"He seems like a pretty cool guy, short-stuff."

"He is."

"Didn't think I'd find anyone that could hate Stephen as much as me and dumb and dumber, but I was wrong."

Dumb and dumber was what the boys all referred to each other as. It didn't matter if it was Floyd talking about Tyler and Louis, or Tyler talking about Louis and Floyd, or Louis talking about Tyler and Floyd. It was always 'dumb and dumber', and it drove me crazy.

"Anyway, I'll let you go; I've got shit to do."

"Thanks, Ty, I really owe you."

He snorted a noise of disagreement before mumbling "Love you."

"I love you too."

————

"All the pics are gone," Jasper stated, looking totally bewildered.

"Oh shit!" Parker leaned forward in excitement. "I forgot to tell you..." He turned to face me. "Your brother has been working on this new thing where he can just *block* an image." He frowned at his lame attempt at explaining it. "He tried to enlighten me with how he did it... but it went way over my head. He somehow does a search of it on the entire web and then it gets blocked." He shrugged.

I giggled. Parker obviously had about as much of an understanding of computer programming as I did.

"Yeah... I don't know what he did." He chuckled. "But they're gone. *All of them*. He said he can't do shit about people taking screen shots or anything that has gone to print already, but every single copy of that image that's on the web, or goes on the web, just disappears... like it ceases to exist."

"It's like magic," J replied.

"That's what I said," Parker agreed.

I was willing to bet that this 'magic trick' of Ty's wasn't all that new. When Stephen had gone to the media back then, it had been surprisingly contained – the whole world had still heard, but publicly, it had died down fairly quickly. I had always had a feeling that Tyler had a hand in that. The real problem back then had been the lies that Stephen had spread personally within the industry... and unfortunately there was no easy way to stop someone talking – not legally anyway.

"We should have called him right at the start. That hacking was badass," Parker mused as he slung his arm over my shoulders and tugged me into him. "I want to meet him, legs."

"You should meet Louis and Floyd too, if you really want to get the full effect of the threatening threesome," Hannah offered helpfully.

Parker raised his eyebrows at me. "The threatening threesome?" he prompted.

I giggled. "Yeah... they're kind of like action men that never run out of battery power."

"Do I even want to ask what the other two do for a living?" Parker asked, looking slightly concerned.

I winced. "Only if you're not going to be intimidated by hearing that they're a professional boxer and a stunt driver respectively."

His eyes widened.

"Actually, I think Floyd's more into that Formula whatever it's called these days..." I thought aloud.

"Your brother is Louis 'The Destroyer' Watson?" Jasper demanded, leaning forward in his chair in anticipation of my answer.

"Well that doesn't sound very pleasant." I frowned. "But yeah... that'll be him."

"Well I'll be damned." Jasper shook his head in what looked like bewilderment.

"You a boxing fan, Jasp?" I prompted.

Parker tugged gently on the strand of my hair that he was playing with. "Jasper gets hard for that shit."

He grinned. "Never seen him as excited as when he's watching two men brawling."

"I get extra hard when 'The Destroyer' comes on," Jasper piped up, not in the least bit fazed by the shade being thrown his way.

"Urrrgghh," I groaned. "That was too much information... I feel sick."

I slipped out from under Parker's arm. "I'll just be in the bathroom throwing up if anybody needs me."

Jasper laughed. "Sorry, Lots. It was just a joke."

I headed for the bathroom. I didn't really need to vomit, but I did need to pee.

"They call Floyd 'The Ghost'," I heard Hannah explaining to the boys as I entered the hallway. "He's pretty big on the legit driving scene these days, but the name and the rep came with him from the old days. Rumour has it he could turn up faster than you could even imagine, and then just disappear into nothing with no trace that he was ever even there. He's got mad skills."

"This is so cool," Parker replied enthusiastically, obviously impressed with my brothers' antics.

I rolled my eyes and grinned.

Trust the adrenaline-junky rock star to be impressed.

"You know, there was news of a gold heist in Rio a few years back... word on the street was the getaway driver was the best in the business – and guess who happened to be holidaying there at exactly that time..."

I laughed. Hannah loved to speculate about my brother's extra-curricular activities. In this particular case, I was pretty sure she was right on the money, but I wasn't going to tell her that.

None of the boys were exactly known for their sense of right and wrong.

They must have inherited something from our parents after all.

But what they were known for was being smart, loyal and loving... and that was more than enough to make them my heroes.

Even though I'll never tell them that.

———

My phone dinged with an incoming message as I walked back into the living room.

"That's probably Ty with the source," I called to Parker as I headed to the kitchen for a glass of water. "Can you check it?"

"Janelle Conrad," he called back. "That's all it says."

I wracked my brain for a few moments, but came up empty. I didn't know a single person by the name of Janelle.

I joined the others in the living room and took my phone from Parker to look at the message myself.

"Does anyone recognise that name?"

Jasper shook his head, Hannah shrugged and Parker replied. "No."

"Well who the hell is she then?" I demanded.

"Google her," Jasper suggested.

Hannah rolled her eyes at him. "Just get Ty to find out. Save us all some time."

I ignored Hannah, instead taking Jasper's advice.

I typed the name into the search engine and hit search.

"Oh shit," I muttered.

Shit, shit, shit, shit, shit...

This was not good. Parker was literally going to hit the roof...

Shit the bed... throw alllll the toys out of the cot...

He was going to lose it *big time*.

"I'm not going to like it, am I?" he ground out through clenched teeth.

I shook my head and bit down on my lip.

I was scared to say the words – not because I feared Parker, but because I was terrified of his head exploding with all the rage.

"Take a deep breath," I instructed. "And sit down."

Somewhere along the line, he had jumped to his feet. His muscles were straining against his t-shirt and I couldn't help but take a moment to appreciate just how damn fine this man really was.

I sighed, forgetting for a moment that we were in the middle of a semi-crisis.

"C'mon, Little Red, you can undress him later, tell us already," Jasper drawled.

I blushed at being caught red handed and screwed up my nose – Parker still hadn't sat back down.

"So, you know how you've had that shitty run with publicists..." I trailed off, leaving him to make the connection between the two things.

I saw the exact moment his brain put it together.

"Nelly?" Parker barked.

I nodded.

"That god damn bitch!" he roared. He flew across the room and into a rage. I was glad as hell that we were at my place and not his – if he were surrounded by his own shit right now, I had no doubt he'd be smashing it all up without a second thought.

At least he can't do that here.

I sighed as my eyes followed his every step.

"I told him it was her," Jasper stated as he watched Parker stomping around the room cursing and swearing.

"Oh Janelle... Nelly... I get it." Hannah narrowed her eyes. "Man... what a biatch."

"Doesn't even cover it," I seethed.

I leapt up off my chair when I saw Parker eyeing up the coffee table. He looked about ready to pick it up and throw it across the room.

"This isn't an antique or anything, right?" he asked when I got closer.

"Don't even think about it, rock star."

He didn't take his eyes off it, but he also made no move to toss it around either, so he'd obviously heard me.

He stood there, his breath heaving, his whole body near trembling with the exertion he was using to keep himself under control.

I approached him slowly – like he was some kind of wild animal I didn't want to spook.

"Parker?" I asked quietly. "Are you okay?"

He laughed humourlessly. "That fucking bitch..." he muttered.

It was pretty clear he wasn't up to talking just now, so instead, I wrapped my arms around him from behind and nuzzled my cheek against his back.

It took about ten minutes of standing silently with me holding him, for him to calm down and relax enough to speak.

He squeezed my hands. "Thank you," he told me quietly as he turned in my arms and pulled me against him, holding me tight and breathing me in. "I just can't believe she'd stoop that low," he said after a few more moments of quiet contemplation.

"I can't figure out *why* she would?" I wondered aloud.

He sighed. "I'm running the risk of sounding like an arrogant, cocky bastard here, but you're aware I'm loaded, right? And famous and shit?"

I sniggered.

And he's back...

Parker acted like a cocky bastard a lot in the

public eye, but never with me – not unless he was doing it in that sexy way that he knew made me weak in the knees. But still, it was pretty sweet that he thought enough of it now to pre-warn me if he was about to say something douche-like.

"You think she's after money?" I frowned. "But how would she get money from doing this?"

He thought about it for a moment. "Yeah I guess you're right... unless someone paid her for the photo... but I don't think Stephen would be that desperate..."

I huffed. "Stephen would be *exactly* that desperate." I wiggled free of him and paced the room back and forth as I tried to think it through. "We've missed something... it just doesn't add up – if she wanted money she would have come to you and demanded some kind of ransom for it, right?"

It just doesn't make sense...

"I hate to say it, but I think we'll need more help from Ty..."

"Maybe he heard we were dating?" Parker suggested. "He would hate that..."

It's possible...

"But who is he out to get? Me or you?"

Truthfully, I didn't give a shit anymore. Stephen's life would be a mess by now – he'd got his karma. But Parker couldn't let it go – I was quickly learning that he was a man that saw things through to the bitter end.

Parker growled deep in his throat and stalked over to where I was standing by the window. "Fuck him being out to get *you*, legs. He even takes a breath in the same air space as you and it'll be his last."

Goosebumps broke out on my skin at the sincerity of his vow.

I had no doubt whatsoever that he meant every word.

———

I blinked drowsily as I woke from a deep sleep. I reached for Parker, but he wasn't there – the soft melody floating down the hall told me exactly where he'd got to.

I glanced around the darkened room, unsure of what exactly it was that had caused me to wake.

My mind drifted back to the dream I'd been having... right back to the statement Jasper had made earlier, and the end of the conversation I'd had with my brother.

There was something that had been nagging at my subconscious all evening, but I hadn't been able to put my finger on it until now.

I lay in bed, listening to the soft strum of Parker's guitar, he was singing quietly too – I couldn't make out the words, but it sounded beautiful.

I swung my legs out of bed and threw on a sweat-shirt of Parker's that was draped over the chair in the corner. It came midway down my thighs so I decided to forgo pants.

I padded down the hallway; a soft light from Parker's studio glowing ahead of me.

I approached slowly, hoping to have the chance to listen to him before he spotted me, or sensed me, or whatever it was that he did that seemed to make him aware of me whenever I was near.

My heart skipped a beat as I realized he was singing one of my songs – not the one he'd serenaded me with on stage, but another that he'd written around the same time. I knew I was the only person in the entire world that had heard this song. Even with his expert sneaking skills, Jasper still hadn't managed to get his hands on it.

I slipped into the doorway and leant my head against the door frame as I took in the sight in front of me.

Parker was wearing only a pair of grey sweat pants, slung low on his hips – his back to the door where I stood. His head was bent low as his calloused fingers strummed at the familiar strings.

His voice glided effortlessly over the verse as he sung about me being the light in his darkened room.

Goosebumps broke out on my skin.

I'll never get used to this.

CHAPTER 35

Parker

I KNEW she was there the moment she stepped into the doorway. She hadn't even made a sound, but I could tell she was watching me. For one thing, I could smell her – her perfume... her shampoo... whatever that smell that followed her everywhere was, it was just *her*, and I knew I'd recognise it anywhere.

But it was more than just the smell, I had this awareness of her – the connection we shared was something I'd never experienced before.

I finished the verse and stilled my hands. I sat silently for a moment – reworking a section in my mind.

When I was satisfied, I sat my guitar down.

"Can't sleep, legs?" I asked her without turning around.

I heard the whoosh of fabric as she padded lightly into the room. She came up behind me and wrapped her tiny arms around me, resting her chin on my shoulder.

"How'd you know I was there?" she murmured against my neck.

"My built-in 'Charlotte radar' buzzed."

She giggled and the vibration of her laugh against the back of my body gave me tingles up and down my spine.

I loosened her arms and turned around on the stool I was sitting on to face her.

God she's beautiful.

I'd never really understood the obsession some men had with seeing a woman wearing their shirt, or some other item of their clothing.

But now I get it.

Holy hell, did I understand it now. The sweatshirt of mine that Charlotte was wearing was more like a dress on her, and it was in no way a revealing outfit, but it was undoubtedly the sexiest I'd ever seen her look. Her hair was loose and wild, just the way I liked it, and her lips were pouty and full, swollen from the hours of attention I'd given them earlier tonight.

Sexy as hell.

I tugged her forward so she was seated in my lap,

her legs straddling me. "You okay, baby? It's not like you to be up at this hour."

Where I could function off a few short hours sleep each night, Charlotte was like a grizzly bear if she got less than a solid seven. It wasn't an exaggeration on my behalf either; both Charlotte and Hannah were sleepers. And for such a tiny little woman, my girl could be damn terrifying if anyone messed with her beauty rest.

"Well... there actually *is* something bothering me..." she confessed, as she nibbled on her bottom lip – what I'd quickly learned to be her nervous tell.

My heart sped up in my chest – my sense of panic rising in an instant. There was nothing in this world that scared me more than seeing uncertainty in her eyes.

She knew me well already. "It's nothing bad," she reassured me quickly, running her hands through my hair in calming strokes. "I probably should have realised sooner, but I didn't..."

I looked into her beautiful blue eyes and waited as patiently as I could for whatever the question was that had caused the centre of my universe to lose sleep.

"Stephen." She stated his name, her tone laced with repulsion. "You two have a history that has nothing to do with me... don't you?"

I couldn't help the small growl that escaped my lips at the mention of that bastard's name.

I'd never told Charlotte about my encounter with

her ex-boyfriend. I hadn't wanted to upset her, and it wasn't like it really mattered now anyway – she already knew he was a prick, so rehashing the past wasn't going to achieve anything. He'd hurt her so much already, I hadn't wanted to inflict any more pain by telling her about what I knew.

But here she was, asking me outright, when she knew I'd never ever lie to her. I'd made that very clear to her – that even when she asked difficult questions; I'd always give her my honesty.

I swept her hair back from her face and pushed it out of the way behind her shoulders.

"Yeah... we do," I confirmed. "Do you want me to tell you about it?" I asked the question with warning in my tone – a not so subtle hint that she wouldn't like what I was going to tell her.

She searched my eyes for a minute, squared her shoulders and nodded. "I want to know."

Well alright...

I launched straight into it.

No point beating around the bush.

"It was about two, maybe three years ago," I began. "There was this awards event; I was nominated for a few things, as were a ton of people in the industry. I took this model as my date, Casey, and she wanted to introduce me to the new photographer she'd been working with – I could tell she worshipped the ground he walked on, and by the time she finally got hold of him and introduced us, it was pretty obvious to me that she wanted a piece of him."

"It was Stephen?" Charlotte questioned.

I nodded. "So, I shook his hand, watched him eye fuck my date, and then I headed for the bar... Casey stayed talking to him. I can clearly remember sipping on my scotch and watching them flirting from across the room."

Charlotte frowned and I could tell she was trying to recall something in her mind.

"Anyway, next thing I see Stephen walk off towards the bathrooms, and no more than thirty seconds later, Casey glances around, before following after him."

Charlotte rolled her eyes.

"Yeah... there were no prizes for guessing what they were going to get up to. And I wasn't having it. I was pretty arrogant and full of myself back then, and having my date go off with another man was not something that was happening on my watch."

Charlotte gasped in mock shock. "You? Arrogant? *No*... surely not." She feigned surprise.

I chuckled.

"So, you followed?" Charlotte prompted, obviously keen to hear the rest of the story.

"You bet your ass I did."

"And you fought over some model?" she asked with an eyebrow raised.

I shook my head.

I wish that was all it was.

"It took me a little while to find where they'd gone, and when I did, somebody else had already stumbled upon them. I'll never forget what I heard that night, legs. I hadn't realised before that moment, but he'd brought his own date with him that night."

I shuddered at the thought of that poor girl, and also for Charlotte – no doubt Stephen had treated her just as poorly as he had treated his date.

"From what I can gather, she must have been coming back from the bathroom and she had stumbled across him getting his dick sucked by the stupid bimbo I'd brought along."

I felt Charlotte tense in my arms.

"It was so fucked up, Charlotte. I heard him instruct Casey to carry on and he made his date watch."

I was looking at the ground as I spoke. I was so ashamed of myself for not stepping in earlier than I had that night.

"I'll never forget the way he spoke to that woman – his date... he told her—"

"You'll watch her suck my dick and then maybe next time I give you the privilege, you'll do a better job," Charlotte cut in.

My eyes flicked up to meet hers in disbelief. Her beautiful eyes were full of tears. My blood ran cold.

It was her...

My mind flashed back to the moment, all those years ago. The minute I'd realized what the hell was happening, I'd snapped.

I'd screamed at Casey to get off her knees, and the tone of my voice must have told her I wasn't messing around. She'd skulked out from the dark alcove, her face flushed red with embarrassment.

She'd tried to speak to me, but I'd silenced her with one look.

Stephen had stepped out a moment later, still zipping his fly like the arrogant fucker he was. He'd glanced back into the alcove and commanded the woman, who I now assumed had been Charlotte, to 'stay', like he was talking to some kind of dog.

I'd seen red. I couldn't believe after what I'd just heard that he was still in control of her, and that she – whoever she was, was still listening to him and following his orders.

I couldn't remember exactly what followed after that, I did remember calling out to the woman in hiding, telling her that I'd help her, and then I remembered punching the bastard when he'd lunged for me.

That was when Sammy arrived and damage control kicked in. I never got to see the woman and I'd accepted that I never would.

I looked at my girl and felt sick to my stomach.

"Oh fuck, Charlotte, please tell me that wasn't you?"

She didn't answer, but just burst into tears, giving me her answer without words.

I'll kill him.

The rage I'd felt at the time was nothing

compared to the all-consuming fury I felt right now, knowing that he'd treated this incredible woman like dirt.

The woman I love.

He was a bastard of the worst kind.

I pulled her in close and rocked her. "Oh, babe, I'm so, so sorry," I repeated the words over and over until her sobs slowed and stopped.

"Oh my god, it was you." She looked up at me suddenly with wide eyes. "*You're* the one who tried to save me."

I nodded slowly, shame creeping in.

I should have saved her.

I could have done more that night... I should have gone back for her... and if I had, I would have met Charlotte then.

"You punched him in the face... you broke his nose." She smiled. "You were my hero that night, Parker, even though I never saw your face... I didn't know who it was that had tried to help me, but it gave me a confidence boost I desperately needed."

"I can't believe he didn't tell you who it was," I muttered in disbelief. I was sure he would have told anyone who'd listen what he thought of me.

She shook her head slowly. "He didn't speak about it again. I think he was horrified that someone knew his dirty little secret." She took a deep, steadying breath. "The next day he was so flustered that when he went to the hospital to get his nose looked at, he forgot to start up the security system like he normally did if he left me in the apartment alone. That was the day I finally got away, Parker... I called Hannah and she helped me get out."

What. The. Fuck.

"He watched you on a security system?" I hissed, totally outraged.

She laughed humourlessly. "Of course he did. He had alerts set up on his phone so he'd know if I left a particular room, let alone attempted to leave the whole building," she replied quietly. "It wasn't that I was never allowed to leave, but he always made sure that he knew where I was going and when I'd be back – I never went anywhere unless him or his driver took me."

Charlotte had talked to me about her time with Stephen before, but never to this extent – she'd clearly sheltered me from the whole truth, I had no idea things had been this bad for her.

If I had to guess, I would say she'd probably never told anybody absolutely everything that went on between them, and she probably never would.

"But you broke the pattern." She smiled.

"Nah, I just broke his nose." I smirked.

She grinned in satisfaction. "Yeah you did, rock star. And that broke the routine... you caught him off guard and he slipped up."

She looked into my eyes and I could see overwhelming admiration shining in the blue pools. "You saved me, Parker."

"You saved yourself," I insisted.

She shook her head in disagreement. "If it weren't for you…"

I didn't even want to entertain the thought. I may not have been the one to actually save her, but clearly things had changed for her that night, and whether or not that was my doing didn't matter. She'd got out.

"Don't even think about it. It's over, he's gone and he'll never hurt you again," I promised her.

She pressed her face against my chest. "Thank you," she murmured. "Just… thank you for caring about a stranger the way you did. You're a good man."

"I can't believe that was you," I murmured in disbelief.

"I can't believe that you never figured it out… I was his girlfriend… you knew I'd been in a relationship with him around that time… I'm not sure why you never considered it."

It was pretty stupid on my behalf, but when I looked at Charlotte, I didn't see her as a victim, I saw a brave, beautiful woman that didn't take any shit from anyone. I also never in a million years considered that the woman Stephen was treating like that was actually in a relationship with him. I'd naively let myself believe that she was just some girl he'd dragged along for the evening. Even when Charlotte had told me the time frames of her relationship, my slow, rocker brain still never made the connection.

And that's not the girl I know…

"I don't see you as the woman that dated a bastard, legs, I look at you and see *my* woman, the woman I love. You've got too much strength and sass to be that woman in the hallway, baby. You're not her anymore."

What I said must have been the right thing, because Charlotte cupped my face in her hands and kissed me softly.

"I'm sorry I didn't make the connection," I murmured against her mouth.

"It's not important now," she whispered back.

"If only I'd gone into that alcove and taken you away... I could have met you then..."

I could have had you all these years...

"That version of me couldn't have handled you," she teased as she kissed me again. "I was broken. I needed the time to become whole again."

I knew what she was saying, but I still couldn't shake the guilt.

If only...

I should have punched him harder.

I was so tightly wound right now. Making the discovery that it had been Charlotte that I'd heard being degraded like that made me feel like I needed to punch something all over again.

"You'll watch her suck my dick..."

"...next time I give you the privilege..."

Bile rose in my throat as the thought hit me like a slap in the face.

Oh god... he didn't... did he?

"Charlotte, babe, I need you to look at me." I gently coaxed her chin up so she was looking into my eyes. "Did he ever... you know... *force* you to do anything?"

She shook her head gently and I felt a deep breath of relief exhale from my lungs.

I didn't expect her to have anything more to say, so I was surprised when she spoke quietly.

"He never physically harmed me. He never hit me, or raped me or even touched me in any way that was inappropriate sexually... but he messed with my mind." She sighed.

I could feel my hands shaking and I tried desperately to make them stop.

"He made me think I needed things that I didn't, he could fool me into thinking he was genuine... that he was sorry... that things would be different.... and then he'd go back to treating me like shit right after he got what he wanted from me. So, no, he never forced me, but sometimes I think that the ability he had to somehow make me believe I wanted him, was nearly as bad."

I held my girl close and made a promise to myself, that if I ever laid eyes on Stephen Miles again, I'd kill him.

———

"Legs?" I called into the bathroom where I could hear Charlotte brushing her teeth. I still couldn't figure out why she brushed them before *and* after breakfast, but it was like what Jasper had told me – women were complex creatures, and sometimes it was best *not* to attempt to figure them out.

I heard her spit her toothpaste into the sink.

"Yeah?" she called back to me.

I fidgeted with my hands.

God I'm nervous.

I still don't know what it was about Charlotte, but she had this unique ability to turn my insides to jelly.

She appeared in the doorway in her pyjama bottoms and a tank top.

"You're sweating bullets." She grinned triumphantly when she noticed how freaked out I was – she knew me like the back of her hand.

"I wanted to ask you something." I patted the space beside me on the bed – indicating for her to join me. "If you could try not to give me shit for two minutes, I'd appreciate it."

"I make no promises," she teased as she sat down next to me.

I ran my hand through my hair. This was a big deal for me – it was a proper announcement to the world that she was mine and that she wasn't going anywhere – even more than dragging her out on stage and singing to her.

"I wanted to know if... I dunno, I just thought it'd be cool if..." I rambled.

Charlotte blinked and waited patiently, apparently trying her hardest to refrain from giving me a hard time.

"Will you come to an interview with me today?

It's for some big shot magazine... I thought it'd be cool for the world to get a little insight into us... they'll have their own photographer and everything..."

Charlotte smiled sweetly and squeezed my bicep – giving me my cue to stop rambling, if I had to guess.

"That's so incredibly sweet, rock star, but I really don't think that anybody cares about me or wants to see photos that I'm in – it's all about you... you're the one everybody wants a piece of."

"*I care*," I replied. "You're important to me, I love you and I want everyone to know it."

Charlotte blushed, the same way she did every time I gave her a compliment. The girl was seriously deluded when it came to seeing herself clearly.

"Please?" I begged, giving her the best puppy-dog expression I could. "It'd be the perfect distraction from all this shit we've got going on."

"Alright," she grumbled eventually. "But don't expect me to get all chatty."

I fist pumped the air.

I'm calling it a win.

———

"Let's start with a nice easy one..." the reporter – Elizabeth, or Liz as she'd asked us to call her, began.

I glanced over my shoulder at Charlotte. She'd insisted upon lingering over by the window rather than sitting her sweet ass down on the seat that was set down right next to me – put there specifically for her.

She gestured with a smirk and a flick of her head that I should get back to my interview.

"She's a little stubborn," I told Liz with a grin, knowing full well that I'd get a rise out of Charlotte.

"That's a bit rich coming from you," Charlotte replied swiftly.

Liz smiled, her eyes flicking backwards and forwards between the two of us. "I'd love for you to join us, Charlotte... the whole world is dying to find out something, actually... *anything* about the woman who has finally tamed the untameable Parker," she spoke across the room to Charlotte.

"No offence intended," she added in my direction.

"None taken," I assured her as I leaned back in my chair, crossing my feet at my ankles. There was no denying that Charlotte had been able to do what the world had decided was impossible. She'd sunk me.

There was no one out there that was like Charlotte. Heading to this very interview was the perfect example.

There had been a ton of paparazzi outside waiting for us when we'd pulled up. Sammy and several of his men had cleared us a path and held back the fifty or so fans that had also got wind of the appointment I had upstairs.

I'd expected Charlotte to shy away – put her

head down and get it over with as quickly as possible – If she even got out of the car that was.

What I hadn't expected was her to stop and talk to a few of the fans that had called her name – she'd even taken photos with a couple of them. And then when someone had played one of my songs on a portable speaker, I certainly hadn't expected her to ask me to dance.

It was one of the most surreal moments of my life. I may have travelled nearly the entire world, and performed hundreds of times, but I'd never felt eyes on me the same way I had as Charlotte and I swayed in each other's arms, in the centre of a footpath – surrounded by burly-looking security.

That was Charlotte for you – shy and reserved in one moment, and open and fearless in the next.

"I'll buy you chocolate on the way home?" I bargained with her.

She narrowed her eyes at me as she weighed up her options.

"The good stuff with those little M&M things in it that I like?" she bartered.

I looked at her and then down at the seat. "Deal."

"Your musical style isn't really defined by one specific genre in the current market... how would you define your style?"

"Well, I'm not really sure... it's just a bit of this

and a bit of that. I just make music that I like." I shrugged, knowing that my answer was a totally useless one.

Liz didn't seem in the least bit deterred. "You're right; you've shown us collaborations with rock, pop, folk, indie..."

"You know, it's like what I told him once... he just doesn't fit in any of the boxes," Charlotte piped up helpfully, a shit-eating grin on her face.

I chuckled quietly but refrained from feeding her the same line I had a few months ago.

"Well I sure do my best to fit in your box, babe."

Liz's eyes flickered back and forth between us again, obviously aware that she was missing out on some private joke – I was waiting for her to begin her interrogation, like most of the reporters I'd ever dealt with would have, but to her credit she just smiled and looked back at her notes for the next question.

"Which musician would you describe as being your influences of this generation?"

"Personally, or musically?" I prompted.

"Whatever comes to mind," she pressed.

I looked to Charlotte for help.

She eyed me up and down. "I'd say... you're kind of an Ed Sheeran, Harry Styles, Adam Levine and Bruno Mars mash up."

"Harry Styles?" I quizzed her.

"Yeah." She nodded. "Definitely some Styles going on... he's got that sexy rocker swag thing happening; especially now he's out of 1D. And have you heard 'Sweet Creature'? I think he might have channelled a bit of you for that one actually..." she mused.

"Well good for him," I deadpanned. "But *I* don't have 'rocker swag'."

Charlotte rolled her eyes. "Well excuse me, Mr. Head-to-toe covered in tattoos."

I chuckled.

"For a bit of old school, throw in some Van Morrison too," she added in Liz's direction.

"Love a bit of Van," I agreed as I tapped out the beat to 'Sweet Thing' on my leg. I suddenly wished I had my guitar to strum the chords.

"Uh oh... you better start wrapping it up," Charlotte told Liz. "He gets all twitchy when his hands aren't busy."

Liz laughed lightly and closed the folder in her lap. "I think I'm about done with you anyway, Mr. Sloan."

"Parker," I corrected her.

"Parker," she amended with a satisfied smile.

She turned her attention to Charlotte. "If you don't mind, I just have one question for you, Charlotte?"

"For me?" Charlotte balked. "What could you possibly want to know about me?"

"It's actually a fan question... and well, they wanted me to ask Parker, but I think I'd rather hear your answer since you agreed to come," Liz answered.

"Well you've piqued my interest now, so let's hear it." Charlotte crossed one leg over the other.

"Well as I'm sure you're aware, every second woman seems to want a piece of your boyfriend."

Charlotte let out a snort laugh. "I hadn't noticed," she replied, her voice filled with light-hearted sarcasm.

"Don't forget about the men," I added with a wink.

Liz laughed. "Well the question is... why *you* out of all the women in the world?"

What?

I jumped to Charlotte's rescue. "I don't think that's really an appropriate qu—"

Charlotte interrupted me with a swat to my arm. "Oh, don't be precious, it's a fair question."

Since when is she into sharing?

She ignored my perplexed expression and gestured for Liz to carry on.

Liz cleared her throat, now seemingly unsure of herself.

"Go on," Charlotte encouraged.

"Well... what is it about you that's different from every other woman that's been vying for his attention for the past five years?"

Charlotte smiled. "Well that's exactly it."

Liz frowned. "What's *it*?"

Charlotte giggled and looked at me with a smile. "I *wasn't* vying for his attention."

"Understatement of the century," I mumbled

under my breath, which got another giggle from my girl.

"Why does anybody end up with the person they're with?" Charlotte looked back at Liz with a shrug. "People meet and fall in love everyday... this is no different. He's just a person, like everyone else... and I've never seen him as anything more than that."

"You know, Liz..." I cut in as I slung my arm around the back of Charlotte's seat. "I think it'd be just as valid to ask... when there are all these other men in the world, why would *she* choose *me*?"

Liz smiled widely at me and I almost got the feeling that this whole thing had been a test, and I'd just gotten myself an 'A'.

CHAPTER 36

Charlotte

"MOVE IN WITH ME."

I froze. This wasn't the first time he'd spoken those words, but for some reason this time seemed different.

I think he expects an answer this time.

I flicked my eyes up to meet his and was confronted with the most sincere expression I'd ever seen.

"All this bullshit is behind us now... I don't want to be alone anymore, not when I could be with you instead."

All this bullshit *was* behind us.

Finally.

I'd called Ty again, for Parker's sake. I hated

seeing him so worked up. He hadn't been sleeping well – he said he couldn't rest when he didn't know who was out to get us and why... and I couldn't sleep if he couldn't sleep.

Ty had done what he did best and hacked into both Nelly and Stephen's computers for another snoop around.

It was actually rather frightening hearing what he'd found on Stephen's end when he'd delved a little deeper.

The man was obsessed. He was worse than a stalker. The evidence was all laid out in black and white. But the weirdest bit was that it wasn't me he had been keeping tabs on for years... it was Parker.

Creepy...

With the details from my brother in hand, we'd eventually come to the conclusion that Stephen had been biding his time to try and find something that could ruin Parker's reputation. Some of the information he had stored on his computer suggested that he had much bigger plans in mind for him... but perhaps when the opportunity had arisen to make a fool out of both me and him together, he just hadn't been able to resist.

Two birds with one stone...

Nelly had provided him with that opportunity. She'd given him everything.

Parker was absolutely fuming to find out that she had been reporting back to Stephen for close to a year

– they had some kind of fucked up little relationship going on.

Gross.

It appeared that Stephen had sought her out when he'd discovered her working for Parker, and manipulated her into giving him what he wanted. I almost felt sorry for her – she was another of Stephen's victims in a way, but she'd dug her own grave, that bitch was as backhanded and dodgy as they came and I knew that Parker was going to take great pleasure in making her pay for betraying him.

Jasper had just been walking around mumbling about how he knew it was her and how he'd never trusted her in the first place – that part of this whole drama was actually quite amusing to watch.

Jasper had put in a complaint with the local police and had been told that they were taking the allegations seriously. We'd all been interviewed within the day, and Nelly had been charged with defamation. I had to laugh at how quickly they'd acted on our information – even cops seemed to bow down to the power and social standing of the famous Parker Sloan.

Tyler had tried to talk us out of bothering with the authorities, he'd assured me that he knew people who could 'handle these kinds of things'. I hadn't asked what that meant. I figured the less I knew, the better.

Stephen wasn't in the country so there was little the police could do with charging him, but I wasn't bothered, I knew he'd get his dues, courtesy of my brother.

Whatever that might be...

What I did know, was that Tyler had left an anonymous message on Stephen's phone, claiming responsibility for destroying his finances, reputation, business and marriage, and warning him that if he made any attempt to threaten either Parker or I, in any way, that he would make him really understand the meaning of being 'ruined'.

Let's hope the warning has been heeded.

For now at least, there was nothing but radio silence from my ex. Stephen appeared to have skulked off into the darkness with his tail between his legs.

Parker had finally relaxed, but apparently relaxing meant that he was back to hounding me about living with him.

I wanted to.

I really do...

But I was scared. The last time I lived with a man, things turned out very, very bad for me.

I knew Parker wasn't Stephen. He would never attempt to control me or hold me back under any circumstances... but I still couldn't seem to make the niggling fear in the back of my mind disappear entirely.

I blew out the breath I didn't realise I'd been holding. "Look, I'm not saying no..."

Parker looked at me intently.

"But I'm not saying yes yet either... I need a few days of peace, okay? I just need to take a few breaths and think about it... is that okay?" I asked him timidly.

I really didn't want to hurt his feelings, but right in this moment, I couldn't say yes to him with one hundred percent certainty, and he didn't deserve anything less.

I shouldn't have been so worried.

Parker chuckled and lifted me up by my waist. "Whatever you need, legs," he replied simply.

———

"I forgot my charger at your place, is it okay if I go back for it?"

Parker chuckled down the line. "I asked you to move in with me, legs. Do you really think I have a problem with you going into my house without me?"

I blushed. "I guess not... it just feels weird not to ask."

"Well consider this your full access pass, whenever you want, day or night; nothing in that house is off limits, okay?"

"Okay," I agreed with a smile.

"And besides, Jasper's never asked once, take a leaf out of his book," he replied. "Shit, I gotta go, babe, they're waiting for me in the studio. Is that all you needed?"

"Yeah, I'm good, I love you," I told him quickly.

"And I love you," he replied before the call disconnected.

I felt terrible for interrupting his studio session. I'd told him time and time again that if he was busy, he could let my call go to voicemail, but short of being on stage, I doubted there was anything that was a high enough of a priority for him to miss my call.

Not since the whole Stephen drama anyway.

I pulled a u-turn and headed back to Parker's place. The only good thing about him not being home was that there wasn't likely to be anybody hanging around outside waiting to take pictures.

———

I unlocked the front door and paused for a moment, trying to imagine how I'd feel if this were the home I came back to every night.

It needed a woman's touch – that was obvious, but it was comfortable and cosy and it housed the man I loved.

Why can't I just say yes?

I still hadn't given Parker an answer, and I knew he was trying his best, but patience was not one of his strong points.

I need to give him an answer... very soon...

I sighed, stepped inside and shut the front door behind me.

I found my charger right where I'd left it, next to what had now become my side of his bed.

I was about to head back to the front door when I heard a soft melody coming from further down the hallway – the opposite direction in which I'd come.

Weird...

I frowned. I was certain that Parker had turned everything off in his studio before we'd both left this morning – in fact I'd watched him do half of it.

I froze for a moment, deliberating about what to do.

Is there someone here?

I heard the strum of a guitar and decided that there was definitely someone inside this house that shouldn't have been there.

It could have been anyone, a stalker, a thief...

Sammy had gone with Parker so he wasn't much help. I cursed myself internally for refusing Parker's offer of my own protection.

Why am I such a stubborn fool?

I knew I should leave. Go back to the safety of my car and then call Parker, or even Sammy directly to sort it out, but my feet didn't seem to get the message, so instead of being the smart girl that walks away from what was bound to be trouble, I headed towards it.

As I crept closer I realized that what I could hear wasn't just music, it was someone singing, and singing damn well.

That voice is incredible.

It could have been a recording, but I doubted it –

that voice wasn't Parker's and he was the only one that used this studio.

Until now anyway.

I paused right outside the door, pulled Sammy's number up on the screen of my phone – just in case, took a deep breath, and peaked my head around the doorframe.

I still wasn't sure what I was expecting to find in there, but it certainly wasn't this.

"Jasper?" I blurted out.

Jasper dropped the guitar he had in his hands as he jumped nearly a foot in the air with surprise.

It landed on the ground with a loud clatter and I winced – that thing was probably worth a fortune.

"Charlotte... Jesus fuckin' Christ." Jasper clasped his hand over his chest as he spoke. "What the hell are you doing back here?"

He let out a deep breath and I felt a tiny bit guilty for scaring the shit out of him. He'd been so caught up in the moment – I'd taken him by complete surprise.

That's when it hit me again. *Jasper* had been singing.

"You can sing..." I pointed my finger at him as I glanced around in bewilderment. "And I have a key... and Parker asked me to live here... why are you here? Shouldn't you be with Parker?" I sucked in a breath at the end of my ramble. "You can sing," I repeated, still completely shocked with what I'd just uncovered about someone I considered a reasonably good friend.

He picked the guitar up and checked it for damage.

He sighed heavily. "I don't suppose there's any way you could not tell Park about this?" he asked, a sheepish expression on his face.

I walked into the room and perched myself next to him on the bench seat he was sitting on.

"I don't understand, J, you're really good... Parker doesn't know?" I inquired softly.

He snorted. "You're being generous. And no. he doesn't know." He shook his head and shrugged.

"Why?" I asked as I attempted to look into his green eyes.

He didn't look at me, instead fiddling with the pick in his hands.

"Singing and playing is his thing, you know? It's just a bit of fun for me when I'm alone." He finally tilted his head to look at me. "Or when I think I'm alone," he added with a smirk.

He was right, music was Parker's 'thing', but that didn't mean it couldn't be Jasper's thing too.

"Jasper, you're really good... you should show Parker what you can do, he might be able t—"

"To what?" he interrupted me softly. "Give me special treatment? Use his contacts and his reputation to get me listened to... to get me signed?" He shook his head. "That's not what I want... did I want a record deal once? Hell yeah I did. Do I want it handed to me because my best mate is the hottest thing in music? Fuck no. But Park would be hurt if I refused his help..." He sighed as he ran his hand through his hair and flipped it back from his face. "It's just easier this way."

My heart broke for him. I could see where he was coming from. Parker would love Jasper's voice – that much I knew already, but he'd do exactly what Jasper didn't want – he'd do whatever it took to ensure that all J's dreams came true.

He wouldn't take no for an answer.

I could understand why Jasper didn't want it like that – there was nothing quite as satisfying as putting in the hard yards and making your dreams happen on your own skills and merit.

There has to be another way...

"It's all good, Charlotte; you can't save the whole world in that brain of yours." He tapped lightly on the side of my head, obviously aware that my mind was going a mile a minute.

"But you're sacrificing your dream for the sake of your friendship, and even though I'd probably do the same thing... that sucks."

He winked at me. "It is what it is, Little Red. It doesn't bother me so much anymore – Parker's like a brother to me and I don't want something as stupid as my average-at-best singing voice to ruin that."

He pushed up to his feet and strolled towards the door.

I picked up the guitar pick he'd left sitting on the bench and twirled it around in my fingers.

He paused near the door. "So, you're moving in here huh?"

"I'm not sure yet..." I confessed. "But he wants me to."

"Well, give me a heads up when you do," Jasper told me, having already assumed that I'd be saying yes. "And I'll make sure I don't walk around here naked anymore."

My jaw dropped and I spun around to face him, but he was gone.

He what?

"Jasper?!" I called out after him. "Why the hell are you walking around here naked in the first place?"

"Because I can, Little Red... a little bit of nudity is good for the soul..."

I shook my head in disbelief.

Unbelievable.

"And also, because I know it pisses off your boyfriend," he added with a chuckle right before I heard the front door close behind him.

Jasper, the dark horse huh.

I sat dumbfounded for a moment, trying to absorb what I'd just witnessed.

I never would have guessed.

I headed to the corner of the room where I knew Parker kept his recording equipment. Jasper was obviously satisfied that Parker never bothered checking if there were recordings other than the ones he'd made – either that or he'd forgotten to delete his song in his hasty exit.

I rummaged in the drawers until I found a USB stick. I rewound the system until I found the moment that it had begun recording – when Jasper had entered the room. I plugged the USB in and listened as the file downloaded.

Jasper was wrong. There was *nothing* average about his voice as he strummed lightly and sang the lyrics of 'Can I Be Him' by James Arthur.

He had a unique rasp to his tone that made for amazing listening.

He's really good…

I didn't know much about guitar playing, but he seemed to be doing a pretty great job of that too.

Parker needs to hear this…

Jasper may have asked me to forget about it – but I'd made no promises.

I was going to make something happen.

CHAPTER 37

Parker

"WHY WON'T she move in with me, man?" I asked Jasper. I was centre stage waiting to run the sound check for tonight's show.

He fiddled with some wiring and checked something off from the sheet on his clipboard. "I dunno, Park," he answered absently. "Maybe she's sick of all your damn whining?" he offered helpfully.

I flipped him the bird, but I knew he was probably right. I'd been asking Charlotte nonstop to move in with me – she was probably getting sick of it.

"Do you think I should stop asking?"

He shrugged and shifted a speaker a foot to the right, giving me no real answer.

"C'mon, J, I'm stuck here," I pleaded with him.

He stopped what he was doing and looked up at me. "I can't do stage manager and shrink at the same time, man, now I know we discussed my role as being 'flexible', but I'm pretty confident this is out of my knowledge base."

I huffed out a breath and kicked the mic stand with the toe of my shoe.

"Jesus, when did you turn into such a girl?" he taunted me.

I didn't even bother denying it – Jasper knew how far gone I was when it came to Charlotte.

"Yes, okay... stop fuckin' hounding her. If she wants to live with you, she'll tell you. In the meantime do your best impression of a non-love-struck, whiny little punk, and get back to the god damn sound check."

He picked up his clipboard and carried on about his business like nothing had ever happened.

I chuckled and ran my hand through my hair.

J was right.

If she wants to move in, she'll let me know

CHAPTER 38

Charlotte

THERE WAS this nervous feeling in the pit of my stomach as I watched Parker tonight. Something didn't feel right with me, but I couldn't seem to put my finger on what it was.

Parker blew me a kiss from centre stage before taking a sip of his water, and the knot in my gut eased somewhat.

Tonight was just another night for me as a musician's girlfriend. I had my spot, my security and my sexy-as-hell boyfriend who was putting on an amazing show.

I glanced over at Jasper as he talked rapidly at one of the crew members. He'd seemed tense tonight, and if I had to guess, it was because I'd snapped him singing at Parker's place the other day.

Jasper played it cool most of the time, but I knew for a fact that he was nervous about what I might decide to do with my knowledge of his secret talents.

Ironically enough, I'd decided I was going to play the recording for Parker tonight when we got home – I had a plan and I couldn't wait to see it play out like I thought it would.

I was also planning on telling him that I was ready to move in with him. I didn't know when or how I was going to do it, but I was finally in a place where I thought it was the right decision.

Maybe that's why I feel so nervous.

"You seem uptight," Hannah observed.

I forgot she was even there – that's how distracted I was.

I shrugged. "I feel weird... I think maybe I'm just really tired."

"Is he still hounding you about moving in with him?"

"If by hounding, you mean asking me every five minutes, then yeah... he's been doing a damn fine job." I smiled as I watched Parker swapping out his guitar for another one.

"You don't want to move in with him?" she quizzed, pulling my attention away from the sex on a stick as he strummed his nimble fingers over the strings.

"Actually..." I blushed. "I wanted to talk to you about something..."

She raised her brows in question.

"I want to know what you'll do if I were to move out..."

Her eyes lit up and her face broke out into a massive grin. "You're going to tell him yes?!"

"Hell yes I am," I told her. "I mean, god, just look at him..." I sighed as my eyes found his gorgeous face and sexy-as-sin body.

"Mmmm hmmmm," Hannah agreed with a hum. "Have you told him yet?"

I shook my head and got back to my original question. "I'm serious, Han, what will you do?"

"Visit you a lot." She smirked.

I rolled my eyes.

I can't just up and leave her.

"I'm serious." She grinned. "I'll be fine. I'll stay in the apartment on my own... or get a flatmate, or move... or whatever the hell works... I don't care, babe, I just want you to be happy, the rest doesn't matter."

There's a reason she's my BFF.

"Are you sure?" I asked her quietly.

She didn't answer me, but instead pulled me in for a hug.

I hugged her back tight. It would be weird not having Hannah around all the time, and we'd have to make some decisions about the in-home business we were running... and then there was the fact that I owned the apartment, but none of that was a big deal.

That's all just little details.

"I'm so happy for you," she finally said as she released me. "But also jealous... actually I'm *mainly* jealous." She laughed.

I was happy for me too – taking this leap with Parker was something I should have done the first time he asked.

"When are you going to tell him?"

"Tonight's the night." I winked. "I'm hoping we'll skip the after party and head straight home to celebrate."

"Good luck with that." Jasper startled me from behind and I jumped.

He was so god damn sneaky, I never knew when he might have been lurking around, eavesdropping and whatever else.

"Why not?" Hannah demanded.

"The label suits are in town... they want the big man at the appearances and the party tonight."

"Dammit," I groaned. I was really looking forward to a night in.

"Sorry, Little Red... you want to see your man, you're gonna havta hit the club." He winked at me before strolling away.

Stupid rock stars and their stupid business...

———

It wasn't that I wasn't expecting it – I was well and truly used to this by now. Wherever Parker went, people followed. He was like a modern-day Pied Piper.

Groupies, paparazzi, media, fans...

No matter where he went, someone was always there.

I'd been to these kind of after parties more times than I could count.

I know the score.

Fifty percent, if not more of these women, didn't give one single fuck that Parker was taken. I could have been sitting right on his knee, and they would still attempt to coerce him into their bed.

I should have seen it coming.

Taking a trip to the bathroom and leaving Parker on his own was like leaving a pot of honey open for the flies.

Bad idea....

There was this one woman in particular.

Malika.

Jasper had warned me about her from day one – she was after Parker, and she was on a whole new level in comparison to the other groupies.

Of course, I hadn't been able to help myself, and I'd asked Parker about her. It turns out they had slept together. *Once...* she wanted more – he wished it'd never happened in the first place. But the fact that she was Jimmy's sister meant that she was *always* around.

Thankfully we didn't spend a lot of time at these kinds of things anymore, but there were certain events Parker couldn't miss, just like tonight.

Stupid record label.

I just want to go home...

Parker's noted absence from the regular party scene meant that when he was around, the vultures were out for whatever they could get.

Like right now, as I watched Malika slide her lithe body right into my boyfriend's lap.

I knew what she was doing. She'd timed her move to perfection. She was banking on me coming out of the bathroom, seeing the scene in front of me and losing my shit.

I wasn't that stupid.

Parker's whole body was tense and uncomfortable and he was trying his best to refrain from throwing the bitch across the room.

I didn't believe for a second that she was a welcome guest on Parker's junk.

I knew him.

I loved him.

I trusted him.

The thing that struck home for me was that *this* was it. It was *always* going to be like this. If it wasn't a Malika, it'd be a Tiffany, if it wasn't a Tiffany, it'd be a Lucy...if it wasn't a Lucy it'd be an Emily... the list would go on and on.

There will always be someone.

The realisation hit me like a slap in the face.

Parker didn't belong to me.

Parker didn't even belong to himself.

There will always be something.

Was this the way I wanted my life to turn out? What kind of future could I possibly have with this man if he would never really be mine?

We couldn't go out for a coffee... we couldn't go for a walk in the park... we couldn't do anything.

He wanted me to live with him... and I wanted to.

God, did I want to...

I was still here waiting to get the hell out of here so I could tell him that I was all set to take things to the next level with him.

But what would my life be like if I lived in his house? Could I walk out the front gate and down the street to go and get a coffee? Or would I have to be driven in a tinted-glass vehicle with my own personal bodyguard?

I'd been making the best of the situation, but it had been wearing me down lately. It was an exhausting life in a lot of ways.

Imagine if we got married...

I couldn't even imagine what life would be like for our children if we had them.

No playing at the playground...

Second guessing the motives of their friends?

My stomach dropped and my blood ran cold.

I knew that I couldn't live my life like this, not the way it was now...

Standing here right now, I knew I only had two options.

I knew I couldn't let Parker give up his career, because I knew he would, if I asked him or if he figured out that that's what it would take to keep me – he'd give it up in a heartbeat.

I couldn't do that to him, hell, I couldn't do that to the world. The thought of being the reason that this immense talent left the industry was unbearable to me – singing was everything to him.

But I couldn't live like this either.

That only left me with one option.

I approached the table slowly, where Parker was still trying to remove the tramp that was clinging on for dear life.

Parker's eyes portrayed sheer panic as he saw me approach. "Legs, it's not what you think."

I gave him a small smile. "I know... can you just get rid of her?" I was suddenly so bone tired; it was like a switch had flicked inside me and I just couldn't do this anymore. I sank down on the bench seat next to him.

Malika huffed and stormed off in a rage, fuming that her half-witted plan hadn't worked.

Keep moving, honey, I've got bigger problems.

"Fuck, babe, I'm sorry, she's out of her damn mind. I just try to be nice to her for Jim's sake. You know that, right?" Parker brushed off his jeans like she might have left some kind of filth on him. It made me want to laugh, but I couldn't seem to remember how.

Tears welled in my eyes. "I know," I repeated.

I lifted my head and met his gaze, letting him see how broken I was.

"Charlotte? What's wrong?" He slid in closer to me.

The tears fell in slow streams down my cheeks at the sheer concern his voice held for me.

I shook my head. "I'm so sorry, Parker."

His eyes widened and he reached for my hands in an attempt to soothe me.

"I just can't do this anymore," I choked out, pulling my hands away before he could make me tingle with the familiar energy his touch created. "I can't live my life under this microscope... I can't deal with the constant stream of women vying for your attention... I just *can't*..."

The pain in his eyes stabbed at my heart. "I would *never*... I love you," he insisted.

"I know you wouldn't... and I love you too," I replied with a resigned smile. "But I can't live like this anymore, and I'm so sorry... I thought I could do it, but I can't." I sobbed.

"Charlotte, please?" Parker begged. "I'll do better. I'll.... I'll step back from the party scene... the performances... I'll give up all of it... *anything*... whatever you need."

The tears fell harder. This sweet, sexy man

offering to give up his whole life just like I knew he would, cut me deep.

"It's not your fault," I choked out. "But even if you wanted to, you couldn't walk away from this, rock star, this is your life."

"Charlotte..." he begged again.

I stood, knowing I needed to get out of there before he convinced me to stay.

I threw him one last apologetic stare and fled toward the exit.

I had no idea if I was making the right decision for my future, or the worst mistake of my life.

Time moved in slow motion as I ran across the room and out the door.

I saw a flash of Hannah and Jasper's shocked faces and a glimpse of Malika's victorious smirk before I burst through the door and into the cool night air. I sucked in deep breath after deep breath, but I still couldn't seem to get enough air.

"Charlotte?" Hannah asked softly from behind me, as she placed a hand on my lower back. It was only then that I realised I was doubled over, crying.

I couldn't even talk, I was sobbing so hard.

"Honey, what's wrong? Talk to me..." Her voice was filled with worry. "Did he do something to you?"

I shook my head furiously. The last thing I wanted was anyone thinking that this was Parker's fault.

I knew he was there the minute he emerged from inside the club; my body was so in tune with his.

"Charlotte!" he called out to me.

On instinct, I looked up at him, right into his light blue eyes that I loved so much. He had liquid pooling in the corners and it took me a moment to realise he was crying.

"I'm so sorry," I whispered as I turned into Hannah's waiting arms and walked away from the only man I could ever see myself truly loving.

CHAPTER 39

Parker

FOR THE SECOND time in my life, I found myself looking at the beautiful girl with the long red hair, with my best friend at my side, as she walked away from me.

"What the fuck just happened?" I choked out, much the same as I had months and months ago when Charlotte had first turned me down.

Only this time, Jasper had no witty remark or laughter and I didn't have a trick up my sleeve to see her again.

He stepped in front of me and hugged me like a brother as I broke down and sobbed in his arms.

CHAPTER 40

Charlotte

IT HAD BEEN five days and I knew my allocated time for avoiding Hannah was well and truly up. I also knew I had to get out of bed, I needed food, and I really, really needed a shower.

I was twenty kinds of messed up over this breakup... I knew it was all my fault, but that didn't change the depressing reality of the situation.

I'd broken up with a man I loved more than anything.

Who does that?

Every time his name appeared on my cell phone as an incoming call or text, or I heard him buzzing our intercom over and over again my heart broke in a new spot... his pain caused it to crack just that little bit more.

I was miserable – stuck between a rock and a hard place.

No pun intended.

I still didn't know if I'd made the right call, but it was done now, and no matter how much I loved or missed him, it didn't change things.

Parker might have been calling and coming over right now, but that wouldn't last forever...

He'll forget about me and move on with his life...

The thought of him forgetting about me caused an intense stabbing pain in my chest. I rubbed at it as I gasped for air and gave myself a mental lecture.

This is what you wanted.

He needs to move on.

You want him to be happy.

I knew I couldn't hold on to him forever – but I wished more than anything that it could be different.

Hannah must have come into my bedroom without me noticing at some stage during my melt down, she touched my arm lightly and I near jumped out of my skin.

"Jesus, Hannah." I clasped my chest and tried to steady my heartbeat.

"You were having another panic attack." She frowned as she sat down next to me. "You can't keep going on like this, Lotte, you need to talk to me... or if not me, then someone, hun, you can't just sit here."

I nodded in agreement. "I need to shower."

It might have been the smallest of confessions, but Hannah's eyes lit up like I'd just made a huge amount of progress.

She made a show of pretending to sniff me. "Yeah... you're right, you kinda stink."

I smiled and it felt weird on my face – wrong somehow.

"I... ah... I brought you this..." She sat the magazine down on my bed.

I knew what it was.

Our interview...

I'd been expecting it earlier.

I scooted further away from it like it was a deadly snake. "I can't look at that." I shook my head vehemently.

"Charlotte..." she pleaded. "Just take one look."

I peered over at the offending object and then back into my best friend's eyes.

"I can't look at those pictures," I whispered, my voice broken.

Parker and I had taken some beautiful photographs together – the photographer had shown us right after he took them – they were the perfect representation of just how much we loved each other.

The thought of them made my stomach churn with guilt.

"Okay." Hannah held up her hands in surrender before reaching for the magazine. "But you need to hear this one part at the very least.

Hearing anything that came from those glossy

pages was about the last thing I wanted to do right now, but Hannah rarely took no for an answer, and seeing as she was at about the end of her patience with me, I doubted she would listen now anyway.

She cleared her throat and I threw my covers over my head in an attempt to hide.

"... I hate to break it to you ladies, but Parker Sloan is very firmly *off* the market... and I doubt he'll ever return. Within only five minutes of meeting Charlotte and Parker, I knew I'd never met a couple quite like this before..." she read the words aloud.

"Stop," I instructed.

"Park—"

"Just stop," I interrupted, throwing the covers back off me.

"Just talk to me, Lotte," she begged. "I just want to understand why you left him?"

"I just couldn't do it anymore," I replied, my voice empty and hollow. "You see all those women throwing themselves at him... I just couldn't do it anymore."

It might not have been all of it, but it was certainly part of the problem.

"You know Parker isn't interested in anybody but you... he doesn't want them, he wan—"

"Just let it go, Han," I snapped. "It's done. It's over... just let it go for Christ's sake."

I felt the thud of the magazine landing on the bed before Hannah turned and left without another word.

Shit. I'm a bitch.

———

I had to admit, the shower was a good decision... I'd even washed my hair.

I could hear Han clattering around in the kitchen as I slinked out into the living room with my tail between my legs.

I sat down on the couch and turned the TV on.

Hannah's head popped around the corner when she heard the noise from the TV. "You're up," she stated, the smile on her face showing me that she wasn't holding a grudge for my earlier behaviour – Hannah was good like that.

I nodded and shot her my best 'I'm sorry' look.

She sighed and walked out of the kitchen and into the living room.

"Damn girl." I let out a wolf whistle. "Where the hell are you going?"

Hannah was dressed up sexy as hell. Her perfect figure was draped in a stunning deep-blue wrap dress which she had paired with a high pair of nude-coloured heels. Her makeup and hair were simple, but beautiful.

She looked amazing.

She waved away my comment.

"I'm serious... where are you going?" I did my best to beat down my panic at the thought of being here all alone now that I was functioning a little more normally.

Pull yourself together...

Hannah had been here for me this entire time, she'd cancelled all of my bookings and made other arrangements for the clients.... she'd taken care of everything and I hadn't exactly let her know how grateful I was for her support. I didn't need to go making her feel bad for taking some much-deserved time out.

"Umm... I have a date..." She smiled brightly, but I didn't miss the nervous expression that she'd covered with that smile.

"With who?" I prompted.

"Oh, just this guy I met a while back... it's just a drink." She shrugged and avoided making eye contact.

She's hiding something...

She seemed reluctant to sit – instead choosing to hover awkwardly near the end of the couch.

"So, what's his name?" I asked her as I tucked my legs up underneath me.

She shifted her weight from one foot to another as she fiddled with the gold bangle she wore on her left arm.

"I don't think you know him."

I narrowed my eyes at her. "Han..." I warned her.

She huffed out a breath. "I can't say, okay?" She finally met my eyes. "I didn't expect you to be up, or I would have done a better job of sneaking out... I'm sorry."

"Why can't you tell me?" I demanded, feeling tears spring in the corners of my eyes for some inexplicable reason.

Damn breakup hormones...

"I just... can't," she finished lamely.

"You're not going out to talk to Parker, are you?" I whispered.

She shook her head quickly. "No, Lotte, of course not... that's not my place."

I breathed out a sigh of relief. I didn't need Hannah and Parker ganging up on me and trying to make me change my mind.

But then who is the guy?

"Oh shit, Han... he's not married, is he?"

She waved her hands around in front of her. "Oh god no," she cried. "He's one hundred and ten percent single."

Thank the lord for that...

She giggled in embarrassment. "We don't need that drama again, now do we?"

I grimaced.

We certainly do not...

Hannah was no home wrecker – she'd been as totally in the dark about her boyfriend's wife as his wife had been about her husband's girlfriend.

But still... no one needed someone's crazy wife knocking their door down twice in a lifetime.

"Oh hell... that was baaaad times..." She

grimaced. "I promise you, this one's not married." She held up her fingers in Scout's honour.

"Phew." I wiped my brow in mock relief.

Hannah shifted her weight again and I could tell she was still nervous – she clearly thought I was going to push her for answers.

I wanted to. But I also knew that I owed it to her to back off – she would tell me when she was ready.

Maybe if I give her some slack about it, she'll return the favour and not grill me about Parker anymore.

"Enjoy your date," I told her genuinely.

She smiled gratefully and turned to get her clutch off the table. "You'll be okay here?" she asked as she paused halfway to the door and turned back to look at me.

"I'll be fine," I promised her.

She gave me a smile and headed for the door.

"Han?" I called after her.

She looked back at me.

"You look beautiful," I told her. "And thank you... for looking after me... I love you."

"No need to thank me, girl..." She blew me a kiss as she opened the door to leave. "I love you too."

"I hope you get laid!" I called after her.

Her laugh floated down the hallway.

I glanced around the living room and took a deep breath. I was out of bed at least.

I can do this...

CHAPTER 41

Parker

THE FACT that I heard the front door slam should have been a pretty big warning sign as to just how pissed off he was with me. The beat was so loud I could barely hear myself think.

That's the whole point.

I already knew it was Jasper. He'd come here every day for the past eight days – that, and he was the only one with a key that was brave enough to use it anymore.

Ever since Charlotte walked out.

I growled at myself and pushed those thoughts back into the dark corner where I kept them. I couldn't afford to think about Charlotte right now –

she wouldn't come to the door... she wouldn't take my calls or answer my texts... it was time to face facts.

It's over.

I pounded out the beat to 'Rebel Rebel' on the drum kit.

The music cut off with a screech, but I carried on hitting the crap out of the drums, taking more and more of my frustrations out.

"You're a shitty drummer," Jasper snarled, dropping himself onto the couch.

I threw the sticks as hard as I could across the room and flipped him off.

"Fuck, man, you've got to stop destroying those classics."

"Go home if you don't like it," I growled as I ran a hand through my hair, now drenched with sweat.

I didn't have a clue how long I'd been in here, taking out my rage, but judging by the look on J's face, it'd been too long.

"I fuckin' have been home, dumbass; you think I can't hear this shit over there?" He narrowed his eyes at me.

"David Bowie would be turning in his grave," I mumbled.

"I wasn't talking about Bowie, I was talking about you murdering those drum solo's for the past three hours."

Three hours.

Well damn.

"Guess I missed that interview then?" I asked sheepishly, ducking my head in embarrassment.

"I've cancelled every interview you've had for the past week, Park, what makes you think I wouldn't have cancelled that one too?"

"You told me it was on." I looked up at him.

"I lied." He looked me dead in the eye.

"Fuck," I muttered under my breath.

"Fuck, indeed," he drawled.

We sat in silence for what seemed like forever.... me trying my hardest to find a way through this fog that had descended within my brain. It didn't seem to matter which way I tried to get out, *she* was always there, blocking my way, making it impossible to move forward.

I knew I'd lost something I couldn't replace.

Trying to get over Charlotte was like trying to get over slamming your balls in a car door – it hurt to even think about it.

I couldn't write, I couldn't play my guitar with any resemblance of talent... I wasn't *me* anymore. I wasn't a rock star... I wasn't anything.

That was the real reason I was in here, making a piss-poor attempt at playing the drums.

"What do you wanna do, man?" Jasper finally asked.

It was a simple question, but I knew exactly what he meant.

Was I done?

Could I go on?

"I... I need..." I choked out. "I just need a break," I finally admitted.

I still couldn't look at him.

"Well thank fuck for that," he replied quietly.

My head jerked up in surprise, my now slightly-too-long hair falling into my eyes.

"You're not pissed?" I asked in surprise.

He shook his slowly. "Nothing to be pissed about, man. It is what it is." He shrugged. "You need a break. That's a fact. No one would want to hear you the way you are now anyway... your heart's not in it."

My chest constricted at his mention of my heart. I wasn't sure that I even had a heart anymore. Charlotte could very well have taken that with her too.

My heart... my sanity... my everything...

Jasper pushed up to his feet and picked up the drumsticks I'd thrown across the room. "I'm taking these fucking things."

"I'm sorry, J," I mumbled, unsure of what else I could possibly say.

"Don't be." He shook his head quickly. "You deserve some time out. I'm gonna make the next three months disappear, and we'll see how it goes from there. Okay?"

I nodded my head. "Okay."

I felt like a total bastard. This wasn't just my life, it was Jasper's too. He was doing his best to sympathise with me, but the reality was, he just didn't understand. He couldn't. He'd never had to lose anything that meant this much to him.

He couldn't possibly understand the soul-destroying pain of watching your life, your future, your whole world, walk out the door and not come back.

I hope he never has to.

CHAPTER 42

Charlotte
136 days later

THE GAPING hole in my chest ripped a little wider at the mention of his name on the TV screen in front of me. I'd done pretty well with steering clear of Parker for these past few months.

I grabbed the remote and hurriedly hit the red 'off' button.

Avoiding him was like trying to avoid the plague. His name was everywhere. In just that one segment I'd heard enough to know that he was still M.I.A. from the music scene.

He'd cancelled all of his shows, tours, interviews... *everything* these past few months.

Word on the street was that he wasn't writing or playing anymore either.

The thought of his talent going to waste threatened to destroy me. Parker lived and breathed music; it was as much a part of him as the tattoos on his skin. I didn't know why he was stepping away from his passion, but it hurt.

Is it all my fault?

I'd thought that maybe it was, but my brain had told me not to be so stupid. There was no way that losing me could cause him to be unable to play.

Or could it?

I think deep down, I knew it was my fault. I'd achieved the very thing I was trying to avoid happening.

I broke him.

I thought about him day and night, no matter what I was doing, he was *always* on my mind, and I knew Parker had loved me as much as I'd loved him, so he was bound to be hurting too.

The situation wasn't exactly helped by the fact that Hannah and Jasper had come out with the news of their relationship about a month ago.

They'd been keeping it quiet this whole time – ever since that first night.

Hannah had explained that it'd only ever meant to be a one-night stand, but with Parker and I causing them to spend so much time together, it'd quickly turned into a three-, five-, then ten-night stand. From there they'd realized that it was so much more than just sex.

Hannah promised me that they had wanted to tell us, but when Parker and I had broken up; they didn't feel like the timing was right. He was the one I'd caught her going on a date with – that was the reason she wouldn't tell me who the guy was.

I got it.

They were stuck between a rock and a hard place.

It still hurts.

It hurt that my best friend had secrets... it hurt that I was the cause of her having to keep them, and shittiest of all... it hurt that she was blissfully happy when I'd never felt more miserable or alone.

I wanted Hannah to be happy... and Jasper too. They were great together. But I was green with envy, and green wasn't a colour I wanted to be.

Hannah had even stopped buying her beloved gossip magazines. Parker dropping off the grid had seemed to make the media want a piece of him now more than ever and it was hard to find even one that didn't have his photo splashed all over the cover. There were endless paparazzi stalking his every move and asking questions of his sudden, unexplained absence from the music industry.

I was grateful for the disappearance of those glossy pages. I made a point of never seeking out news about him, but if it was put in front of me, I rarely had the willpower to resist.

That man still called to me like nothing I'd ever experienced.

I was torn. Nearly every day I regretted my decision to end our relationship. I'd pulled his number up on the screen of my phone more times than I could count, but I couldn't bring myself to hit call.

I was pathetic. Stuck on a man I'd chosen not be with.

He'd have moved on by now...

That's what I tried to convince myself of anyway.

CHAPTER 43

Parker

I KNEW Hannah was talking to me.

Asking me something maybe?

I just couldn't make myself focus long enough to listen – that, and I wasn't sure I even cared. I didn't care about much these days.

"That's it!" Hannah screeched at Jasper.

I flinched, there was no missing that level of noise.

"I'm not pussyfooting around him any longer. We're sorting this shit, and we're sorting it right god damn now!" she yelled at the top of her voice.

Uh oh.

"Yes, ma'am," Jasper drawled, grabbing a hold of

Hannah and pulling her back against his front, a giant smile on his face as though he loved it when she got all crazy and riled up like this.

They were an interesting mix, those two, where Hannah was fiery and full on, Jasper was chilled and relaxed. They were like night and day in a lot of ways.

"You want Charlotte back, right?" she demanded, turning her crazy-ass rage on me now.

Shit.

I flinched at the off-limits topic, but this time, instead of withdrawing and running away, I took a deep breath and decided it was time. They say time heals all wounds, but I was beginning to think that that theory was nothing but a crock of shit – I wasn't any happier now than when she'd walked away from me months ago.

Time to face the music.

Do I want her back?

"More than anything," I told her honestly.

Hannah gaped at me. The woman put on a brave façade, but I could tell in that moment that she hadn't expected me to be honest with her.

"Right...well, good..." She stumbled through her words. "We need a plan." Hannah wiggled free from J and began to pace the room.

She had obviously realised that this was an opportunity she needed to pounce on and she was intending to do exactly that.

"Is there anything she ever said that hit a nerve with you? Anything you think was really important to her?"

"I don't know," I mumbled unhelpfully.

"Seriously?"

"I don't know..." I shrugged. "She said a lot of things..."

"She's the one who ran; maybe I should be having a talk with her instead," she threatened.

I knew she was just trying to spur me into action. Any form of threat towards Charlotte and I'd do whatever it took to stop it from happening. Hannah knew that as well as I did.

"Hannah..." I warned. "This isn't her fault."

It was my crazy life that had been the problem, but I could change that... and it was time I took responsibility and tried to get her back instead of just sitting around like a loser.

Hannah huffed out a breath. "Well she's as miserable as you are, if not more so, so get thinking," she demanded.

I'd insisted that neither Jasper nor Hannah speak to me about Charlotte... *at all*, I didn't even want to hear her name. I was terrified of hearing that she'd moved on, or that she was happy without me.

But she misses me too...

It was unfair of me, but I was thrilled to hear that Charlotte wasn't coping without me either.

I might actually have a shot at getting her back.

I had to hand it to Hannah; she was a fucking good friend to Charlotte... and to me. Jasper was too, he'd put up with my mood swings, cancelled gigs, and he'd managed to sweep my public outbursts under the carpet.

Jasper and Hannah had both been so patient with me.

Even before they came out as a couple.

It was fuckin' cute that they'd thought they were hiding their relationship. I'd known those two were a thing before even they did. They'd made sexy eyes at each other from day one... it was obvious. That, and their piss-poor attempts at sneaking around next door were a pretty good indicator that there was something more than friendship going on between them.

I was happy for them, and it was a relief that they'd finally just come out with it... but witnessing their happiness made me pine for Charlotte even more.

I missed her more than I would have thought possible.

"Seriously, Park, there must have been something?" Hannah demanded, pulling me from my thoughts.

I closed my eyes and allowed myself to picture Charlotte for the first time in months.

I thought about her eyes, her long red hair, her voice, her scent, the sway of her hips, her laugh...

I sighed in contentment.

Charlotte...

She's so funny... and beautiful... and smart... and insightful...

My eyes flickered open.

All of a sudden, I knew what to do.

CHAPTER 44

Charlotte

I HAD A PRETTY good feeling that Hannah was up to something. She wasn't exactly known for her stealthy skills or her ability to keep her emotions off her face. So, when she'd slunk in earlier, doing a piss-poor job of appearing casual, I'd gone on high alert.

Nothing had happened yet, but I wasn't ready to accept that I was in the clear.

My eyes darted towards the door for the fiftieth time in the past hour. I dropped my book down on the couch with a sigh. I was so on edge, I'd read the same page ten times and I still didn't have the faintest idea what it said.

"Want some popcorn?" Hannah asked as she strolled into the room, a big bowl full in her hands.

"You watching a movie?" I asked.

She checked the time on her watch. "I was just gonna see what was on," she answered vaguely.

"Okay," I agreed, sliding over so she could sit down.

She grabbed the remote and sank down next to me.

I grabbed a handful of popcorn as the TV screen flickered to life.

Oh. My. God.

The popcorn slipped through my fingers and went all over the couch as I stared at the screen in front of me.

It was Parker. And not some old footage from one of his concerts like I'd accidently witnessed a couple of weeks back.

This was Parker *right now*. The 'LIVE' label on the bottom of the screen was testament to that.

He looked scruffy, like he needed a trip to the barber to sort out his hair and his whiskers, but it was him. And it was even better than I remembered.

"Hannah," I whispered, unable to look away.

I squeezed her thigh when she didn't answer. "He needs a haircut," I mumbled.

"He wouldn't let me," she whispered back.

"Hannah..." I said again, totally unsure of what the hell I was seeing.

"He had to do something," she replied quietly.

What exactly that *something* was hit me like a ton of bricks.

This is for me.

He was back on his old street corner.

Where it all began...

He was there, his favourite acoustic guitar in his hands and he was playing *my* song.

He's showing me how far he's come.

I hadn't heard this song in months and my eyes prickled with tears hearing the perfection of it now.

"Han, is this..." I choked out half of a sentence.

Hannah reached for my hand and squeezed. "He's lost without you, Lotte, he did this for you, because he wants you back."

I let out a whimper, still staring in disbelief at the screen.

"You're not happy without him, Charlotte, in fact you're miserable. And I know you said you can't live with the fame and his life, but, hun, I think you have to figure out a way, because it seems like you can't live without him either."

She was right.

So right.

I'd spent all these months convincing myself I couldn't live my life under a microscope, but I'd been ignoring the fact that I didn't know how to be me without him anymore. He made me lighter, happier, and somehow, he made me feel free – even with the constraints of his life bearing down on us.

"How do I fix this, Han?" I asked, finally pulling my eyes from the image of the man I loved.

She smiled and let out a relieved breath, as

though I'd just said the words she'd been waiting to hear. "There's a car downstairs."

I gaped at her. "He sent a car for me? What if I didn't change my mind?"

She shook her head quickly and her expression turned all gooey. I knew then that it was Jasper's doing. Hannah had never made that face about anyone other than him.

"Jasper organised the car," she confirmed my hunch. "Parker's plan was just to make you see that he wasn't all sold out stadiums and groupies."

We were both on our feet by now; I grabbed my bag and hustled out the door, Hannah hot on my heels.

"I never thought that about him," I argued. "I just couldn't find a way to deal with it, Han."

Hannah hit the ground floor on the elevator and we began our descent.

"Just talk to him," Hannah encouraged. "You're my best friend and I love you, but what you did last time damn near killed him. I know you didn't set out to hurt him, but you never even gave him a chance to try and make anything right," she told me softly, speaking the words that I knew she'd felt, but had never actually said.

She blames me... and she's right.

My eyes burned with tears. "I know," I whispered as we arrived on the ground floor.

The doors opened, but neither one of us moved.

Hannah held her finger on the button to keep the doors open.

"Why'd you run, Charlotte? I never understood. You loved him more than anything..." she asked.

"I still do," I told her honestly, the tears welling again.

"Then why? Was it really just because of the attention he gets from women?"

I shook my head. "It wasn't all of it, but it played its part. Mainly, I was scared to tell him that it was too much for me..."

A tear slid down my cheek and I wiped it away quickly.

"Can you imagine being the one that Parker gave up this... *life* for? Gave up music, performing... fame..." I asked her. "Because he would have... I know that man, and I know he would have done that for me."

I looked into Hannah's eyes, willing her to understand why I'd done what I did.

"*I* couldn't handle it. *Me.* And I know without a shadow of a doubt that he would have given it all up for me if that's what it took. I couldn't do that to him. Music is his life, Han, it means everything to him. I couldn't let him give it up for me."

She shook her head gently in disagreement, but her eyes were soft with understanding.

"Look, I get it... I understand what you were trying to save him from," she acknowledged. "But you're wrong. Music wasn't his life anymore... *you* were. He would have given it up because he loves you more than he loves the music," she told me softly.

I was his life...

He loved me more than he loved the music...

The words bounced around in my mind.

I'm an idiot.

I could feel myself teetering on the edge of a breakdown.

What have I done?

"I've made such a terrible mistake," I whispered, my voice was so broken I didn't even recognise it as my own.

"Breathe, Lotte, let's just get you to Parker. Okay? It's not too late." She put her hand on my back and urged me to walk forward; towards the car that would take me to the man I loved.

I sucked in a breath and nodded.

Parker...

He was all that mattered now.

Parker

I WASN'T ENTIRELY sure that playing a serenade on live television was the best idea I'd ever had – since my fame was the thing that had forced Charlotte and I apart in the first place, but it was a gesture, and it was grand.

That's what my Nona had always said.

"A woman loves a grand gesture."

Well, this was the best I could come up with. If this didn't say 'grand gesture' then I had no idea what would.

These past months had been the longest I'd ever gone without playing or singing since I'd first started at five years old. And I was coming out of my lull, for her.

Charlotte.

My entire consciousness absorbed the sound of her name, the thoughts of her seeping into every part of my body.

I'd deprived myself for too long.

I picked my guitar up off the seat of the car and gave Sammy a nod that it was time.

He'd been watching me carefully for the past few minutes. I knew this wasn't his preferred way to spend the afternoon – having to fend off the hordes of fans that were bound to show up was going to be no small feat, but he was here and he hadn't complained once – other than the frown that had been permanently etched into his brow since the moment I'd filled him in on this plan.

Screw it – I pay him enough, he'll get over it.

Sammy had called in a whole team of security on this one, there were at least a dozen guys out there, all dressed just like Sammy – black suit, black shirt, black tie and dark glasses.

The whole thing was a bit James Bond meets Men in Black for my liking, but I would have been a fool not to agree to having their protection.

If this whole thing played out, and Hannah was able to get Charlotte to watch it, I didn't want her seeing me getting trampled and mauled by a bunch of bat-shit crazy fans. That wasn't going to help the situation in the slightest.

I took a deep breath and swung open the car door

that would lead to my old stomping ground – my old street corner.

"Sir?" Sammy called before I could get my ass off the seat. He'd driven me here himself – I had no idea what Kelvin was doing, but Jasper had asked to borrow him for the day.

Who knows with Jasper...

I shot him a death glare. "For God's sake, Sammy, you've worked for me for five years, call me Parker," I snapped.

"Certainly, sir." He nodded, and I swear I saw a slight twitch in the corner of his mouth.

Smart bastard...

I ground my teeth together. It didn't matter how many times I told him – his answer was always the same.

That's about to change.

I knew I hadn't been the easiest guy to work for lately. I was moody, aggressive and fucked off at the world. Sammy had worn more than one of my temper tantrums in the past couple of months, so I couldn't exactly blame him for the use of formal greeting, but this had been going on for years. 'Sir' was for old boring people.

This stops now.

"Call me Parker, or you're fired," I bartered with him, my face as deadly serious as I was.

He narrowed his eyes at me for a few beats before finally cracking. "Well fuck... nicely played, *Parker*."

I chuckled. "About time."

And keep it that way...

"Now what do you want?" I demanded. I wanted to get this show on the road.

"I just wanted to say that... I hope you get her back, she's a great girl and I know she makes you happy."

Just how much I was putting on the line hit me again. This was my chance to get her back – she was everything... without her, this life was all just a big lot of nothing.

"Me too, Sammy." I nodded. "And I owe you an apology. I've been a prick lately... when this is over I'm giving you a bonus and a compulsory vacation."

He waved away my apology, but I could tell he wasn't going to argue about the time off – he'd more than earned it.

He reached his hand out and I shook it firmly before grabbing my guitar and stepping out of the car.

A few of Sammy's team were lingering around outside, sweeping the area with their eyes and doing a piss-poor job of blending in.

Sammy was right behind me – so close he damn near walked into me when I paused to look around.

"Calm your shit, Sammy, there's no one here yet," I told him with a chuckle.

"I give it fifteen minutes," he grumbled back.

Fifteen was generous – it'd probably be more like five.

My fans might have been crazy as hell, but they

were resourceful, I'd give them that. The minute this thing went live, they'd find a way to get here.

I gave Snitch the nod to signal I was ready to roll. I went over to the stool and mic that Jasper had set up for me earlier.

The man himself was leaning against the side of the closest building, taking a drag of a cigarette. Jasper didn't even smoke anymore, but for some reason he still carried around a pack and lit one up about once a month. He didn't even smoke the whole thing. It was odd really – but that was Jasper for you.

I lifted my chin in his direction and he mimicked the action back to me.

Here goes nothing.

I glanced around and took a deep breath before running my fingers over the strings.

————

I'd expected it to feel awkward, but it wasn't.

It had been so long since I'd played at all, let alone played well. I didn't really want to blow my own trumpet, but I was killing it.

Toot toot.

I had a whole backlog of songs that I'd written about Charlotte, and they were all coming out now... I was currently on song number six and I was feeling these songs, the melodies and the lyrics like they were coming straight from my soul.

This level of connection couldn't be faked or

impersonated – this was heartbreak... it was raw and painful.

It was love.

There was a huge crowd surrounding me now, watching as I poured my heart and soul out to the entire world.

To her...

She's my entire world.

Snitch's live feed had lit up social media, and the world was going crazy apparently. People were turning up by the car load and piling out onto the footpath, their cell phones already in their hands ready to film this new, unheard material.

I didn't care how many people saw or turned up as long as *she* saw... that was all that mattered. I wasn't ungrateful for my fans and their support – it was actually quite the opposite... but my whole career had been for the fans and for myself, this here and now was about Charlotte.

I looked up and nearly missed my lyric with the shock at seeing the size of my growing audience. More and more people were flooding in by the second. It was crazy.

It should have been a total scream-fest night-mare... but instead, there was something going on here that I couldn't explain.

Maybe it was me – maybe I was exuding an *aura* of some sort that just told everyone to calm the fuck down...

I don't know what it is...

Whatever it was, it was bizarre. The crowd had made no move to come too close to me. They'd formed a wide circle directly around me, metres of clear space surrounding me. Sammy and his team hadn't had to restrain or warn even one single person.

Maybe they know...

I hadn't said the words, but I think it was obvious this was about more than just playing music. I was a man on a mission, and for once, the beast seemed content to just be along for the ride.

The crowd applauded and whooped and hollered as I finished my song.

I took a deep gulp from my water bottle and hung my head down – this was exhausting, I was more emotionally drained than I could ever remember being.

This was it.

This is my last chance.

If this didn't get me the girl, then nothing would.

Sure, I had more songs *about* her that I could play, but this was the only song I'd written *to* her.

Here goes nothing.

CHAPTER 46

Charlotte

"HOLY SHIT," I muttered as we approached the
spot where Parker was singing.

When I'd seen him on the TV screen, there were
maybe thirty people watching him – now there was
probably about five hundred.

Maybe more...

It was madness. There were cars and people
everywhere – I couldn't even see Parker at all, he
must have been totally surrounded.

Hannah had been on the phone to Jasper on and
off during our drive downtown, but I couldn't focus
long enough to figure out what she was saying, or
what scheme the two of them were cooking up.

The car pulled to a stop. "Here we are, miss," Kelvin called from the driver's seat.

I'd been surprised to see Kelvin driving this car – I'd assumed he would have been with Parker. I was grateful for the familiar face of someone I knew I could trust – it was sweet of Jasper to have sent him to pick us up instead of some stranger.

"Thank you, Kelvin, I really appreciate it."

He tipped his non-existent hat in my direction.

The door next to me swung wide open and nearly gave me a heart attack.

Jasper's blond head appeared through the door.

"Jesus, Jasper." I clutched my chest. "You scared the shit out of me."

"Hey, baby," Hannah crooned.

"Hey, barbie." Jasper winked at her.

I sighed. They really were so cute together.

"Glad you could make it." He grinned at me and I could already tell that he had a plan. "Out you get," he prompted.

"Thanks for this, J, but what now? There's too many people... maybe I should wait," I murmured nervously as I peered around Jasper and looked at the hordes of people that were standing between Parker and me.

"Not a chance, Little Red, c'mon, days a-wastin'," he announced.

I felt my heart speed up in my chest.

I can't go out there.

My panic must have been evident on my face.

"Charlotte," Jasper soothed. "Just listen to him..."

I took a deep breath and leant out the door. Now that I'd calmed down, I could hear his voice.

He was singing something I'd never heard before.

"You're all I want... all I need... I'm empty without you... it's nothing, without you and those sexy legs..."

I could only catch snippets over the noise of the crowd, but it didn't take a genius to figure out he was singing this song to me.

"There's nothing that can keep me from you... only you..."

My feet moved of their own accord in the direction of his voice.

Jasper slipped in behind me, his hand on my arm so I was close. He let out a loud, shrill whistle and out of nowhere, about half a dozen burly-looking men in suits appeared and flanked us on either side, clearing a path through the crowd as we moved.

"This is so cool," Hannah squeaked from somewhere behind me.

I hadn't even realised she had come out of the car behind me, but I should have known she'd want to be right in the action.

Jasper tugged on my arm and pulled me to a stop as the crowd thinned and Parker's voice became clearer.

He's right there.

I may not have been near him in months, but my body hadn't forgotten how to react to him. My heart sped up and my whole body hummed with awareness.

"You ready?" He turned my shoulders in an attempt to get me to look at him.

My shoulders moved but my head stayed trained on where I knew Parker was. I couldn't look away.

I nodded dumbly as Parker's voice turned husky and low.

"Your blue eyes, they haunt me at night... I can't do this without you, I've lost my fight."

My eyes blurred with tears.

"Everything is nothing without you..." His voice was thick with emotion and it nearly broke me in two.

Jasper must have signalled someone because suddenly there was nothing standing between me and the man I loved.

And there he was.

I let out a sob as I laid eyes on him for the first time in what felt like forever.

He was even more handsome than I remembered... more beautiful than what any screen or photo could portray.

With that guitar in his hands and his eyes closed in concentration, he really was sexy as hell.

His fitted grey t-shirt hugged his toned body in all the right places, and even though he'd clearly lost some weight, his muscles still bulged and strained in the most delicious way.

I took a step forward out of the safety of the crowd.

I could hear whispers of 'oh my god, she's here' and 'is that her?' starting up around the circle as Parker strummed the final chord and stilled before me.

There was nothing but silence. I didn't know if that was due to the emotional turmoil that had just played out before the crowd, or because I was here, taking another tentative step towards Parker.

I watched him take a deep breath and with a sigh, lift his head.

His ice-blue eyes opened and he looked right at me – directly into my eyes.

His face transformed into an expression of utter disbelief. He blinked once, twice, three times before he seemed to believe what he was seeing.

"Charlotte?" he whispered, his voice hoarse.

I nodded. I wanted to yell out to him, tell him that I was here and how sorry I was... but nothing came out.

"You're here?" he croaked out.

I nodded again and a tear slipped down my cheek. I still couldn't seem to speak, so instead I told him with my eyes.

I'm sorry...

I should have stayed...

I love you...

God I miss you...

I sobbed again and the noise spurred him into

action. He was in front of me, his strong, familiar arms wrapping around me in a flash.

The crowd went wild.

He held me so tight I was torn between worry that he might snap me in half, and my desire to be held tighter.

"Legs?" he questioned, as though he still didn't quite believe what he was experiencing. "You're here..."

"I'm here," I choked out, my voice muffled against his chest. "I never should have left." I whimpered at my own stupidity.

I was a fool to think I could live without him. In his arms was the only place that felt like home anymore.

"Shhhh." He soothed me as he rubbed slow circles on my back. "I can't believe you came."

"I can't believe you did this for me."

He pulled back and held me at arm's length so he could look into my eyes. "I've told you once, and I'll tell you again, I would literally do *anything* for you, Charlotte."

If it weren't for him holding me up, I probably would have crumbled to the ground. He looked deep into my soul with his beautiful eyes and promised me with nothing more than a look that he was dead serious.

I didn't deserve this man, but if he would let me, I was going to keep him anyway.

"I'm sorry," I whispered.

He shook his head. "*I'm* sorry."

I opened my mouth to argue but he cut me off. "It doesn't matter anymore, legs, all I want, is to make this work... whatever it takes. Can we do that?"

I bit down on my lip and reached up to wrap my arms around his neck.

"Whatever it takes," I agreed in a whisper before his lips met mine.

CHAPTER 47

Parker

I COULDN'T BELIEVE she'd come to find me.

Even now, hours and hours later I still couldn't believe she was really here, in my arms and back in my life.

Jasper was right... I am one lucky son of a bitch...

I couldn't explain how I was feeling in this moment.

I'd accepted that I was never getting her back. It didn't stop me dreaming about her... or barely being able to function in normal day to day life... but I'd come to terms with it as best I could.

It was like all my Christmases had come at once.

She laughed at something Jasper had said, and the vibration of her laugh moved through my whole body and I smiled – really and truly smiled for the first time in months.

I had no idea what she was laughing about, or heard a single word that had been spoken since we'd arrived back at my house – and I couldn't have cared less what they were discussing anyway.

I was perfectly content just to look at her, hold her, breathe in her perfume and run my fingers through her hair.

She'd been doing much of the same. Her hands had run through my scraggy hair numerous times, her fingers tracing over my nose and along my prickly jaw… she was committing me to memory as much as I was.

There was still so much we needed to say to one another – but we had all the time in the world for those conversations.

Right now, all that mattered was that she was mine again.

I'm never letting her go.

———

"I mean this in the nicest way possible, but get out of my house," I instructed J and Hannah.

There was no mistaking where my head was at so I didn't even bother denying it when they teased and catcalled me for wanting to take this party to the bedroom.

Damn right I do.

Charlotte blushed at the obvious longing in my eyes.

It had been far too long since she'd been underneath me and I wasn't waiting any longer.

I stood up and bent down to scoop her into my arms. Jasp and Hannah had barely made it out of the living room and I was already carrying her up to my bedroom.

She didn't say a word as I carried her – just looked into my eyes with a million unsaid words.

I walked her straight to my bed and lowered her gently onto the mattress.

"Parker..." she whispered, reaching up to cup my jaw. "I love you."

I'd seen and heard a lot of things from women in my time, but never anything that looked or sounded this perfect.

"God, I love you too, woman."

"I'm so sorr—"

I cut her apology off. "I told you, I don't want to hear it... I meant it, legs... you have nothing to be sorry for."

She hadn't done a thing wrong. She couldn't live with my lifestyle and I couldn't blame her for that.

That was why I was giving it up. All that was left was to tell her... and then the rest of the world.

"I'm done with it all," I whispered. "I can't risk losing you again," I told her as I dragged my shirt over my head and then began work on her jeans.

She gasped. "No...you can't give it up."

I reached for the hem of her shirt and she let me lift it over her head.

"I can, and I will," I answered as I shoved my pants down my legs.

The sight of my hard erection seemed to shut her up.

She made a hum of appreciation deep in her throat.

I reached for a condom, but she reached out and grabbed my hand.

I looked at her in question.

"I got the pill before we broke up... and you and me...this is forever, right?"

Oh fuck yes.

I nodded and tried to downplay just how elated I was. I'd been fantasising about taking Charlotte bareback since I'd first been inside her.

My right hand and I had got pretty well acquainted these past few months, but that wasn't going to be nearly enough to stop me blowing my load like a teenage boy losing his virginity right now.

"I'm not giving you up for anything," I confirmed as I lined up to push inside her.

I didn't need any foreplay and I knew she didn't either – looking at her creamy skin was all the prep work required today.

"I'm not enough," she panted as I pushed deep inside her.

I groaned loudly. I'd forgotten exactly how tight

and perfect she felt, and the lack of barrier between us only magnified that tenfold.

"You're everything," I ground out as I desperately tried to keep my composure.

She dragged her nails down my back, hard enough that she would leave a mark, and I nearly lost it.

I was so damn close to falling over the edge.

"You... need... the... thrill," she choked out between thrusts and breathy moans.

She was getting close, I could tell.

"You're my biggest thrill," I argued through clenched teeth.

I knew what she was doing – she was testing me. If there was ever a time a man was going to say something stupid, it was during sex. Lucky for me, I didn't have a single thing to lie about – she could grill me about anything she liked.

"Oh god," she cried out.

I thrust harder and deeper.

"The thrill of the stage or the thrill of—"

"You," I growled, interrupting her question with a hard thrust of my hips. "Always you."

She fell apart beneath me, her body sagging from the pleasure we'd both created.

I followed right behind her.

Charlotte kissed the picture of her, right over my fast-beating heart.

"You're not giving it up, Parker," she whispered as she looked up at me through her long lashes.

"I promise you I won't run again because of the fame."

I kissed her forehead.

"But I need you to give us a chance to make this work, please," she begged.

I dropped my forehead to hers and sighed. "Okay, I'll think about it."

CHAPTER 48

Charlotte

"I HAVE A SURPRISE FOR YOU," I told Parker as I jumped off his lap.

He'd been back in my life for two weeks and the fact that he hadn't yet returned to music or any of the commitments that went with that life, meant that he'd spent every minute he could with me. If I wasn't working, he was there. He'd even come onto the set of a movie with me one day – but his presence had proved to be too much of a distraction for some of the extras, so he'd had to go home early – albeit kicking and screaming.

I laughed lightly at the memory.

That's Parker for you... always causing a stir...

I handed him the USB stick and gestured

towards the stereo system in the cabinet in front of us.

"What's this?" he asked with a frown as he turned the stick over – looking for a sign of what might be on it.

I'd held onto this thing the entire time we'd been apart. I'd considered mailing it anonymously to him, but I knew he'd never see it that way; he got more fan mail than I'd thought would have been possible.

I hadn't even showed this to Hannah – but she was about to hear what her boyfriend was capable of.

I glanced nervously over at Jasper and Hannah snuggled on the couch.

Let's hope J has a good poker face...

"So... you know how we talked the other night, and you mentioned that you would have loved to be up there alongside someone when you perform? That you wished you had that duo thing going, rather than always being a solo artist...?"

He nodded, no doubt thinking back to our conversation. We'd been having some serious talks about him returning to his music career, and while he wasn't dead set on giving it up anymore, he wasn't exactly jumping at the chance to get back into it either.

When he'd mentioned the idea to me, I'd pushed him hard for more information on what he wanted.

Parker wanted to share the spotlight. He'd decided that he was over being the centre of attention – he was tired of it all being solely focused on him.

He'd expressed his disappointment at the idea probably never becoming a reality – Parker didn't trust many people and there was no way he would bring someone into his music career that he didn't trust.

That was where Jasper came in – he didn't know it, but I had the perfect person in mind. This was exactly what Parker needed.

Now to let his voice do the talking.

"Yeah... what has *that* got to do with *this?*" He held up the stick in question.

"Plug it in and tell me what you think," I instructed.

"But wh—"

"Oh, for God's sake, rock star, just do what you're told for once," I snapped.

He chuckled. "Alright, legs, I'll behave." He held up his hands in mock surrender.

I rolled my eyes. "Like hell you will," I muttered under my breath.

"What did you say?" he asked over his shoulder as he slid the stick into the port on the sound system in his living room.

"What did you hear?" I raised my brows at him.

He chuckled again. "Nevermind."

He hit play and sat down on the floor in front of the speaker.

He held his hand out for mine and tugged me down to sit between his legs.

I glanced over at Hannah and Jasper again, they weren't paying one scrap of attention to us right now, but I knew that was about to change – even the uber relaxed Jasper would struggle to stay chilled about this particular experiment.

Parker ran his hand through my hair, fiddling with the long strands.

The recording kicked in and the strum of the guitar filled the room. Parker dropped the strand of my hair and turned his attention entirely towards the music.

Jasper's raspy voice swirled around me, transporting me back to when I'd first heard him.

Goosebumps covered my skin as I closed my eyes and let myself enjoy the melody.

I heard Jasper cuss and Hannah shush him.

Parker hadn't moved an inch, and without opening my eyes to check, I guessed that he was totally enthralled with what he was hearing.

I'd half expected Jasper to have come over and switched it off by now, but as far as I was aware, he hadn't moved from his spot on the couch.

I've got your back, J... just trust me.

The song finished and the recording cut off abruptly – I'd had to chop off the part where I'd busted in and yelled Jasper's name.

Might have been a teeny tiny giveaway.

My eyes fluttered open as I peeked up to look at Parker's face – his eyes were still shut, his expression serene.

"Well?" I prompted with a whisper.

CHAPTER 49

Parker

THAT VOICE.

Have I heard that voice somewhere before?

I wracked my brain, but came up empty.

It was good. Hell, it was damn good.

It was really unique, and whoever owned it knew exactly how to use it. I hadn't heard control like that in years.

Whoever that guy was – he deserved to be absolutely killing it in the charts, but I was fairly confident that that tone didn't belong to any of the artists who were in the top one hundred alongside me.

This was someone new.

"I want him," I blurted out.

"Excuse me?" Charlotte raised her brows at me, fake outrage written all over her face.

I chuckled. "Oh c'mon. You knew what I meant... I want to sing with that dude."

She grinned gleefully.

The possibilities raced through my mind.

"Who is he? How'd you get this? Who do I need to contact? Do you think he'd be interested in jamming with me? Do you know if he writes his own material?" I fired question after question at her without giving her time to answer.

That rasp would be the perfect accompaniment to my voice.

I knew a good mesh when I heard one – and if I could get this guy to agree, we could make some seriously good tunes together.

"Remember to breathe," Hannah called helpfully from the couch.

I looked up at her and took a deep breath.

"But seriously, Lotte, who the hell was that? His voice is HOT." She shot Jasper an apologetic glance. "Sorry, babe, but it's true."

Jasper didn't reply, but I couldn't help but notice the daggers he was shooting at my woman.

I was about to hit him up about it, but Charlotte spoke first.

"It's just someone I stumbled across," she replied vaguely. 'He's kind of... shy... I guess you could say he wasn't too keen on having someone of your... *status* hearing him sing."

"Why the hell not?" I demanded with a frown.

What the hell was wrong with this guy?

I had power in the music industry. Certain record producers would yell 'how high' when I told them to jump. I could give this guy the start he would need in such a competitive market.

Toot toot – blowing your own trumpet much?

She pointed her finger at me like I was in trouble. "Because... he wants to make it off his talent – not because of your contacts, rock star," Charlotte explained, almost as though she could read my mind. Actually, at this point I was willing to believe that she could read my mind – she knew me better than I knew myself most days.

I absorbed her words for a few beats. "Okay... I get that." I nodded. "I can respect a guy for that... but if his talent wasn't what it was, then I wouldn't be willing to put my ass on the line for him, would I?" I shot back, hoping like hell that she'd see where I was coming from.

Charlotte grinned triumphantly. "That's exactly what I was hoping you'd say."

I furrowed my brow in confusion.

What is she playing at?

"So, let me get this straight... you think this guy has what it takes, right?" She jiggled with excitement.

Her breasts bounced, and for a moment I forgot all about the voice I'd just heard.

She's so damn sexy.

Charlotte cleared her throat, disrupting me from

my ogling. "Eyes are up here, rock star." She pointed to her eyes with a smirk on her lips.

I shook my head to try and snap out of it.

Damn Charlotte...

The voice... think about the voice...

"If he can nail every track like he did that one? Then yeah, I know he's got it. This is what I need. I need a guy with a voice like that... but there's still the fact that I don't know or trust him, so it wouldn't be a done deal," I explained.

"But *if* you could trust him?" she prompted.

I thought about it for a minute. "Then I'd offer him the deal of a lifetime."

I wished more than anything that she could magic up someone with a perfect set of lungs that I knew would have my back. That was exactly what I wanted going forward.

I wasn't sure when the loneliness had set in – it was probably around the time Charlotte had left. I didn't feel as confident anymore – I'd done some harmonies with Pete lately and it was the most fun I'd had with music since before my hiatus, and while he wasn't too bad of a singer, he didn't hold a flame to the talent I'd need to make this duo idea work.

Talent like I just heard.

Raw talent.

I needed raw talent that I could trust.

"You'd want him to be your wing man?" Charlotte pressed, anticipation building in her eyes.

I nodded, unsure of where she was going with

this. Trust took time to build; there was *nothing* she could say that was going to make me trust this guy in an instant.

"Hell yeah I would, in a perfect world, if someone would offer me a guy with a voice like that, that was down to earth and could be trusted in my life, then I'd offer him whatever he wanted."

"Well then you're in luck." She grinned, her excitement palpable.

"Charlotte..." Jasper warned.

Charlotte snapped her head around to look at him.

I frowned in confusion as I looked between the two of them – locked in a silent standoff.

Hannah must have picked up on the tension too. "Alright, which one of you two is going to tell me what the hell is going on here?"

"C'mon, J..." Charlotte begged.

Jasper stared hard at her, and I could tell he was debating internally with himself. What he was debating, I had no idea, but it was clear he was struggling with it.

"Pleeease, Jasper," she whispered into the tense silence.

J balled his fists tight and groaned. He threw his head back onto the back of the couch and muttered a string of curse words. "Fine," he mumbled more coherently.

Charlotte squeaked out some type of ecstatic noise that I'd never heard her make before.

"But if it all turns to shit, it's on you, Little Red," Jasper added in warning.

Charlotte nodded furiously in agreement. "I'll keep him under control, I promise."

I didn't know what was going on here, but I was starting to think that my girlfriend and my best mate had been doing some type of scheming together behind my back.

"Oh fill us in already," Hannah snapped, looking between the two of them. She nudged Jasper in the ribs. "You know I hate secrets."

"Well you're going to be thrilled with me..." he muttered.

"You know who it is, don't you?" Hannah replied in a pissy voice. "You better tell me, Jasper Jones, or I swear I'll—"

"It's me," he interrupted her with a resigned sigh.

My jaw dropped.

It's him?

He turned to face me, his expression guilty as hell. "Charlotte snapped me having a jam in your studio," he explained.

Jasper?

Jasper can sing?

Jasper can play?

I opened my mouth to speak, but no words came out. Even Hannah was silent – and that was a fucking never-before-seen event.

Charlotte took my hand in hers. "I know what's going through your head, rock star, and yes, he can sing... *and* play the guitar, and who knows what else... I've heard him in person, and he's really that good."

It didn't matter which way I swung it in my head, I just couldn't make this information fit with what I knew about Jasper.

We'd been friends forever – since we were kids.

He'd been by my side, supporting my music career for years, and he'd never shown any inclination towards singing.

"Are you serious?" Hannah shrieked.

I winced.

Jasper was in for it now. Hannah was bound to rip him a new one for keeping this a secret from her.

"This. Is... AWESOME!" She cried.

What the hell?

Did I just hear that right?

Charlotte giggled – at Han's reaction, or my bewildered expression, I wasn't sure.

"My boyfriend is sweet, sexy, tattooed *and* can sing like a God. Oh you wait till the girls hear about this!" She bragged, clearly thrilled with herself. "It's like a girl's wet dream," she added with a content sigh.

I couldn't help but laugh at the expression on Jasper's face. He looked like someone had just crowned him king of the world.

Proud as punch.

He was smitten as hell with that crazy-ass girl, and it was clear as day that her praise was worth everything to him.

"He's pretty incredible, right?" Charlotte whispered to me.

I looked down at her and nodded in agreement. "How long have you known he had that in him?"

She grimaced sheepishly and screwed up her nose. "Since before we broke up... I always planned to tell you – even though Jasper asked me not to... but then, you know..." She shrugged. "Life got in the way."

"Why didn't he want to tell me?" I asked her, surprised by the hurt in my own voice.

Jasper and I were like brothers, and for whatever reason, he hadn't wanted to share this side of himself with me. I'd be lying if I said it didn't wound me a little bit.

We could have had so many jam sessions together; we could have made new music... I would have put him in front of the producers that gave me my big break... he would be a signed artist by now...

Reality hit me.

That's why he didn't tell me...

He didn't want a free ride.

It didn't explain how I never knew he had that voice when we were kids, but it sure explained why he hadn't told me since I'd made it big.

Jasper was so relaxed he was basically horizontal. We were different like that. I loved the attention – or at least I did for the first few years. I was all about the big parties and events, where J had always preferred to have a few quiet beers at home with a good group of mates.

He'd come out of his shell since he'd agreed to become my manager, but he'd been forced into that for the most part. These days he was comfortable in clubs, on the stage doing the intro and dealing with his own fans.

But could he handle hitting it big?

I thought about it for a moment, and knew that with me here to support him, he could do whatever the hell he wanted.

Charlotte was watching me quietly with a satisfied smile – she knew I was figuring it all out inside my head.

I kissed her forehead before turning back to my best mate.

"Alright, man... I'm just gonna lay it out there. I'm gutted you didn't tell me. You're the closest thing I've got to a brother, and you should have been able to talk to me."

Jasper nodded his head, a shameful expression on his face like he'd seen my disappointment coming.

"But I can see why you didn't... because you know me well, and you knew that I'd make a massive deal about this."

He nodded again, his eyes fixed on mine.

"So, I won't do that," I told him simply.

Charlotte squeezed my hand and I knew she was proud of me.

"But I will tell you that your voice is good, man. It

deserves to be heard, and hell, I'd love to have you up there with me if we could make it work somehow. I think a duo is exactly what I need... but there's no pressure. I'm not gonna push you into something you don't want, and I'm also not going to offer you anything you haven't earned."

"I appreciate that, Park," he replied, his voice thick.

"How would you feel about starting small... just a few jam sessions in my studio?"

He nodded and grinned. "As long as you don't attempt to drum, I'm there."

I chuckled.

Charlotte looked at me in question, but I just shook my head.

I'm never touching those damn drums again.

CHAPTER 50

Charlotte
Three months later

I SWAYED SLOWLY in my spot on the side of the stage.

This was the fourth show I'd been to this month alone, but it still felt like I was experiencing it all for the first time.

Parker had come back with a renewed passion for his music. Already he had pumped numerous new releases, all of them hits.

Most of them about me...

It was like he couldn't do a thing wrong if he had a guitar and a mic in his hands.

He first reappeared on the scene on his own, before bringing Jasper in on a few collaborations about a month ago. He'd wanted to ease Jasper into the industry and they hadn't even promoted their songs, so no one was more surprised than us when those singles had turned out to be the most popular of all.

Their first song together had debuted at number one all over the world and still remained there now, four weeks later.

I had a pretty good feeling that over the next few months they would transition into a duo entirely.

I looked out at Parker and Jasper now as they belted out another of their newly released songs. They looked right up there together – this was a change that was going to be good for the both of them.

I'm so glad he's back.

I still felt guilty to my very core about causing Parker to take a step back from his music career, but at the same time, it was as though he'd needed it – the break seemed to have given him more inspiration than ever and the songs he'd written since then were exceptional.

They were honest and raw and real. Some of them were truly heart-breaking – those were the hardest for me to hear. Parker said they were the hardest to perform too, and the tears that could be heard in his voice when he sang some of them showed that he wasn't being insincere in the slightest.

I sighed as I watched them up there, two best

friends doing what they were born to do. It was so satisfying to witness.

Hannah nudged her elbow against mine.

I looked over at her and smiled. She may as well have had giant hearts in her eyes as she looked at Jasper.

My best friend was so in love, it was beautiful to watch.

"They're on fire tonight," I called to her over the deafening volume of the music. They were magic together. They were already so close, and that translated into their music; they flowed together perfectly and they could read one another like they'd practised it their whole lives.

She nodded in agreement. "I've got goosebumps!" she yelled back, gesturing to her arm.

The song came to an end, and as the crowd exploded into cheers and whoops, Parker turned to catch my eye.

Uh oh.

I knew that look.

That look was trouble.

Oh shit...

I backed up in what I already knew would be a futile attempt to get away from him as he began to prowl towards me from the centre of the stage.

Hannah clapped her hands together enthusiastically. "I *love* it when he does this," she cried gleefully.

Traitor.

"Parker..." I warned as he got closer.

I'd backed up as far as I could – my back was hard against the sectional wall.

He had a giant smile on his face and that gorgeous dimple of his was on full display.

I sighed, hearts of my own in my eyes. Even I knew it was all over for me – I'd do anything this man wanted when he smiled at me like that.

"Hey, baby." He grinned. "I'm sure you can figure out what's gonna happen next." He slung his thumb over his shoulder in the direction of the stage.

I groaned.

"C'mon, legs, let's just get it over with." He pressed his body against mine, his guitar slung around the back of him.

He kissed my neck, just below my ear. "I'll make it worth your while..." he whispered suggestively.

"Just go already you party pooper," Hannah demanded from somewhere behind Parker.

"Fine," I muttered in defeat.

Parker chuckled. "You'd think you just agreed to your own execution."

"May as well have," I grumbled.

It wasn't that I didn't love him singing to me – but he could do that at his house, or mine... or anywhere really... anywhere where we weren't being watching by thousands of people.

But as per usual, I let him lead me out from the safety of my hiding space and onto the stage. I just didn't seem to be able to deny him something that clearly made him this happy.

The crowd went absolutely bat-shit crazy the moment they saw him towing me out. I should have been used to that by now – Parker had been making a habit of bringing me out on stage and singing to me, but the all-encompassing volume of noise still nearly knocked me backwards.

I glanced around and frowned. The crew normally set up two chairs facing each other, one for me and one for Parker.

But not today... today there was just an empty stage – even Jasper had made an escape.

"What are you doing?" I hissed at Parker.

If it weren't for the slight twitch from the corner of his mouth I would have thought he didn't hear me. Either way, he didn't answer – instead tugging me by the hand out into the very middle of the bright lights.

"So, you all know my girl, right?" His husky voice boomed out into the packed arena.

The screams picked up volume.

"Now I know I've been singing to her lately, but in the spirit of mixing things up, I'm not going to do that tonight."

Half of the crowd booed in disappointment, the other half screamed in excitement of the unknown.

I looked up at him, questioning his intention with my eyes.

He glanced down at me and ran his finger over the crease between my eyes that my frown was causing.

"I actually brought her out here because I've got a

bone to pick with her," he announced, his eyes only leaving mine as he finished speaking.

The crowd let out a few collective gasps.

I may have joined them.

I didn't know what this damn rock star was up to, but I didn't like the chances of me escaping without a bright red face.

I heard a few calls from the crowd, and surprisingly, it wasn't the usual females asking Parker to defile them in vulgar ways. It was still strange to me that I could actually hear an individual over the general noise of the masses.

One stood out most, a male this time. "I'll take her off your hands, man!" he yelled.

Parker chuckled. "I'm sure you would, man... she's beautiful, isn't she?"

The crowd erupted into screams and applause.

Damn it.

There goes that blush.

Parker slung his arm over my shoulders.

"I'm going to share with you all the grief she's been giving me," he told the crowd with his shit-eating grin back in place on his face.

I nudged him in the ribs and shushed him, entirely forgetting that half the world was probably watching my reaction.

The laughter of the crowd reminded me of where I was.

I blushed even deeper.

Parker chuckled again, but otherwise ignored me.

"So now, you see, I've been asking Charlotte here to move in with me..." He trailed off.

My heart accelerated into overdrive.

Parker may have been hounding me to move in with him before we broke up, but he was yet to mention it again since we got back together. It was ironic really, I'd hesitated before when I should have agreed, and now that I was finally ready to say yes, he'd stopped asking.

Parker interrupted my thoughts. "I've asked her fifteen times, can you imagine that?" He played it up to his audience.

"You would only have to ask me once," a call came from the front row.

I refrained from rolling my eyes.

"I've always had to be... *resourceful* when it comes to impressing Charlotte." He glanced down at me again and smirked.

I had to laugh at that.

"Is that what we're calling stalking and theft these days?" I teased.

My words rang out over the crowd and I cringed. I hadn't realised I was so close to the mic. "Shit," I muttered as Parker laughed loudly along with the crowd who were apparently hanging off our every word.

"See?" He shrugged, totally unembarrassed. "*Resourceful...*"

Something like that.

"Now I figured if I asked her again, in front of all

of you, that she'd be less likely to turn me down... gotta work with what you've got right?"

Cheers rang out.

He turned to face me entirely – his attention focused solely on me now.

"So whatdya say, legs? Move in with me?"

I pretended to ponder the question for a moment.

Parker waited nervously.

"I've got two conditions," I bargained with him.

He smiled the biggest smile I'd ever seen, and nodded. "Alright, let's hear it."

I wrapped my arms around his middle and held him tight. "Number one, if you decide you want to marry me one day... you do *not* do it on a bloody stage," I told him with a smile.

He threw his head back and laughed.

God I love him.

"Deal," he promised through his laughter. "What else?"

I shot him a sassy smirk. "I don't know how many times I have to tell you to use your damn manners..."

"Please move in with me," he cut me off quickly. "Please, please, please, please, please." He chuckled.

"Do it, Little Red!" Ricky's voice boomed through the speakers.

I laughed; he was such a smart-ass, wherever he was.

Parker smiled at me with his gorgeous dimpled cheek.

"Hell yes," I told him.

He fist pumped the air to the cheers of the crowd before kissing me like there was no tomorrow.

―――――

"Well this is new," Jasper drawled as he looked around the bare apartment, lit only by candles – the power wasn't out or anything, we were just trying to be romantic.

It was weird seeing the place empty again. It had been home for Han and I for a long time now, and in a lot of ways it was the only place I'd ever truly felt at home.

Until Parker came along...

Now I was home whenever he was near.

All of my things were now mixed in with all of Parker's stuff and we may not have been married, or even engaged, but I knew that they'd stay that way forever.

"Would you just let us surprise you for once?" Hannah whined when Jasper tried poking around under the blanket we'd set out.

Parker sauntered up behind me and wrapped his arms around my middle.

"Is she still pretending to be pissed off with him?" He chuckled.

"Looks that way." I grinned.

Hannah was still acting like she was bothered with how Jasper had asked her to move in with him. The smart bastard had literally waited until all of my stuff had been moved out, he'd walked into the half empty apartment, glanced around and announced to Hannah, 'pack your crap, barbie, you're moving in with me'. I'd thought it was hilarious. Hannah, who I knew was genuinely overjoyed at moving in with Jasper, hadn't stopped comparing the way Parker had asked me to live with him, with the way Jasper had asked her.

If you asked me, I thought she got the better deal.

"What's all this about anyway?" He kissed my cheek.

I shrugged. "A girl can't treat her man?"

"It's my job to treat you."

I rolled my eyes. "It's twenty seventeen, rock star, come out of your cave."

———

"Now that we've lured you here under the false pretence of food and romance... we actually wanted to talk to you about your team of staff."

We'd all stuffed ourselves full on the platters that Hannah and I had put together and were onto our second bottle of red wine.

Time to get down to business...

"I told you we'd hired Snitch as our private photographer and to do some videos and shit, right?" Parker asked before stuffing another stack of food into his mouth.

He had told me, and I was excited about him

joining them; Parker already trusted him, so it really did make sense to bring him on board.

I really liked him too, he was sweet. He and his wife had been so genuinely thrilled about the amount he made off my fake pregnancy photos that he'd sent me a bunch of flowers as a thank you.

He's a good guy.

He'd also been a big part of Parker's public 'get Charlotte back' plan too, and Parker had been really impressed with his work.

"You told me," I confirmed.

I shot Hannah a nervous look. We were both a bit freaked about this, but we were hoping the guys would be on board with our ideas.

She gave me a thumbs up.

"So, we were thinking... that you need to hire a new publicist."

Parker and Jasper groaned in unison. Hannah laughed.

"I would like to never, ever have to have a publicist ever again," Parker stated.

"I second that motion," Jasper agreed quickly.

"Pipe down, we're not done," Hannah scolded them both like spoiled children.

Parker smirked and Jasper gave her a salute.

I cleared my throat. "And then there's also the small issue of the manager turning into a singer and joining the madness..." I gestured to Jasper. "So really, you need a manager *and* a publicist."

"Shit," Parker mumbled.

"I thought this date was meant to be fun." Jasper scowled.

"You'd think we'd just told you both you needed a tooth pulled, not that you need to hire some extra help." Hannah shot them both a look of disbelief.

I wasn't surprised at Parker's reluctance; he hated bringing new people into his circle.

That's why our plan is so perfect.

"Now I know you just *love* the whole interviewing process and having new people in your space..."

Parker grunted at my obvious sarcasm.

"So how about we just skip all that instead... and you give me and Lotte the jobs..." Hannah cut in.

Parker's mouth opened and then snapped shut again without him saying anything as his eyes darted from me to Han, and back again.

A slow grin broke out on Jasper's face. "For real?" he asked.

"For real," I confirmed. I could tell he was already sold on the idea.

"But... but..." Parker stuttered. "But what about your business... we can't ask you to give that up."

I knew that was what he'd say. That was why we'd already eliminated the problem.

"As of yesterday, C & H styling has officially been restructured," I told him.

Hannah nodded. "Yep... we decided to give it a shakeup... the two of us are retaining only a handful of high-end clients who we couldn't seem to get rid of." She rolled her eyes dramatically. "You celebs... you're so needy."

It was true. When we'd informed our clients that we wouldn't be working in the same capacity any longer, there were a few that wouldn't take no for an answer. They'd thrown more and more money at us until we'd come to the conclusion that even if the guys turned us down, we'd still be making the same amount of money we had been making previously, with less than a quarter of the time spent doing it – that, and we both still actually loved our work, just not full time.

It was a no-brainer.

On top of that, we'd hired two makeup artists and two hair stylists to take over and expand on our little, more low-key business. We'd been training them ourselves for the past month and were confident in their abilities and the fact that they wouldn't run our reputation into the ground.

Working together, we figured we'd have more than enough time to attend to our existing clients, keep an eye on our new team, and manage and run PR for our men.

"Legs, you can't give it up for us," Parker argued.

"It's not just for you," I insisted. "It's for us too... I can't speak for Hannah, but your life is crazy busy, and adding my work into it just makes for a near impossible situation. I just want to be with you, Parker, whenever I can be... and if that means that I don't apply as much makeup to strangers, then hell, where do I sign?"

"What she said," Hannah agreed. "That, and you guys are going to pay us really, really well." She grinned.

"You're serious about this?" he asked me, his ice-blue eyes full of concern.

"Deadly serious," I promised. "I'll tell you all of the ins and outs later, but if you don't agree to this pretty soon, I'm probably going to get offended and start getting emotional."

"You're hired," he replied without missing a beat. "Oh, that's unless my partner has any problem with it?"

I looked at Jasper.

"You had me at 'for real'." He grinned.

"This does not mean you get to boss me around," Hannah warned him, her attitude all bark and no bite.

"Oh c'mon, babe, don't be like that..." he teased her.

Parker's hand reached out for mine and stole my attention entirely with one touch. "Do you know how much I love you?" he asked me with a beautiful smile on his face.

"Probably as much as I love you?"

"You know what; I think the bad luck streak with the publicists is going to continue," Jasper interrupted our little love fest with his taunting. "This one has a bad attitude."

I giggled and sighed as I looked around. I had my best friend by my side – and literally living right next door; she was madly in love with an amazing man – even if he did like to push her buttons, and I had the love of my life in the bed next to me every night.

Life doesn't get much better than this.

CHAPTER 51

Parker
One month later

"I WAS PERFECTLY content until you came along, you know that?" I told her as I tugged gently on the hem of her shirt.

It was a lie – I'd only thought I was content, but really, I was running on empty – my life before her was nothing compared to now.

Charlotte made me a better person, she had this way of bringing me to my own attention – she made me see things about myself that I didn't know, or perhaps didn't want to see, and then without even saying a word, helped me become the person I could be.

I wasn't me without her.

"Me? What'd I do?" Charlotte asked as she glanced up at me from where she was painting her toenails on the end of our bed.

Our bed...

"You made me want *more*," I told her, my voice already shaky with nerves.

"You've got the entire world eating out of the palm of your hand, rock star, what more could you possibly want?" she asked absentmindedly as she applied another coat of black polish with the tiny brush.

"You," I stated. "Forever," I added in a voice so quiet I wasn't even sure she'd hear it.

She heard. She froze mid-stroke of the brush. Her wide, blue eyes coming up slowly to meet mine.

Yip... she heard alright.

"You want what now?" she asked in a breathy voice.

"You heard me."

We stared at one another for a beat, with her too scared to ask, and me too scared to repeat the words that were hanging between us.

"Do you still have that music box I gave you?" I finally asked her.

"Of course I do," she breathed, her expression turning tender.

She loved that thing – I knew she wouldn't have gotten rid of it under any circumstances. It was the gift I'd bought for her when I was out of town, back before all that shit had gone down on social media. We'd well and truly moved on from that scandal, but I knew Charlotte would cherish the antique wind-up music box forever.

"Can I see it?"

She pointed at her toenails. "They're still wet."

"I'll get it," I offered.

She smiled gratefully. "It's in the top drawer."

I retrieved the box and sat it down in front of her on the bed. "Open the back," I instructed.

My heart was beating a million miles an hour as I watched her carefully screw the lid back on the nail polish and set it down.

I'd never planned how this was going to go. I'd half expected her to have discovered what I'd hidden in the back of the box of her own accord. But she hadn't, and here we were.

"Okay..." she replied, uncertain about why she was doing this.

She opened the back slowly, revealing the cogs and mechanisms that made the whole thing work.

She was moving so slowly I had to resist the urge to grab it out of her hands and do it myself.

She was nervous. I could tell. Her eyes were wide and her skin was flushed.

"Okay... now what?" she asked quietly.

"Tip it," I instructed.

She looked right into my eyes for a brief moment

before turning her attention back to the box. She slowly tipped it up on its end.

Nothing happened.

"Shake it."

She gently shook the box and I heard the clank of loose metal bumping against metal.

She bit down on her bottom lip as she shook it again.

It was like it happened in slow motion. The two-carat, antique diamond halo ring fell from the small hole and dropped onto the bed between us.

"Is that..." Charlotte trailed off.

Hell yes it is.

"That music box wasn't the only thing I bought for you that day."

She looked at me, shock written all over her face.

"Whaaa... what?" she stammered. "I don't understand? You bought me this box months and months ago, Parker..."

I nodded. "I knew I wanted to marry you within two weeks, legs."

She gasped.

"You're lucky I waited this long."

She picked up the ring in slow motion, like she was afraid it wouldn't really be there when she reached for it. She clasped it between her thumb and finger and brought it up to her face to look closely at it.

"Charlotte, look at me," I commanded.

Her lip trembled as her eyes met mine.

I got up from my spot and slowly rounded the bed as she watched my every step like a hawk.

I stopped at the edge of the bed and grabbed hold of her to turn her around gently so she was facing me.

Her first sob broke free as I dropped down onto one knee before her.

I may not have been willing to ask her father for her hand in marriage, but I was going to do this thing as old fashioned as I could.

If I had my way, this would be the one and only time Charlotte was proposed to, and she deserved it to be like they did in all those chick flicks she loved to watch.

I reached for her hands and held them gently in mine. I could feel the ring in her hands.

"Charlotte... I don't even know where to begin. I don't know how I could possibly tell you everything that you mean to me..."

There aren't enough words in the world.

"I read something once, it said that perfection was not achieved when there was nothing left to add, but when there was nothing left to take away."

I paused for a moment and watched as a tear slid down her face and fell into her lap.

"And I've realised how true that is about life. Life isn't about seeing how much you can get, it's not about wanting more and more... it's about realising the things you can't live without."

I reached out and wiped away her tears that were now falling freely.

She smiled gratefully at me.

"You're it, legs. You're my point of perfection. *You* are the thing I can't live without..." I kissed her hand. "I know I'm meant to ask your dad for permission, but I thought, well to be honest... *fuck that...*"

She laughed through her sniffles.

"So, I did the next best thing," I told her with a smile.

I knew that she wouldn't be expecting this. I reached into my pocket and pulled out my phone.

Charlotte looked at me in confusion.

I grinned and hit play on the voice recording.

"Short-stuff!!" the chorus of men-children began.

Her eyes flashed up to meet mine. "You asked my brothers?" she whispered.

I nodded and tried to force down the emotions that were threatening to spill out. Watching her realise that her life was changing forever was the most incredible thing I'd ever been a part of.

"Lover boy came to see us..." One of the twins made kissing noises in the background – I couldn't tell which one, they were the most identical twins I'd ever seen or heard.

"You know what we told him, Lots? That if he wanted to marry our baby sister, he had to go one round with each of us."

Charlotte groaned and I chuckled.

"Please tell me they're kidding?" she demanded.

I shook my head. "I'm afraid not."

"Sweet baby Jesus," she muttered as the boys started up again.

"So, he went for a spin in the car with Floyd…"

"Scariest three minutes of my life," I interjected.

"Then he went a few rounds in the ring with me," Louis piped up.

I grimaced as I remembered how easily he'd kicked my ass. They didn't call him 'The Destroyer' for nothing – I was sure he'd broken at least one of my ribs.

"And well, my job isn't all that scary," Tyler jumped in. "So, I fucked with him and told him I needed him to be my inside man, and then I tripped the alarm."

Charlotte's eyes widened. "I'll kill them," she stated, matter of factly. "All three of them."

I chuckled again.

"Don't get your knickers in a knot, sis, it was a set up," he added.

"I take it back… *that* was the scariest three minutes of my life." I chuckled.

"Seriously though, short-stuff, he's a good guy, even dumb and dumber can see how much he loves you." There were noises of a scuffle in the background and if I had to guess I would say that Louis and Floyd were involved in some type of wrestling match.

Charlotte sighed and looked right at me with so much love in her eyes. I could see how much she really appreciated me doing this for her – even if her brothers did drive her crazy.

The scuffle ended with a groan from one of them.

"You're a smart girl, Charlotte, so we already know you're going to say yes, but we wanted you to know that you've got our blessing... all three of us."

Another tear slid down her face. I reached out and wiped it away with my thumb before cradling her face in my hand.

"We love you, short-stuff," one of the boys told her, his own voice thick with emotion.

"Love you," the other two joined in.

"Just make sure you have some hot bridesmaids," Floyd, if I had to guess, chimed in before the recording ended.

"You really let them do all that stuff to you?" she asked with her eyebrow raised.

I nodded. "I'm really that crazy in love with you," I confirmed. "That...and they're kinda terrifying. Tyler seems to have a head on his shoulders... but those twins." I grimaced. "They haven't got an ounce of fear between them; I thought they might go easier on me if I went willingly."

Charlotte giggled between her sniffles and I took her hands back in mine.

"So, what do you say, legs, you want to try for a lifetime with a rock star?" I asked her in the same cocky voice I had that very first night when she'd shot me down – I just hoped that this time she had a different answer for me.

She laughed loud and free and I knew that she was remembering that night where it all began too.

I sucked in a deep breath in anticipation of her answer.

"Hell yes I do."

Charlotte

ALL OF THOSE celebrity couples that people read about in the magazines, they all seem to be getting divorced or separated... or re-married... or arguing over money... or fighting fierce custody battles over their children.

They say the pressure of fame puts an immense amount of strain on a relationship – that they're much harder to sustain in the public eye than they are in private.

I'd have to agree that there is some truth to that.

It's been hard.

Even now, with twenty years of marriage and four children under our belts, it's still hard sometimes.

Parker stopped releasing new music about five years ago now, but people still, to this very day, stop and scream his name in the streets. They snap our picture and ask him to sign everything and anything.

Women haven't stopped throwing themselves at him either.

He may have dropped the 'bad-boy rocker' tag, but he picked up the 'D.I.L.F.' one in the blink of an eye, and I'm still undecided on which one is worse.

But it's worth it.

He's worth it.

Parker is the kind of man that can be bossy and cocky in one moment, then sweet and seductive in his very next breath. He's the kind of man that left a crowbar sitting in the middle of the dining room table when our oldest daughter brought her new boyfriend over to meet us for the first time, but he's also the kind of man that let our twins colour in the tattoos on his back like a colouring book.

He's the kind of man that taught each of our children to play the guitar with incredible skill and who beamed with pride when our youngest daughter won the school talent quest with the amazing voice she'd inherited from her father.

He's also the kind of man that purchased an obscene amount of land on the outskirts of town and created an entire gated community, complete with a playground, skatepark, stores and a pool, intended for families just like ours, and Jasper and Hannah's, who sometimes just needed to feel like they weren't always being watched by the world.

He's the kind of man that cares fiercely about the people he loves.

He is so worth it.

I knew he thought I was worth it too. I was still the only person he saw in a crowded room – always had been, always would be... the tattoo on his chest still testament to that.

His ice-blue eyes still looked at me with the same intensity they had on that very first night, and I still shuddered under the feel of his kiss.

We both knew we'd found something that most people could spend their whole lives searching for, and we were eternally grateful.

I'd walked away from him once before, and I knew now, without a shadow of a doubt that I would never, ever make that same mistake twice.

Parker Sloan, *the* Parker Sloan, the 'sexy rock star', was the love of my life and I wouldn't give him up for the world.

ALSO BY

Love like Yours Series

Rushed – Book 1

Pierced – Book 2

Hunted – Book 3

Chased – Book 4

Love like Yours Box Set – Books 1-4

Rock Games Novels

Paper, Scissors, Rock: Vol. 1

Hide and Seek: Vol. 2

My Heart Duet

My Heart Needs

My Heart Wants

Every Last Beat – The Heart Duet Box Set – Books 1 & 2

Calendar Boys

Mr. January

Mr. February

Mr. March

Mr. April

Mr. May

Mr. June

Mr. July

Mr. August

Mr. September

Mr. October

Mr. November

Mr. December

Calendar Boys Box Set – Books 1-4

Calendar Boys Box Set – Books 5-8

Calendar Boys Box Set – Books 9-12

<u>Standalone Novels</u>

Master Manipulator

The First Rule

ACKNOWLEDGMENTS

This might sound a little strange, but I want to thank Ed Sheeran for helping me write this book. Those who know me know how much I love that man's music.

I saw him perform live a year or so back and I'll never ever forget it. He was incredible. I witnessed the very last show on his tour before he took an extended hiatus from music and the world in general.

He gave everything he had in that show and even now, the feels are real.

He was a big part of the inspiration for the way I imagined Parker's performances and for his love of music. I think that he'd feel the music just like Ed does.

So, thank you, Ed, you're awesome.

It's a bit scary stepping outside of my current series and writing about a new group of characters, but I'm so glad that I did. This story came to me one day when I was folding washing of all things; I had to stop and grab my phone where I hastily typed down a ton of notes. When I later transferred it to my computer, I'd already written over 1000 words of what turned into this story.

Parker, Charlotte, Jasper and Hannah have been so fun to write about, and I only ever intended to write the one book, but I'm not sure if I'm quite ready to part with Jasper and Hannah just yet. There's also the three unexpected brothers of Charlotte's who have intrigued me more than I thought they would.

So, who knows? Never say never!

ABOUT THE AUTHOR

NICOLE S. GOODIN is a romance author and mother of two from Taranaki in the North Island of New Zealand.

In mid-2015, she started to write about a group of characters who wouldn't get out of her head. Her first book, Rushed, was published in mid-2016.

Nicole enjoys long walks on the beach, pillow fights and braiding her friends' hair. She dislikes clichés, talking about herself in the third person, and people who don't understand her sense of humour.

Please feel free to contact her either via her website, email, Instagram, Twitter or on her Facebook page, she would love to hear your feedback. If you're feeling really game, you can even sign up for her newsletter.